PUMPKIN SPICE MELTDOWN

KATE MINTY

First paperback edition October 2024

Book design by Donna L. Rogers, DRL Cover Design

ISBN 979-8-9914-2700-5 (paperback)
ISBN 979-8-9914-2701-2 (ebook)

www.kminty.com

To Jessica.
i carry your heart (i carry it in my heart)
-e.e. cummings

PUMPKIN SPICE MELTDOWN

The Text

A gate agent handed Natalie a pair of airline slippers as she exited the plane. Natalie couldn't remember the last time an airline had given her anything since a pair of wings on her first flight when she was six years old. Upon closer examination, she saw the reason they were being so generous today; when they'd embroidered the name of the airline across the toes of the slippers, they'd used two Is in the word AIR. But free was free, and she wasn't going to complain because this company swag seemed nice.

She held the plastic-bagged slippers to her chest and looked around for a place to untangle her purse and carry-on from her body. While walking down the little aisle of the plane, her purse had somehow gotten jumbled in her carry-on, and everything seemed to be precariously balanced on her body now. The airport was packed and all the seats she passed were filled with travelers waiting to board their planes.

As she looked down the terminal, she saw a coffee kiosk with a few little tables that would be the perfect spot to stop, reconfigure her bags, and dig out her phone. Plus, a tasty, caffeinated beverage would help perk her right up. Even though she'd slept for most of the flight, she was still exhausted. More emotionally than physically—selling most of her belongings to move across the country so she could live with her boyfriend had been taxing. But she was here and ready for the next step. The two of them were going to officially start building a life together, and that made of her sacrifices worthwhile.

Natalie used the recently washed ten-dollar bill she had found in the pocket of her hoodie that morning to pay for her pumpkin spiced latte. She placed the slippers and coffee on the table and began to unwind herself from her constraints. When she was free of everything, she rummaged around in her carry-on for her phone, which she'd tossed in there during landing. Once found, she took a coffee pic she could use to let her mom know she had landed.

Her heart started beating so fast as she switched off airplane mode. She had really done it; she had really moved, and today was the first day of her new life with her boyfriend. Tonight, she would fall asleep next to him in his apartment. Their days of long-distance were now a thing of the past. She paused to savor the moment and remind herself that as hard as it was to leave her job, her apartment, and everything else familiar, this move was worth it. He was her person, and if they didn't take their relationship to the next level, she would always wonder *what if.*

Goosebumps covered her arms because she knew she was exactly where she needed to be when she needed to be there. She clicked on the text icon and was delighted that he had already sent her a welcome text. She wondered when she would change his name in her phone from *Boyfriend* to *Fiancé.*

Boyfriend: Natalie, I couldn't bring myself to say this to you, so I have to text it instead. Now just wouldn't be a good time for you to move in with me. I'm married. I didn't know how to tell you. I'm sorry.

Natalie fell into a chair and gasped for breath. She felt like she was going to throw up and suffocate at the same time. The world around her disappeared, and she was spiraling. She didn't know how long she'd been sitting staring at the table before her phone dinged. With a shaking hand, she unlocked the screen to see if he had sent her another message saying, *just kidding!* But he hadn't messaged. Instead, there was a text from her Great-Aunt Lindy.

Aunt Lindy: Hello Dear, I hope you had an easy flight. I know we are having dinner later this week, but I wanted to remind you that if you need me for anything, just let me know. I am beyond delighted to have you in the same city as me! Having you so close makes my heart happy.

Lindy was the only other person she knew in the city. Natalie slowly typed out her response.

Natalie: I need you.

CHAPTER 1

Natalie lay on the couch and wondered how the hell she had gotten there. The past week had been terrible and a complete blur. She wished Lindy enjoyed sleeping in. But why would that be the case? Nothing else seemed to be going Natalie's way. The banging noises coming from the kitchen were sending her over the edge. It took all her willpower to swallow the tears about to form behind her eyes. Crying again over her married ex-boyfriend was the last thing she wanted to do.

A week ago, she'd happily gotten on a plane to start a new life with her on-again, off-again, long-distance boyfriend. She'd thought this move would be the fresh start they needed to finally remain squarely in the 'on' category. In an instant, her world had shattered. She couldn't go back home because she'd quit her job and gotten out of her lease. And her parents had downsized to an RV and were driving around the country, so she couldn't even run to the safety of her childhood home.

However, at least two aspects of her life hadn't completely disintegrated the moment she stepped off the plane. The first was that her new job as a social media manager started in a few days. The second was that she knew one person in the city—her Great-Aunt Lindy. So now she lived in a retirement home with an overly active eighty-year-old. Natalie's thirty-fourth trip around the sun was not turning out how she had planned.

Trying to drown out the noise from the kitchen, she pulled the blanket over her head. This helped slightly, but not much. She could still hear Lindy clearly from the kitchen when she called out, "I can't remember if you like creamer in your coffee or half-and-half. I know you like it sweet, but I can't remember how sweet."

Natalie reminded herself she was lucky to be able to stay with Aunt Lindy. If it weren't for her great-aunt, she would blow through her savings in no time flat, and then she would really be up shit creek without a paddle.

So, even though she longed to sleep her heartache away, she yelled from underneath the covers, "Pumpkin spice creamer, please."

Attempting to summon the will to live, Natalie reluctantly threw the covers off and sat up. Folding the blanket barely did anything to help the chaotic state of Lindy's living room. Thankfully, Lindy hadn't said a word about how Natalie's clothes had exploded around the room. The only clear memory Natalie had since her arrival at Montrose Retirement Village a week earlier was when she'd walked into the living room, threw her suitcases in a pile, and fell onto the couch. The rest of her stay had been a blur. Her days had fused together.

Lindy walked in with two mugs of coffee. She handed one to Natalie and took a seat in the overstuffed armchair next to the couch. "So what's on the agenda today?" Aunt Lindy asked.

"More apartment hunting," Natalie replied. Since she'd arrived, she'd been consumed by looking for a place to live. Natalie had sold her car as part of her fresh start and could only view rental listings online. But every search had led to a dead end when she called the leasing offices. "I heard back from my HR rep at my new job. I told them my original plan fell through, and she's putting me in touch with a real estate agent next week. With this housing crisis right now, I'm having a hard time finding anything in my budget. I have a feeling I'll have to go with something more expensive and get a roommate. I don't even know how to go about finding a roommate. I haven't had one since college."

Lindy listened intently to everything Natalie uttered and, in a soothing tone, said, "Well, you are welcome to stay with me as long as you need to. I enjoy having you here."

Natalie felt instantly guilty about any negative thoughts she'd had about living in Montrose. Lindy had taken her in without a second thought and had enveloped her with love from the moment she arrived. So what that Lindy's neighbor had just celebrated her ninety-fifth birthday? She was a cool old lady who zoomed down the halls in her motorized scooter.

"I know, and I'm so thankful for everything you've done for me. I don't know where I would be without you."

Lindy blew on her coffee. "Fiddlesticks. We come from strong female stock, and you would've figured out what to do.

You still will. Right now, you're simply in transition. You are adjusting from one expectation to another. Bigger and better things are coming your way."

The tears she had suppressed now ran free. As much as she wanted to stop crying, Natalie couldn't. She felt lost and out of control. Deep down, she knew Aunt Lindy was right, but getting a handle on her life again felt so far away.

Lindy handed Natalie a tissue. "Okay, sweet girl. I'm going to give you five minutes to cry. And I want you to cry hard. Then you are going with me to water aerobics. The exercise will be good for your soul, and the warm water will be very soothing. Your back can't feel great after sleeping on the couch for a week."

Natalie was caught off guard. She didn't want to go to water aerobics, but she also didn't want to be rude. She ached all over, and she didn't know if it was from her depression or from not sleeping in a real bed. "I don't know where any of my bathing suits are. I don't have one in the top suitcase." Natalie tearfully looked over at her stack of luggage. Her life had been condensed into three suitcases. She had put a few boxes in her parents' storage unit, and once she got settled, they were going to mail them to her, but those were mainly sentimental items and school memorabilia.

"Don't worry about that. I have plenty of suits, and I'm sure I have one that will fit you. Now you cry while I go get you a towel and pick out a suit for you." Lindy got up and headed to her bedroom.

Natalie followed directions and wept so hard it felt like she couldn't breathe. When she finally gained control of herself, she saw Lindy had laid out a suit and a towel for her on the armchair. She headed to the half bath off the living room to change because she didn't have the energy to protest. Plus, if she stayed in the apartment, she would cry more, and at this point, she worried about becoming dehydrated.

It did not surprise Natalie that the suit fit. She and Lindy had similar frames. They were both tall and carried a few extra pounds. Most of the women in her family had the same curves. Lindy had picked out a suit for her that was more dress than bathing suit. As she looked in the mirror, she didn't recognize herself. Sure, there stood a woman staring back at her who had her same brown hair and blue eyes, but that woman looked lost, and that wasn't how Natalie usually appeared. She sighed and tried to accept her current dismal existence.

She walked back into the living room, where Lindy waited with a quilted front-zip robe for her. Natalie took it and put it on.

That week, she'd only had the physical capacity to open the top suitcase. Each day she declared she would get into the others, but every time she talked herself into it, she decided that action would be too taxing. The top suitcase held all her work clothes, so Natalie had been rotating between what she'd worn on the plane, her pajamas, and the spare set of clothes she always put in her carry-on. Natalie had sandals in one of the other bags, but instead of retrieving them, she opted for the slippers the airline gave her.

"Let's go!" Lindy exclaimed.

Natalie followed her out the door and took the elevator to the lobby, where the staff was busy taking down the Halloween decorations and putting up the Thanksgiving ones. By removing the spiders and witches' hats and replacing them with cornucopias and pumpkins, the whole feel of the room had changed.

As always, Lindy filled her in on the gossip surrounding the different residents as they walked. Unfortunately, Natalie wasn't in a place where she could retain this information.

Whenever Lindy introduced her to her friends, she said she had insisted Natalie stay with her until her new job started and her apartment became available. Aunt Lindy never once indicated to anyone that Natalie's life had fallen apart and that she was currently having a complete meltdown. Lindy passed her great-niece's stay off as a planned visit and blamed her memory for not having told the other residents sooner.

"Now, over there is Jean. Her nephew has just been arrested for insider trading. Jean said he was always up to no good, even as a little boy." Lindy slyly nodded toward a woman sitting at a table in an alcove working on a jigsaw puzzle.

"Have I met Jean before?" Natalie asked. Her grief-stricken mushy brain couldn't keep anyone straight.

"Yes, briefly, last night at dinner. She told us about her new Jell-O salad recipe."

Natalie did remember snippets of that conversation. "Right, she decided to add walnuts instead of pecans, and it was a game changer."

Lindy opened the door to the indoor pool and said, "Exactly."

They were early for the class and the first ones there. Natalie set her towel on a chair. The stillness of the surface acted as an invitation, drawing her to the pool ramp. Walking into the water felt like entering a warm bath. The water embraced her, and for the first time in a week, she felt her tension start to ease. Lindy was, as always, spot-on with her recommendation to get off the couch.

Natalie lowered herself in until her chin skimmed the surface. "This feels amazing."

"I know. Just wait till your arthritis kicks in, then it'll feel even better," Lindy said as she slowly twisted and stretched in the pool.

"Something else to look forward to." Natalie closed her eyes.

"I told you how my friend Charlotte was getting back from her cruise late last night. Normally, she is here with me. But I don't know if she'll feel up to it this morning. If she's not here, I want us to run by her room on our way back so I can introduce you."

Natalie nodded in response and tried to tune Lindy out. She felt peace and wanted to savor the weightlessness as long as she could.

As more women got in the pool, Natalie was forced to join the world again. Lindy gave introductions when needed, and Natalie attempted to pay attention and remember their names. While Natalie talked to a woman who used to be a geologist, she heard Lindy squeal with delight.

"Welcome back, stranger," Lindy said to a stunning woman about Lindy's age who had perfectly coiffed hair and wore a ruched red bathing suit. The woman waved as she walked down the ramp.

Lindy leaned over to Natalie and whispered, "That's Charlotte. She used to be on the beauty pageant circuit."

Natalie struggled to corral her skirt, which had decided to float up to the surface of the water, and whispered back, "That makes sense."

Lindy made her way to Charlotte, and Natalie followed.

"You are a sight for sore eyes," Charlotte cooed as Lindy approached.

"I am so surprised you made it. I was sure you'd be knackered," Lindy said.

"Trust me, I am. But after all that flying yesterday, I knew I would regret it if I didn't come, so here I am. And who is this?" Charlotte asked as she waded into the pool.

Natalie knew Lindy had already told Charlotte about her moving to the city; Charlotte was, after all, her best friend. Per Lindy, she and Charlotte were the Laverne and Shirley of the community. But Charlotte didn't know about Natalie's new living arrangements.

"This is my niece, Natalie. She's staying with me until her apartment's ready."

The two older women exchanged a glance that said a thousand unspoken words. Natalie watched realization wash over Charlotte's face. The compassion Charlotte had in her eyes made Natalie want to cry again. Luckily, the instructor started the class before the floodgates opened.

* * *

There was nothing mellow about the workout. Natalie was not prepared for how rigorous the water aerobics class would be. Other women causally chatted as they exited the pool; Natalie tried to act like she hadn't gotten her ass kicked.

Aunt Lindy and Charlotte stood in the middle of the pool and waved her over. "How'd you like our class?" Lindy asked.

"You guys really go all out," Natalie replied.

"You'll get used to it. Just remember to go at your own pace," Charlotte said.

These women were at least forty years older than Natalie and were telling her to go at her own pace. Natalie kicked herself for not going to the gym more before today. Never in a million years had she dreamt she'd need to work out to keep up with the golden girls.

"Let's walk some laps. This way, we don't have to wait forever at the elevator when we head back to our apartments," Lindy said.

Natalie fell in line with the two women as they walked the length of the pool. They amicably talked about the cooling weather until the room cleared.

When it was just the three of them in the water, Charlotte turned to Natalie. "Sweetheart, I know something big must have happened for you to be here and not at your boyfriend's. Are you okay?"

Natalie didn't know this woman, but it didn't matter. Charlotte felt like a safe haven. Being with these two ladies made Natalie feel like she was being sheltered from a storm.

"I'm okay at this current moment," Natalie said, staring down at her hands. She needed to look anywhere but at their faces. Seeing any expressions of sympathy would make her start to cry.

"If you don't mind me asking, what happened?" Charlotte inquired.

Lindy hadn't asked many questions, and Natalie hadn't felt like talking much. But there was something about Charlotte that made it seem okay to open up. "When I got here, I found out my boyfriend is married," Natalie answered.

"He sent her a text message. She read it as soon as she got off the plane," Lindy added.

"No!" Charlotte exclaimed.

"Yup," Natalie said, still unable to look up.

"I mean, I have never heard of such tomfoolery. Of course, you didn't know he was married, but why on earth would he ask you to move out here if he had a wife?" Charlotte asked.

The three women continued to walk laps around the pool. Natalie finally looked up but purposely kept her gaze away from Lindy and Charlotte.

"I keep replaying everything in my head. We'd been together for three years. He was in town all the time for business, so I never traveled to see him. Every time we'd plan a trip for me to see him, we broke up. Then when he came back to town, we got back together. That should've been a red flag, but I didn't see it. My job had gotten stale and my parents were moving away. All my close friends had one by one moved across the country, so I didn't have any real ties left back home. I floated the idea of moving closer to him, and he didn't say no. If he had said no, I would've found out he was married because

I would've asked a thousand questions as to why not. And I never would've moved." Blood rushed to Natalie's face as her exasperation grew.

"Of course you would've sussed it out if he had been honest with you. Also, red flags are nearly impossible for those in love to see," Charlotte consoled.

Natalie slowed her pace and continued her story. "He kept getting more distant, but I thought it was nerves." When she felt her anger reaching its breaking point, she stopped and looked at Lindy and Charlotte. "I wasn't even the one who suggested I move in with him. He did that."

She applied pressure to her tear ducts with the tips of her fingers and sighed as she peered up at the ceiling. "But again, with the gift of hindsight, I can see the night that the discussion happened more clearly now. We'd both been drinking and were lying in bed when he said something like, 'It'd be fun to live together.' My tipsy brain took that as we were going to live together. The next morning, when I brought it up, he didn't say no. I can't believe I didn't notice I was the one leading the conversation." She shook her head and pointed to her chest. "I put together a budget for half of the utilities, for god's sake. I feel so stupid." She closed her eyes and wished she could melt into the warm water and disappear.

Lindy took Natalie's hand. "Look at me, child." Natalie reluctantly opened her eyes and looked at her aunt. "You are not stupid. You were having conversations with your boyfriend about taking the next step. Not once did he stop you from going down this path. He is a coward and should have said something."

Natalie's chest ached and her eyelids felt so heavy. "I thought we would get married. I thought we'd have kids. Moving out here was going to bring us closer. In my mind, distance was the only thing that kept getting in our way. What am I going to do now?" Natalie looked from Lindy to Charlotte.

Lindy hooked her arm through Natalie's. "Well, first things first, we need to find you a place to live. You have a job already, so that's one big hurdle already crossed."

"Everything is so expensive here, and the places I can afford have giant wait lists," Natalie said in a quiet voice.

"Well, Charlotte and I know tons of people. We will put our feelers out," Lindy said with encouragement.

"My grandson knows all kinds of people too. He's coming for lunch today. You two should join us. We'll pick his brain and figure out a plan. You're not in this alone," Charlotte said, taking Natalie's other arm.

Lindy squeezed Natalie's hand. "Know you have a place here with me until we get this all worked out."

Tears ran down Natalie's face. She nodded, grateful to have her Grand Dearies looking out for her.

Chapter 2

All Natalie wanted to wear was sweats and a hoodie. But sweats weren't in the top suitcase. Natalie thought about borrowing something from Lindy but decided against it. She struggled to put on jeans after getting out of the shower and questioned all her life choices, making a mental note to find her elastic-waist pants after lunch. Besides, everyone knew that no one should wear structured clothing when their life was in shambles.

Natalie pulled her sweater over her head and wondered why she had bought everything so form-fitting. Obviously, she hadn't anticipated her current implosion and desire to stay in the fetal position forever.

After finally coming out of the bathroom, she saw Lindy waiting on her bed. Lindy patted the spot next to her, and Natalie sat down.

"Sweetie, I feel it's time to call your parents," said Lindy.

Natalie felt dread build up inside. "I know, but I don't want to. Telling them makes it real." Up until today her parents had been at a state park near the Great Lakes and didn't have great cell phone coverage, but now they were en route to her brother's house, just a few hours' drive from the park.

"You need to rip the bandage off. You can't keep Susan and Bill in the dark much longer," Lindy said.

She knew this needed to be done; she just didn't want to. Lindy patted her leg before Natalie reluctantly stood up and headed to the door. "You're right. I need to do it before I lose my nerve."

"Good girl. I'm going to take a shower and get ready, so you will have plenty of privacy."

Natalie nodded and left for the living room, closing the door to her great-aunt's bedroom. No matter what she did, her parents were always supportive. But telling them about her predicament meant she'd have to admit she'd read all the signs wrong. She felt like a failure. She pulled her phone out and clicked on her mom's contact information before she talked herself out of calling.

Her mom picked up after the second ring. "Hello, my darling! How's my precious girl?"

Hearing her mom's voice melted her. Any resolve she had mustered was completely gone. Natalie burst into tears and told her mother everything. Her mom patiently listened and gave the appropriate responses when necessary. She also occasionally stopped the conversation to fill her dad in, who was driving.

"Natalie, your dad wants to know what excuse Mr. Slime Bucket gave for not telling you he was married," Susan said.

Natalie wished her mom would put the call on speaker, but technology was not her parents' forte.

"Nothing. I tried to call him after I got the message, and it went straight to his voicemail. I sent him a couple of frantic texts, which he read but didn't respond to. Aunt Lindy suggested I block him, so I have."

"Bill, she said she called him, and he wouldn't answer, and she also sent him texts. I think he's ghosting her. Lindy told her to block him, so she did." Natalie wondered where her mother learned the word *ghosting*.

Natalie heard murmuring in the background. "Your father thinks that's best, and I do too," her mom said.

Neither one of her parents had ever gone through a break-up themselves. Her parents were *the* couple. They'd been high school sweethearts and had been glued to each other's hips ever since. They were Natalie's ultimate relationship inspiration. Even with their lack of personal heartache, they had always been supportive and understanding through all of Natalie's.

"Oh, lovie, we both wish we were there with you right now. I want to hug you so bad. I'm glad you have Aunt Lindy to lean on."

"Me too," Natalie replied.

"And don't even worry about Thanksgiving. When we get to your brother's house, we'll talk to them about hosting this year. You know Jenny will be thrilled by this idea," Susan said.

Natalie almost dropped the phone. She had totally forgotten about Thanksgiving. Usually it was held at her parents' house, but with their recent downsizing, the big family Thanksgiving celebration was now going to rotate between the whole family. Natalie had volunteered for the first year. Her married ex-boyfriend's apartment complex had a stunning lounge residents could use. He had even told her he'd reserved the room for them. Natalie wondered why on earth he had kept up this charade for so long.

In any case, there was no way Natalie could host Thanksgiving for all her extended family now. It was a little less than a month away and she lived on a couch. But the idea of her sister-in-law lording this over her for the rest of her life was unacceptable.

Most people described Jenny as being a pleasant-enough woman. Susan and Bill thought her delightful, and Jenny loved Natalie's brother Kevin a ton. The only problem was that Jenny was a closeted bitch to Natalie. Her sister-in-law made passive-aggressive digs at Natalie every time they were together. Most of the things she said to Natalie started with, "No offense, but," which was, of course, followed by an offensive statement or, "But don't take this the wrong way."

Jenny also made sure to point out all of Natalie's shortcomings by passing them off as compliments. The only two people who had ever picked up on Jenny's treatment of her were Natalie's grandmother and Lindy.

Natalie would rather give up coffee forever than let Jenny host Thanksgiving this year. "Don't worry about Thanksgiving. I still want everyone to come here. I'll figure it out," Natalie blurted.

"Are you sure? That's a lot of people to host. Honey, everyone will understand. You'll do it next year. I think you need time to heal," Susan said.

If Natalie let Jenny host first, Jenny would become the savior of Thanksgiving. All she'd hear the whole weekend would be how Jenny had graciously offered to switch years, how she didn't mind taking on this last-minute burden, and how poor Natalie needed Jenny to save her. With her world crumbling all around her, Natalie needed Thanksgiving. She needed this win.

"Hosting Thanksgiving will be good for me. It gives me something to focus on. Plus, people have already made their travel arrangements. It needs to stay here," Natalie insisted.

"Bill, she said people have already bought their plane tickets." Natalie heard more murmuring on the phone, then, "Your dad said he'll help cover the cost of people changing their travel arrangements if this turns out to be too big for you."

Natalie needed to get her parents on board, and she had one last ace to play. "I can handle this. Plus, I have Aunt Lindy to help me." Natalie knew with this card played, the game was won.

"Okay, I'll start spreading the news to the family about your updated situation, so you won't get a million questions during the holiday weekend," Susan said.

In Natalie's family, everybody knew everything. This had never bothered her, because she also wanted all the details about everyone else. It wasn't until Natalie reached adulthood that she learned every family didn't behave this way.

"Thanks, Mom, and drive safe. Text me when you get to Kevin's house," she said. They proceeded to say their goodbyes and hung up.

Natalie paced the room and kicked the air to try and stretch her jeans out. Mid-kick, there was a knock at the front door.

She took one step in that direction when Charlotte let herself in and waltzed into the living room. Natalie couldn't remember the last time she'd known someone well enough to let herself into their house.

"Are we almost ready?" Charlotte asked, tidying a stack of mail on Lindy's counter.

"Almost," Lindy hollered from the bedroom.

Natalie sighed, knowing Lindy had to have heard most of her conversation with her parents.

She'd thought about putting on makeup for their lunch date, but what was the point? The odds of her crying it all off were high. "I'm as good as I'm going to get," Natalie said as she adjusted her sweater again.

"You look beautiful," Charlotte said.

Natalie knew Charlotte was lying, because she hadn't bothered to brush her hair after getting out of the shower and had thrown it up in a messy bun on top of her head. With her puffy eyes and splotchy face, she felt anything but beautiful.

"You are very sweet," Natalie replied. Calling a kind, older woman a fat-mouth liar didn't seem like the right move.

Lindy walked out of the bedroom in an outfit Natalie wished she was wearing—a matching tracksuit. Now, she regretted not borrowing clothes from Lindy. "Let's head down and snag one of the good tables by the window," her great-aunt said.

Retirement home dining hours were not something Natalie ever thought she'd get accustomed to. Breakfast and lunch were at typical times, but dinner started at four fifteen. Luckily, Lindy enjoyed eating later, at five thirty or six.

On her first day at Montrose, Natalie had learned all about the table hierarchy. The ones by the bay windows were the most coveted, and if you got to the dining hall late for lunch, you'd be stuck with a table by the front door, and apparently that part of the room had a dreadful draft. Natalie couldn't attest to the draft yet because they always arrived thirty minutes before lunch opened to get one of the good tables. And at dinner, they were one of the last people to eat, so seating was never an issue.

Per usual, when they arrived in the dining room, all three bay window tables were open. But she knew they wouldn't be for long.

"Quick, Charlotte. I see Janet coming down the hall—she'll get our favorite table," Lindy said, quickening her steps through the entryway of the dining hall. All three window tables were fine, but the farthest one from the entrance had a perfect view of the fountain in front of the gazebo so it was the most coveted.

Natalie looked around to see who Lindy was talking about and saw a woman on a motorized scooter with her eyes set on their table. Without thinking, Natalie sprinted to her aunt's favorite table. She needed to lay claim to it before this Janet woman. Natalie ran like she hadn't run in years. She had just barely thrown herself into a chair before Janet arrived.

As Natalie clutched her aching sides and struggled to breathe, she raised her fist into the air. "It's ours! I got here first."

Janet breathed a sigh of annoyance and headed to the bay window closer to the entrance, which was the second-best in the room. Natalie looked at her aunt, who beamed with pride. Twice today, Natalie's lack of gym time had humbled her.

"That was very impressive," Lindy said as she approached and took a seat.

"Thank you," Natalie said while her breathing normalized.

"Janet has such an advantage with that scooter. She's always speeding up to get to things first. One time, she ran over poor Arnold's foot and didn't even apologize," Charlotte said, pulling out her chair.

Lindy leaned forward and softly said, "She's such a bitch."

"You said it, I didn't," Charlotte replied, and nodded in agreement.

Natalie enjoyed seeing these two women interact with each other. She knew they had met when Lindy moved into the community, but a bystander wouldn't have known that. The two of them got along as if they had grown up together.

Lindy had always planned on moving in with her sister, Ruth, Natalie's grandmother, so they could live out their golden years together. But cancer had other plans for Ruth. At the funeral, Lindy was a shell of herself. When Ruth died, a part of Lindy died too. Once Lindy decided she didn't want to live by herself anymore, she went on a cross-country tour to find a facility that had everything she wanted.

Lindy said she knew Montrose Retirement Village was the place for her because they had a bar in the lobby and a stunning library. One of the reasons Natalie had decided to move in with her married ex-boyfriend was that she'd be close to Lindy. Lindy didn't have kids and had always treated Ruth's like they were her own. Natalie had had two grandmothers for the price of one. She called Lindy on a regular basis, but being able to see her in person was a big selling point.

"I love these gourd centerpieces. It's not that I don't love Halloween, because I do. But Thanksgiving has always felt so cozy to me," Lindy said.

Charlotte adjusted a gourd and said, "Same. Fall has always been my favorite season."

"I love fall too. Charlotte, what's your grandson's name?" Natalie asked.

"Brian. And he should be here any minute," Charlotte replied.

Natalie and Lindy craned their necks to look around. Natalie didn't know why she bothered; she had no clue what he looked like. But she kept an eye out for anyone under the age of seventy.

Lindy spotted him first. "He's coming in through the side entrance."

Natalie and Charlotte both turned in that direction. Walking toward them was a tall, catalog model of a man. Charlotte's genes ran strong in her family. This man not only looked like brands were knocking down his door to get his endorsement, he also appeared to be strong enough to throw someone over his shoulders and save them from a burning building. Natalie felt her breath catch in her throat.

"Brian, over here," Charlotte lilted, and waved her grandson over.

Brian's dark hair was perfectly disheveled, unlike Natalie's, whose was carelessly messy. But at this moment, she was thankful she hadn't opted to wear something from Aunt Lindy's closet because sitting across from a beautiful man in a pastel tracksuit would have made her want to shrivel up and die. Natalie sat up straight and tried not to appear like the depressed sack of potatoes she felt like.

Brian came to the table and bent down to kiss his grandmother on her cheek. He nodded to Lindy and took the seat opposite Natalie. She could tell he was surprised to have two additional guests for lunch.

Lindy jumped in before Brian could ask any questions. "Brian, I'd like you to meet my niece, Natalie. Natalie, this is Charlotte's grandson, Brian."

Brian extended a hand and Natalie took it. She noticed his firm, but not crushing, grip. She didn't know what to say, and was afraid if she said anything, her story might come rushing out of her mouth, and she wouldn't be able to stop herself.

"It's nice to meet you," Brian said, giving Natalie a quizzical look.

"Same," Natalie finally replied. She was pleased with this response. She'd have been pleased with anything that wasn't "My life's a giant dumpster fire, and I have nowhere to live."

Brian squinted at Natalie, and she was sure he was wondering if she was there to recruit his grandmother into being part of a pyramid scheme or something equally nefarious. He shook his head a little before turning to Charlotte. "Gigi, tell me all about your cruise."

"Oh, it was delightful. They always are. I ate too much, as always, but I can't help myself. The food is just so good," Charlotte responded.

"Mom said the whale-watching was the highlight of the trip," Brian said.

"It really was. Just spectacular. I have never seen anything like that in my whole life. We really had the best time. Your cousin Kelly even won five hundred dollars at the casino one night. It was thrilling. And there was this lounge singer named Burt who could sing anything you asked for. Next time, you'll have to join us." Charlotte placed her hand on his arm.

He gently patted his grandmother's hand. "I'll try, but you know it's hard for me to get away."

"I know, you are so busy with all your endeavors. Speaking of your endeavors, Natalie here needs a place to live and is having the darndest time finding an apartment. I was hoping you could help out with this," Charlotte said, sweetly eyeing her grandson. Natalie recognized this was a woman who knew how to get what she wanted.

Brian looked at Natalie and then back at his grandmother. "I don't know how I can."

Charlotte was clearly not pleased with his response. She raised her eyebrows and said, "You know everybody. Surely you know someone with a reasonably priced apartment for rent."

Brian shook his head. "I can't think of anyone. You're asking for a needle in a haystack." Charlotte didn't drop eye contact with her grandson, and he added, "But I guess I can put some feelers out for you."

"That's all I am asking for." Charlotte turned to Natalie. "Brian remodels buildings. He does beautiful work. Recently, he bought an old office building downtown and is remodeling it into apartments. It is going to be fantastic." Charlotte straightened in her chair and focused on Brian. "Hey, are any of the apartments in your building done?"

Brian sat back in his chair, scratched his head, and said, "No, it's kind of a disaster over there right now."

"Do you have any that are close to being done?" Charlotte asked. This woman was persistent.

Brian thought about the question for a moment, then replied, "I guess I have one that could be done in about two weeks. But even if I did finish it, she'd be living in a construction zone. There'd be constant noise."

"Well, I think that sounds perfect. Because it's a construction zone, you will, of course, give her a discounted rate. And getting her monthly rent will help you financially, I'm sure. And you aren't working all the time. The crew leaves in the evenings, which will be when Natalie arrives home." Charlotte folded her hands on the table, indicating the decision had been made.

Everything happened so fast that Natalie wasn't sure what to do. This apartment didn't sound like the ideal situation, but it could be better than a couch. However, what she thought about it didn't matter because Brian clearly didn't want her to move in.

Natalie straightened in her chair. "Fixing up the apartment sounds so complicated. I will figure this out on my own." She tried her best to sound confident when she added, "I am sure I can find something affordable, and if not, I'll get a roommate. Charlotte, I'm so appreciative of your asking, but please don't worry about me."

"Even with a roommate, you'll be hard-pressed to find a reasonably priced apartment in this city. I'd love to help, but it isn't feasible right now," Brian responded.

"But it will be in two weeks," Charlotte added.

Natalie and Brian started talking at the same time. They stopped and looked at each other, and Natalie waved for him to go first. Brian folded his arms across his chest and did little to hide his frustration. "I'm not saying I can, but if I could get this apartment together in two weeks, you need to know when I say construction zone, I mean it. And it will be that way for at least a year."

She hoped he realized she wasn't pushing for this.

Charlotte gave her grandson a stern look. "Brian, Natalie needs our help. She moved halfway across the country, and the rug was pulled out from under her when she arrived. Now that I know we have a way to help her, this is what we need to do. She belongs to Lindy, which means she is one of our own, and we take care of our own."

Charlotte's words made Natalie want to cry again. She felt an odd combination of belonging and being lost.

"Okay, I'll do what I can. Would you like to see the apartment before you say yes?" Brian asked.

Natalie couldn't tell if he was looking at her because at that moment, if she took her eyes off her place setting, the tears would start rolling.

Lindy had been watching this whole exchange and answered on Natalie's behalf. "I think that sounds like a fine idea. When would you like us to come over?"

Brian sighed and asked Lindy, "Do you have time tomorrow morning? This way, if the apartment doesn't work for her, I don't have to rush to start working on it."

"Tomorrow morning sounds great. Natalie and I will be there," Lindy replied.

"I will too," Charlotte quickly added.

"Great. Can we go through the buffet now? I'm starving," Brian said.

The two older women responded with affirmations about going to get plates. Natalie gave a silent sigh of relief that the focus was removed from her, at least for a little while.

* * *

Montrose was known for their terrific food. All the residents raved about the kitchen crew and the magic they performed. As good as all the meals had been, Natalie still missed cooking for herself. Being in the kitchen was a form of therapy, but it would have to wait. Cooking and Lindy did not mix. Her kitchen had one pot, a spoon, and a smattering of cheese knives.

Today's selections were as delightful as always, but Natalie craved tomato soup and a simple grilled cheese sandwich.

"The kitchen crew did it again. I am going to have to write them another note. I don't know what they put in their macaroni and cheese to make it so delicious, but it's the best I have ever had," Lindy exclaimed as she placed her napkin on the table.

"It was tasty. Not as tasty as yours, Gigi, but still very good," Brian said after wiping his mouth.

"My cooking days are behind me. The most I want to do now is make cinnamon toast for breakfast every once in a while," Charlotte said, leaning back in her chair.

"The food here is fantastic. But I can't wait to cook for you both," Natalie added. She leaned over and squeezed both Lindy and Charlotte's hands.

"You'll be in your own kitchen before you know it," Charlotte stated.

Brian pushed his chair away from the table. "I hate to eat and run, but I need to head back to work. I'll see you all tomorrow morning." He looked at Natalie with a straight face and said, "Natalie, it was nice to meet you." She got the distinct feeling he, in fact, did not think it was nice to meet her.

"Same to you," Natalie replied.

Brian stood up and gave his grandmother a quick peck on the cheek before heading for the door.

"He is such a nice young man," Lindy said, as she watched him walk away.

"Thank you, I think so too. And how wonderful would it be if this apartment worked out? It would be beneficial for both of you," Charlotte said, patting the table.

"It'd be great." Natalie turned to Lindy. "Aunt Lindy, I've one more issue I need your assistance with. My mom reminded me that I signed up to host Thanksgiving this year. She told me I didn't have to, but I think it'd be good for me. I told her I still wanted to host, and I need your help figuring out where."

"I forgot all about that too. That is not an issue. We have a grand private dining room here. It's where I am planning to host when it's my turn, and you'll do it there too," Lindy replied.

"Perfect!" Natalie exclaimed.

"Everything is coming together. I have a feeling you'll sleep better tonight than you have all week," Charlotte said.

"I sure hope so," Natalie said.

"Let's gather our things and head out. People are starting to eye our table," Lindy said.

The three women got up and walked to the elevator. Lindy pulled out her cell phone and sent an email. Natalie made sure her aunt didn't trip or run into anything while she was on her phone. By the time they reached the elevators, Lindy had put her phone away.

"I have sent a request asking if we can reserve one of the shuttles to take us to Brian's new building in the morning. Since I don't know when we'll be done, we'll have to Uber back, but that's not a big deal. I've also sent an email to the catering manager about reserving the private dining room for Thanksgiving," Lindy said.

"That all sounds great," Natalie said and wondered how Aunt Lindy could be more adept at using a cell phone than her mother.

Natalie didn't cry for the rest of the day.

Chapter 3

27 Days till Thanksgiving

When Charlotte said Brian's property was an office building, that was like someone saying the Mona Lisa looked like a doodle. Before disembarking the Montrose Retirement Village shuttle bus, Natalie's jaw had already hit the floor of the van. Natalie stood on the sidewalk and stared up at a gorgeous art deco masterpiece that needed to be on a postcard. Brian didn't appear to be much older than her, yet he owned this piece of history. Natalie felt sure they were at the wrong address; they had to be.

Lindy and Charlotte didn't act surprised to be in front of such a nice building.

Natalie walked to the structure to get a better look inside. As she peered in a window, she saw what seemed to be an old pub. The wooden bar appeared to have intricate hand-chiseled details and took up a good portion of the room. She'd put money on it having an old-fashioned brass footrail. The rest of the room was filled with stacks of boxes, buckets, and drop cloths.

"Brian just said he will be down any minute," Charlotte stated as she stood next to Natalie. They both looked in the window. "This is going to be something special when it's all done," Charlotte said with a gentleness in her tone.

"It's already something special," Natalie said.

Brian opened the front service entrance door and waved them over. Walking toward him, Natalie wondered if she had been looking into the correct building, but as they made their way down the hall, they passed a glass door that opened into the pub.

The hallway gave off sterile office-building vibes. It reminded her of a poorly remodeled doctor's office. Brian started the tour when they reached the elevator. "On the ground floor, we have the old bar." He pointed further down the hall. "Back there's the storage room, the kitchen, and the building manager's old office."

They rode the elevator up to the first floor, and when it arrived, Brian held the door open for the three women to exit. "Head left. It's the first door down that hallway."

Charlotte led the way. Piles of wood and boxes of tiles stood along the walls. Dust coated everything the eye could see. Brian made his way to the front of the pack and opened the door to the apartment.

The apartment did not look like it was two weeks away from being completed. Tarps covered the floor, and a table saw was set up in what Natalie assumed would be the living room.

The kitchen did not have a sink, countertops, or appliances. She peeked around the corner of the kitchen and saw a small hallway, which led to what she assumed was the bedroom. There, sitting in the middle of the hall, was a toilet.

"There's still a lot to do, but all of the major stuff is done," Brian said.

Lindy looked at Natalie with rounded eyes. Natalie felt better knowing Brian's words hadn't had a reassuring effect on her either. "And you really think this will be done in two weeks?" Lindy asked.

"The rest of the stuff is finishing touches. I wasn't planning on working on this apartment again until the end. But my crew can do it," Brian said as he stacked boxes so they had a clear path around the space.

Charlotte was the only one unfazed by the state of the apartment. "It's going to be great. Now show us the bedroom. Will this unit have a washing machine?"

They walked down the hall and Brian opened the door to the bedroom. Charlotte barreled in, with Lindy following close behind. Natalie wasn't as anxious to check out another room. Looking around the space made her sick to her stomach. What had she gotten herself into? If her options were between sleeping on her aunt's couch in a retirement home or living here, she'd pick Montrose every time.

Lindy and Charlotte were deep in conversation by the time Natalie joined them.

"It'll be just like the Boxcar Children books. We can clean this place up and make it look brand new," Charlotte said, running her finger along the window seal.

"You guys are acting like this is how the apartment will be when Natalie moves in. It's going to be clean, and the toilet will be installed. I'll have my tile guy start on the bathroom today, if this is what you guys want. Gigi, give me more credit that I can do better than a boxcar," Brian said.

All three women looked at him with surprise. Natalie realized if the apartment were cleaned and the walls painted, it might not be so bad.

"Will we have a say on finishes?" Charlotte asked.

Currently, the top priority on Natalie's wish list was a bedroom with a door. The apartments she had found online were carbon copies of one another, so the opportunity to have a say in how the apartment would get completed was more than Natalie could have hoped for.

Brian shrugged. "I guess. There are a few decisions left to make, but not many. We're going to use tiles left over from old projects. Since this apartment is a one-off, I was gonna customize it a little more."

"What does one-off mean?" Lindy asked as she walked out of the bedroom.

Brian hurried behind her and said, "It was the only apartment already in the building. This was the building manager's apartment. We aren't touching the layout at all. It's also the only one-bed, one-bath apartment."

Natalie was glad Lindy and Charlotte were asking all the questions she wanted to ask. She stepped away from the group and, for the first time since entering the apartment, let her mind fantasize about what to do with the space. She continued to explore the apartment silently.

It wasn't a large place, but plenty of room for one person. It was open concept, and she stood near the front door and imagined how she'd lay out the space. The kitchen was to the right of the front door, and while it felt a little odd to walk straight into the dining area, the unit had a big picture window on the other side of the room that let in nice light. Natalie could imagine herself reading next to it. She decided then and there the living room area would be next to the window.

As Natalie inspected the apartment, she thought there might be enough room for a good-sized couch, a TV stand, and a dinette table. It seemed like Brian had added an island that could accommodate barstools. She stood in the kitchen and imagined Lindy leaning against the counter while she made them dinner.

Her mind traveled outside the apartment and into the rest of the building. She tried to imagine herself carrying groceries up to her apartment. Brian was right about it being a construction site. It wasn't ideal, but she might be able to make it work. With her savings, she could buy a few pieces of furniture. She purposely didn't think about all the other things she needed to buy to make a house a home, like dishes. That would be a worry for another day.

She was so lost in her thoughts she hadn't noticed Lindy and Charlotte were still talking. She rejoined the group, milling around in the kitchen.

"Great, the three of us will come by again on Monday after Natalie gets off work to finalize paint colors, light fixtures, and faucets," Charlotte said.

Brian rolled his eyes. "You only have three options for the light fixtures and faucets."

"Options are options," Charlotte stated, and headed back to the elevator.

Brian walked across the room and stood by the front door. Natalie took this as the cue to exit the apartment. As she left the space, she realized she had barely spoken a word; she had been too busy taking everything in.

Lindy's phone dinged, and she dug around in her purse to retrieve it while Brian struggled to usher Charlotte out the door. Lindy read the message, looked up at Natalie, and said, "Well, the private dining room is booked for the whole Thanksgiving weekend."

Before Natalie could jump into panic mode, Charlotte walked out of the apartment and said, "We'll just have to find a restaurant in the city that has a private dining room. That won't be hard to do."

Charlotte was right—a private dining room was a private dining room. And since she wasn't sure she'd have access to a kitchen to prepare the meal, if they held the dinner at a restaurant, she wouldn't have to worry about how to feed her whole family. Plus, there'd be room for everyone. There was no way Lindy's apartment could accommodate everyone coming, and even if Brian got her place ready, she'd be lucky to get her immediate family in there. She would simply host Thanksgiving at a restaurant. When they got back to the retirement village, she'd make some phone calls.

"Brian, can you show us the bar downstairs?" Lindy asked as she pressed the elevator call button.

Brian nodded and held the door to the elevator open for the women.

As she stepped out onto the ground floor, Natalie heard someone whistling. She could whistle, but not that well. The tone and clarity she heard were impressive.

"And that's my foreman, Henry Valley," Brian said. He headed in the direction of the melodic tones, leading them into the pub through the glass door they'd passed when they first walked into the building.

Next to the bar, sorting a box of tile, stood a stout older man who resembled Santa Claus. He wore headphones and was oblivious to anyone listening to him. Brian gingerly tapped him on his shoulder, clearly hoping not to scare him too much.

As Henry lowered his headsets, he looked at the group and smiled. Natalie liked how gentle his eyes were. "Hello, lovely ladies. How are we doing today?" he asked.

Lindy and Charlotte acted like flattered schoolgirls and giggled at his kind words.

"Henry, this is my grandmother Charlotte, her best friend Lindy, and Lindy's great-niece, Natalie. Natalie might start living in apartment 102 soon," Brian said.

Henry frowned and looked at Brian. "Are you sure that's a good idea? That place is a mess."

"Well, I'll start the finishing touches on it this evening to get it livable before she moves in," Brian said.

"I can help with that. I'm almost done on the third floor," Henry added.

"Great." Brian turned toward the women. "Ladies, this is the pub. Right now, it's a catch-all for our supplies and materials."

"It's like a chaotic Home Depot," Natalie said. The words burst from her mouth without her permission.

Brian gave Natalie some serious side-eyed before continuing. "For now, it is, but I'm hoping to eventually turn it into a restaurant. The building was built in 1919, and the previous owner did a great job at restoring the bar, but covered up a lot of character pieces in the rest of the space, like the tin-tile ceiling. The kitchen and bathrooms are going to need a total overhaul, but everything else is in pretty good shape. Our last step in this whole project will be to bring it back to its original state as best we can."

Natalie looked around the room in awe, ignoring the boxes of screws and tubes of caulk. "It's going to be incredible." She couldn't fathom someone wanting to cover anything up. Old pubs like this gave off such a comforting feeling.

"Thank you. I think so too," Brian said.

"I'd definitely eat here," Lindy said.

"Well, good. I know nothing about restaurants and hope I can find a good one that will be as excited by this space as I am."

"A space like this deserves something wonderful," Natalie said.

Brian smiled before he led them farther into the pub. "Over here is the back room. The previous owner used this as storage space." Natalie and the Grand Dearies all peeked inside the room while Brian talked. "I haven't decided if we're going to keep this as storage or knock down the walls to make the dining area bigger. It doesn't match up with the aesthetic, but I'm waiting on that decision for later. As I said, the bar is the last area to be touched, since it's mostly cosmetic issues that need to be fixed."

"I don't know, a kitchen and bathroom overhaul sounds like a pretty big job to me," Lindy said. They followed Brian as he led them to the kitchen.

Brian waved her off and said, "By the time my guys get to this kitchen and bathroom remodel, they will be able to do it in their sleep. Remember, we are converting this whole building into apartments."

* * *

When the tour was over, Charlotte gave her grandson a hug. "Brian, we're going to get out of your hair now. You've so much to do. Thank you, sweetie, for taking the time to meet with us. I'll call you later."

Natalie took out her cell phone and requested an Uber. There was one only a few minutes away. She knew she needed to say something to Brian before she left. It was as if she wanted to say everything and nothing all at the same time. Natalie couldn't believe the lengths Brian and Charlotte were willing to go to help her. She decided to simply speak from the heart. "Brian, thank you so much. This really means a lot to me."

Brian nodded at her and walked them outside.

Chapter 4

24 Days till Thanksgiving

Monday morning, Natalie clung to the fact that at least she felt confident about starting her new job. She had the normal new-job nerves but knew she was a good social media manager. Making catchy social media posts had become second nature to her. Being quick on her feet, creative, and having a little sprinkle of ADHD were apparently the perfect combination needed to succeed in her field.

In her last job, she'd worked for a small barbecue restaurant chain. She loved their smoked chicken, but no one ever ordered it, which kind of made sense to her because their ribs were legendary. However, she still thought the chicken needed some love. One day, she ordered a cheap chicken costume and had the chicken sit in the restaurant, sad and alone, drinking a soda. The Sad Chicken video went viral. She made more videos of the Sad Chicken riding the bus, reading a book at the library, and buying wine at the grocery store. The chicken became a mascot for the restaurant, and several new smoked chicken dishes were created to help with its newfound popularity.

When she'd decided to move halfway across the country, she applied for several positions and received four job offers. Everyone wanted to recreate the success she'd had with Sad Chicken. Mom and Pop Soda Brewery won out in the end. They were a small soda company with unique flavors. Their head-quarters—and therefore Natalie's new office—had turned out to be only one tram stop away from her married ex-boyfriend's apartment. Since Natalie hadn't known where she was going to keep her car in a crowded city, this became a big selling point in the soda brewery's favor and the deciding factor in selling her SUV. She'd live close to work, and her married ex-boyfriend had a car, so why did she need hers?

As Natalie got out of her Uber, she looked up at the building in front of her—a modern tower with an all-glass facade. It dazzled so brightly she couldn't look at it for long.

At her last job, her office had been close to the test kitchen, so the air always smelled sweet and smokey. By the looks of this building, she doubted her office would smell like syrup.

She had never worked anywhere big enough that she needed to check in at a front desk to be let up to her floor. This building felt larger and posher than she had been used to. Natalie stepped into the lobby bathroom to collect herself before getting on the elevator. The barbecue company's headquarters were small and attached to a glorified factory. This building had marble floors. She took a second to remind herself that she could do her new job and that she belonged in this building even though the lobby bathroom had the fanciest paper towels she had ever seen. On the elevator ride up, she repeated that she was good at being a social media manager, companies coveted her, and she had a choice of places to work.

An energetic young woman greeted Natalie at the elevator bay when the door opened on her floor. "Good morning, you must be Natalie."

"That's me," Natalie said as the doors closed behind her.

"I'm so excited to meet you. My name's Lisa, and I've been asked to help you get acclimated today and be your tour guide." Lisa started to raise her hand for a handshake, then she changed her mind and let her arm hang down at her side.

Natalie decided to help Lisa out and extend her hand first. "It's nice to meet you, Lisa, and I'm looking forward to working with you."

Lisa enthusiastically shook Natalie's hand. "You might, maybe. That's really up to you. I'm an intern and work with the marketing department. But if you need help, I can be assigned to you. But maybe you won't. I don't want to presume. So, like, no pressure."

The joy radiating from Lisa was infectious, and Natalie couldn't help but smile. "Why don't we start with my office first so I can put my stuff down?"

"OMG, of course. It's this way." Lisa led her through giant double glass doors.

The whole floor had a light and airy feel. All the walls being glass helped with that. Natalie wondered how much window cleaner they went through in a month; it had to be a ton.

Mom and Pop Soda headquarters was not at all what she'd expected. The company's website exploded with color, and Natalie anticipated seeing vibrant hues when she arrived. Instead, she'd walked into a very meditative environment. If it weren't for the logo hanging over the main door in the elevator lobby, Natalie would have thought they were an aromatherapy company or a meditation space.

Natalie thanked Lisa for holding the door to her office open as she walked through. She stood next to her desk to take in the view of downtown. The whole back wall of her office was one giant window.

"Don't worry, it doesn't get hot in here," Lisa said as she took a seat in the visitor chair.

"What? Oh, I didn't even think of that." Natalie said and sat down behind her desk.

"There is some kind of special tinting or something on them. I don't know. All I know is I expected it to be crazy hot up here this summer, and it wasn't at all," Lisa said. "Plus, if it's too bright in here, you can always close the blinds."

"Cool," Natalie said as she looked around and wondered where she should put her purse. She didn't want to get up and put it on the coat rack next to her door, so she opted for a drawer in her desk for the time being. Her office continued the natural feel of the entire floor. She had a tan oak desk, which made the space feel modern, but not cold. There were several tall plants placed around the room, so she didn't feel too exposed by the glass walls, but she still made a mental note not to scratch her butt while in there.

Once her purse was in the drawer, Natalie looked at Lisa. "I think I'm ready to continue the tour."

"Great," Lisa said and charged out of Natalie's office.

As they worked their way around the floor, Lisa stopped several times to introduce Natalie. One of the downsides of starting a new job was learning everyone's names. She wished they all wore nametags.

The rest of the office looked like a Zen paradise. However, the breakroom looked the way Natalie had thought the whole office would: colorful and bright. Glass-door refrigerators full of soda stood along one wall, while on the opposite side of the room was a soda bar with at least fifteen different kinds of drinks on tap.

Lisa opened all the cabinets to show Natalie where everything lived. "This is where the plates and bowls are kept. The soda cups are in the dispenser on the bar, and the extras are kept down below." Lisa pointed to everything like she was a host on a gameshow, showcasing a huge prize.

"Outside of a convenience store, I don't think I've ever seen so much soda," Natalie said as she walked over to the closest refrigerator. She loved how each drink had a unique name, like Zazzle Berry and Tropical Tutti Fruity. The soda name she loved the most was called Marv's Choice. She wondered what that one tasted like. Seeing Marv's Choice gave her so many ideas. What kinds of other things did Marv choose?

"Sometime soon, I want to come back in here and try all the different flavors," Natalie said, admiring the soda bar. Mom and Pop Soda Brewery was a regional brand, and Natalie hadn't been able to try them until now.

Lisa walked over and stood next to Natalie. "I recommend trying only a few at a time and sticking to a flavor theme. When you jump around, you can't tell the difference between Midnight Classic and Soday Pop."

* * *

In the HR office, Natalie signed all her new-hire paperwork and scheduled a meeting to go over her benefits package later that week. She also let them know she might have a lead on an apartment but would let them know if she needed the number of a real estate agent.

Lisa gave a very thorough tour. Everyone Natalie met seemed very friendly. Based on first impressions, this company seemed like a good fit for her.

En route back to Natalie's office, a tall, older curvaceous woman with kind eyes greeted them both in the hallway. "Good morning, Lisa, and you must be Natalie." The woman extended a perfectly manicured hand to Natalie. "I'm Donna, the Director of Marketing. It's nice to finally meet you in person."

Natalie shook Donna's hand and marveled at how confident she appeared. She had video-chatted with her new boss several times before being hired, but a screen didn't do Donna's perfect posture any justice.

"Likewise," Natalie said.

Donna looked at Lisa. "I can take it from here."

Lisa nodded and headed toward the marketing department, which was located on the other side of the floor.

"I wanted to get you an office closer to the marketing department, but none were available," Donna said as she pointed in the direction Lisa had walked. "I don't want you to feel like you aren't a part of the team, because you are. We're all glad you're here."

"Don't worry about it. Walking over there will give me a reason to stand and stretch my legs. I already feel so welcome," Natalie responded.

"Good," Donna said.

Donna walked with Natalie to her new office. Once there, they had the usual get-to-know-you chat. Natalie learned Donna and her wife owned three corgis.

"I don't have any pets." Natalie thought about how she barely had the capacity to keep herself fed, much less take care of another living creature. And if she were being honest with herself, Lindy was the one making sure she was eating and staying hydrated. "Maybe someday."

"I couldn't live without mine," Donna said. She checked her watch. "Let's talk shop for a little bit."

Donna proceeded to fill Natalie in on the different people in the marketing department and the role each of them played. "I'm not sure who you met during your tour, but you'll meet your team today during lunch."

"Great, I look forward to getting to know everyone," Natalie said. She opened the notes app on her phone before asking, "Who has been putting together your social media schedule?"

"There's been no schedule. As I'm sure you have seen, our social media presence is inconsistent at best. There are so many platforms out there that posting has been an afterthought. It's started to take more time than my team can spare," Donna said, crossing her legs.

"Plus, there is the engagement aspect," Natalie said.

"Exactly. We have found there is way more to posting on social media than just throwing something out there," Donna replied.

"I am glad to see you understand the scope of my position," Natalie said. Donna had been a major factor in why she'd picked Mom and Pop Soda. A few of the places she had interviewed had impossible expectations. However, Donna knew they'd be building their presence from the ground up, which would take some time.

"We've been overwhelmed and are glad you are here to take it over," Donna said. "Have you had time to turn your computer on yet?"

"No, but I can," Natalie said, and pushed the power button.

"I am going to have you pull up our drive, so you can see what we have been up to." Donna guided Natalie through the login process and their folder system.

Until it was time to meet the rest of the team, Donna gave Natalie an overview of the current and upcoming marketing campaigns.

After lunch, Lisa led Natalie back to her office and filled her in on the next phase of the tour, which was to drive to the soda kitchen and bottling facility. "It's about an hour away from corporate, so I vote we stop by the bathrooms before we head downstairs," Lisa said while opening Natalie's office door.

"I'm on board with this plan." Natalie took her purse from her desk. "That's a hefty drive when you want to visit the factory." She made a mental note that without a car, she'd never be able to visit the bottling factory alone.

"Yeah, it's a trek," Lisa said as they headed to the bathroom.

* * *

Being in a car with someone she didn't know well could have been awkward, but Lisa was easy to talk to and Natalie enjoyed her chattiness.

"This is my first job after college, and I think I'm pretty lucky to get an internship that pays a livable wage," Lisa said. "I know I'm just an intern, but I feel like I'm really part of the team."

"That's awesome," Natalie replied. "During my first internship, I felt like an indentured servant. I learned a lot, but I wasn't paid, and several people took advantage. When they offered me a full-time position, it was the easiest no I ever gave."

"I have a friend who is feeling that way now," Lisa said.

Lisa exited the highway and drove through the outskirts of the city. The GPS said they were still forty-five minutes away. It took all of Natalie's self-control not to pull out her cell phone to see if any restaurants had returned her calls about private dining room availability for Thanksgiving. So far, she had had no luck.

"I know you are new to town. If you need any help settling in, I'm happy to offer my assistance. Since your housing fell through, I can call apartment buildings and look for availabilities," Lisa said.

Natalie's ears perked up. "I think I have an apartment lined up. I should know this evening." She really wanted to ask for help in finding a restaurant, but they had just talked about interns being taken advantage of. She didn't want Lisa to feel uncomfortable, but she also could use her help. "I do have one project that I could use some assistance with. But there is no pressure to say yes. If you say no, it's not a big deal."

"Just depends on what it is," Lisa said, shrugging her shoulders.

"I'm supposed to be hosting my whole family for Thanksgiving. The place I had lined up fell through. Now I'm desperately trying to find a restaurant with a private dining room. I've called a ton of places already, and everything is booked up. Would you mind helping me call different restaurants?" Natalie asked.

Lisa scrunched her face up, and Natalie knew she should have only asked the intern to help with work stuff. "I'd love to help, but you're going to be hard-pressed to find anything available on Thanksgiving. We are a destination location for Thanksgiving because of the Turkey Trot."

Natalie looked at Lisa. "What's the Turkey Trot?"

"It's a big marathon that's held every year by the river. People dress up as turkeys and, you know, run," Lisa said.

"I thought every city had a Thanksgiving run."

"They do, and if there are costumes, it is because of us. We were the first and are by far the biggest. This place goes wild for Thanksgiving. Hotels are booked up at least a year in advance."

Natalie slumped down in her seat and looked out the window, completely dumbfounded. In all her research, how had she not known she'd moved to Thanksgivingpalooza?

Jenny had already started texting her, telling her how it wouldn't be a big deal to move Thanksgiving to their house and how she'd be happy to host on Natalie's behalf. Jenny had even suggested they could be cohosts, since Natalie couldn't do it on her own. Natalie figured Jenny would show up with a T-shirt saying, *Savior of Thanksgiving*.

Hearing Lisa talk about all the events that went on around the city felt like the death blow to Natalie's plans of hosting. There was no way she'd find a location that could hold her whole family so close to Thanksgiving. Continuing with the charade of pulling this off was pointless. Natalie had lost, and she could add this L to the growing list of things that had gone wrong with her move.

Natalie took a deep breath. Admitting defeat needed to wait until she got home from Brian's that night. Right now, she needed to focus on her new job. She pushed all her thoughts about her family to the side and asked Lisa more questions about Mom and Pop Soda.

CHAPTER 5

When they got back to the office, Natalie barely had time to gather all her things before the Montrose Retirement Village shuttle bus arrived to pick her up from work. The bus was parked at the curb when she exited the building. Inside, waiting patiently, were Aunt Lindy and Charlotte. As soon as Natalie stepped on board, they inundated her with questions about work. Natalie felt like a kid coming home from the first day of school.

"I thought you might be peckish, so I brought you a snack," Lindy said, and handed her a baggie of baby carrots and a stick of string cheese.

Natalie did a little shoulder dance as she took the baggie and started to eat the carrots. "Work is going to be great. Everyone seems so nice. I've already got a million ideas, and I didn't cry once today."

Lindy and Charlotte both erupted in cheers.

"That's marvelous news. You're so clever! They're lucky to have you," Lindy said.

"Thank you, that means a lot. It's nice to know there's one area of my life that isn't a disaster right now," Natalie said.

They wanted to know all the details, and Natalie was happy to oblige. She told them about everything from the breakroom to the soda kitchen at the bottling facility. She'd just finished telling the Grand Dearies about the labeling machine when they pulled up to Brian's building. Henry Valley was in the bar again and ran out to greet them.

"The lovely ladies are back," Henry said as he held the building door open. Lindy and Charlotte swooned over his compliment. "Brian is upstairs waiting on you. Do you remember how to get there?"

Charlotte patted Henry's upper arm and said, "We do, thank you, kind sir."

As they walked to the elevator, Charlotte linked arms with Natalie and whispered, "I love younger men." Natalie smiled at this idea and hoped when she was Charlotte's age, she'd flirt with younger men too.

The apartment door was open, and a light was on inside. As soon as Charlotte walked into the room, Brian started talking. "Okay, Gigi, here are the options for tiles for the bathroom and backsplash." He didn't even bother with a hello. He was clearly focused on getting these decisions made as quickly as possible. He had set up a makeshift table with plywood and sawhorses in the dining area.

The difference in the apartment's appearance since they'd last been there was like night and day. The layers of dust were almost completely gone. The toilet had been installed in the bathroom, and neat piles of tile were stacked around the room. Even so, the state of the apartment today still did not look like it could be finished in two weeks.

Natalie and Lindy hung back in what Natalie thought would become the living room area while Charlotte went to inspect Brian's offerings. "What color of grout are you going to use?" Charlotte asked.

"Grey," Brian answered.

"Hmm, what shade of grey?" Charlotte asked, picking up one of the tiles.

"Gigi—stop! We're not going to nitpick this whole project. I'm not going over budget on this. It's a standard grey that matches everything. It's what I have, and I'm not buying anything else," Brian scolded.

Charlotte held her hands up in submission. "I hear you. Grey sounds lovely." She motioned for Natalie to come over to the table. "I'm thinking the hexagon tiles. The big ones for the shower, and the small ones for the kitchen backsplash. What do you think?"

All eyes focused on Natalie. Brian was doing her a huge favor, and Natalie was grateful for anything. As a renter, she didn't feel comfortable giving her opinion. But it so happened that Charlotte's picks were her favorites too. Natalie said to Brian, "Those work for me. I also like all the tiles. Whatever is easiest is what I like."

"Hexagon is fine," Brian said, rubbing the back of his neck. Natalie had a feeling he'd have sounded put out by any of the decisions made. She wondered how many phone calls he'd received from Charlotte over the weekend about this apartment. He motioned for them to follow him to the kitchen. "Tell me what faucets you like."

Charlotte picked out brass faucets and light fixtures. In all honestly, all the options were beautiful. Natalie could only imagine what his finished work looked like if these were the leftovers from other projects.

"What about window coverings? When will those be installed?" Charlotte asked.

Brian glared at his grandmother. "They won't be. I'm ordering for the whole building at the end of the project."

Charlotte was rubbing all his nerves, and she did not seem to care. "Can you please measure the windows for us so we can figure out curtains?"

Brian patted down his body and looked around the room. "I must've left my measuring tape downstairs. Hold on." He got his phone out and sent a quick text.

Within a few minutes, Henry strode into the apartment waving the tape measure. Brian thanked him and walked with Charlotte to the main window to start measuring.

Natalie turned to Lindy. "This apartment is going to be amazing, but I don't know how I'm going to furnish it. I have savings, but the idea of blowing it all right now makes me so nervous."

Henry was walking out of the apartment when he stopped in his tracks. "My mother's church is having their annual rummage sale at the end of the week. They'll have everything from dishes to bedding, and especially furniture. It's open to church members for a presale on Friday and then the public the next day. I bet I can even get you in at the end of the presale. That is, if you don't mind waiting till all the church members have gone through."

Natalie looked at Lindy and let out a little squeal. A rummage sale sounded perfect and could really save her bank account.

"I don't mind at all. Thank you, Henry. And if I can't get in early, that's okay too. I appreciate the heads-up."

"Yeah, no problem. I'll call her and let you know what she says." Henry checked his watch. "You ladies have a great rest of your night. I'm heading home." He waved at them and walked out of the apartment.

"Well, that's a stroke of luck. Now you have two unexpected things that have gone in your favor—this apartment and being able to furnish it. You know good things come in threes," Lindy said as she gently bumped Natalie with her shoulder.

"I'm not pushing it. I'm happy with two," Natalie replied.

After Charlotte and Brian finished measuring the bedroom, Natalie ushered the ladies to the hall so they could leave. Brian followed silently, clearly needing a break from all the questions. Once downstairs, Lindy and Charlotte decided to stop in the bathroom before their Uber arrived. Natalie leaned against the wall while Brian messed around on his phone. As she looked around, her eyes landed on the door to the bar.

Natalie walked over to the glass door, trying not to put her nose directly against it.

Brian put his phone away and asked curtly, "What are you looking at?" She wasn't a fan of his tone but figured he had already hit his patience quota for the day.

"Your bar. It's empty," Natalie said with her face still glued to the door.

"That's very observant of you," Brian said.

"And it will be empty for Thanksgiving," Natalie said.

Brian stepped forward and stood next to Natalie. "And the Thanksgiving after that. What are we looking at?"

Natalie took a deep breath in and said, "I need to borrow your pub."

"What?" Brian folded his arms across his chest.

"For Thanksgiving," Natalie said. She stepped back and stood squarely in front of him.

"I don't understand what is happening."

"You told us the other day the bar was in good shape. You were just going to do cosmetic changes. I see the tables and chairs in the back all stacked up. All that needs to be done is to reorganize the boxes and piles of stuff. And give everything a good deep cleaning," Natalie stated matter-of-factly.

Brian narrowed his eyes at her. "I'm not pulling my crew away to clean the bar up. I'm already doing that for your apartment. Also, the bathrooms in the bar are unusable."

Natalie knew she'd pushed the line, but people did crazy things when they were desperate. Having Brian frustrated with her was better than cohosting Thanksgiving with Jenny.

"I'll do it. I'm great at organizing. Plus, there's plenty of room in the storage to hold all this stuff. I can come over after work and on the weekends. As far as bathrooms go, there's one off the manager's office that Lindy and Charlotte are using right now, and my apartment will have a working bathroom by then," Natalie pleaded.

He took a deep breath through his nose before saying, "I know where everything is. You can't shove it all into the back room. I need to be able to access those materials."

"I won't shove the boxes willy-nilly. In the end, you'll have a great system that works better than what you have right now." Natalie almost believed what she said. With her organizational skills, she knew she'd come up with an efficient system for him, but she didn't know for sure if it would be better.

Brian furrowed his brows. "Even if you move everything out of the way, there is still so much grime on everything. There's no way this space is gonna be ready by Thanksgiving with just you cleaning it. Everything needs to be scrubbed down."

Natalie was frantic now. "Brian, I need this more than you can imagine. I know you are going out of your way to make the apartment work, and I am so thankful. But I didn't ask you to do that. I promise I'll stay out of your way, and I'm not going to ask another single thing of you. You won't even know I'm here. What's the harm in letting me try?"

She watched his face. Even though he rolled his eyes, Natalie knew she had won him over.

"Fine," he said. "But you can't ask me or my crew to help with anything."

She held three fingers up in the air. "Scout's honor." Natalie had no idea if that was the actual gesture or not, but it was close enough to count.

"Fine," Brian scoffed as he threw his hands up and walked away from the bar door.

Charlotte and Lindy approached and stood on either side of Natalie. "What's fine?" Charlotte asked.

Natalie straightened her back and said, "I'm going to host Thanksgiving here."

"Oh, what a marvelous idea!" Aunt Lindy exclaimed.

The three women huddled together and brainstormed a checklist of everything that needed to be done.

Brian rolled his eyes as he held the front door open for them. No one seemed to mind that he didn't wait with them on the street for the Uber. They were too wrapped in their plans to even care.

Chapter 6

23 Days till Thanksgiving

Moving to a city that had excellent public transportation was a real bonus for Natalie, especially since she didn't have a car. But living in a retirement village on the outskirts of said city without a walkable bus stop in sight was starting to wear thin. Plus, she could only reserve the shuttle if a resident would also be using it, and even then, there were no guarantees one would be available, since Montrose was full of active retirees. Furnishing a whole apartment and paying for rides to work every day were two things Natalie hadn't factored into her original budget.

Now that the dust had started to settle, Natalie needed to get serious about her finances. Charlotte had negotiated with Brian that she could live in the apartment for a reasonable rate, but no one had actually mentioned numbers. Tuesday morning, before she reached out to Brian to discuss her rent, she did some research. Natalie knew apartments in the downtown area were way out of her budget, and she took that into consideration when calculating what she was willing to pay. She looked at comparable apartments and came up with a number she thought was fair and not too far off from the lower asking range.

Since this would be her apartment, she had decided to take over asking the questions. Charlotte gave her a list of things to find out, and Natalie pared it back to the need-to-know questions. She sent Brian a text about her potential rent and was prepared to back up her number, but he just replied with "Okay." There was no feedback at all. No *that seems fair*, or *that's too low*, or *you are overpaying*. Just *Okay*. In fact, every text response from him that day had been one word, and it drove Natalie bonkers. She knew she it bugged him when she sent him so many texts, but it was his fault. If he bothered to elaborate on any of her replies, she'd have fewer questions. When she sent him a text message with two questions, and he replied *Yes*, it almost drove her over the edge. Natalie wanted to scream.

Natalie had told Lindy she'd get a ride after work. She needed to make a stop at Target to pick up a few things before she went to the bar to put together an organizational plan and cleaning schedule. The idea of going to Target filled her with joy. All this upheaval in her life had worn on her, and she longed for a little slice of normalcy. Target was the perfect solution.

The minute she got the text from Charlotte telling her she had made arrangements for Natalie's after-work transportation, Natalie felt a twinge of annoyance. She appreciated the kind gesture, but for one evening, she wanted to feel like an average adult doing normal adult things. A thirty-four-year-old woman getting a ride from a retirement home shuttle was not normal.

Natalie stopped in her tracks as she exited the building that evening. Instead of seeing the familiar Montrose bus, there was Brian, standing next to his truck. The wind blew some of his hair into his face, and when he tossed his head back, he looked like he was posing for a photo shoot. She tried so hard to keep the annoyance she felt from showing on her face. Fingers crossed, she hoped the smile she plastered on masked her frustration. Not once during their last excruciating text exchange did Brian mention he'd be picking her up. If he had, she would have told him not to bother, and she'd be sitting in the back of a comfortable rideshare right now instead of walking toward a man whom she was pretty sure—based on their texts—disliked her as much as she disliked him.

Before opening her mouth and saying something she might regret, she reminded herself this man, who might be a terrible communicator, had bent over backward to help her out. After she got her mind right, she said, "I wasn't expecting to see you here."

Brian leaned against his truck with his arms crossed and a scowl on his face. He practically growled, "I wasn't planning on being here. But Gigi insisted I pick you up and take you to the store before heading back to the apartment building."

"You don't have to do this. I can get another ride." Natalie reached for her purse to dig her phone out.

"Tell that to Gigi. Also, I didn't bring you a snack, because you are an adult." Brian abruptly headed to the driver's side.

Natalie got in the truck without saying a word. The energy radiating off Brian didn't inspire her to try any kind of small talk. She wanted to tell him this wasn't how she wanted to spend her evening either. The night she had been daydreaming about now wasn't going to happen at all. She'd no longer be able to leisurely peruse the aisles and ponder which set of felt-tip pens she wanted. She wouldn't be able to check out what the elastic-waist pant options looked like, or deliberate which kind of candy to buy that wasn't shaped like a ribbon or had an annoying little wrapper. The very last thing she wanted to do was shop with a man.

Brian's silent treatment continued into the store, which was fine with her. Natalie snagged a cart and went straight to the office supply area. The first item on her list was a notebook. Natalie loved notebooks of any kind, but the pretty ones held a special place in her heart. Her eyes lit up when she saw the variety of decorative options available. Natalie picked up one to see how it felt and to check out the weight of the paper.

Brian didn't bother walking into the aisle. He just stood in the main thoroughfare, looking at her. "I have notebooks," he said in a curt tone.

"But I want my own notebook," Natalie said, deciding between two hard-cover, spiralbound options.

He picked up a small spiral notebook from the end cap with a black cover. "This one's only a dollar."

"But this one is prettier," Natalie said as she held up the floral-covered notebook she had decided on. She didn't bother looking at him for his reaction. She simply headed to the pen section.

As Natalie stood in front of the display, she took a few seconds to decide if she wanted a pack of colorful pens or just black ones.

"Here," Brian said, tossing a pack of cheap ballpoints at her.

She barely had time to turn and catch the package. Those were her least favorite pens. "Thank you, but no thank you. I don't like this kind," Natalie said, and she returned them to their original location.

"It's a pen. What's not to like?" Brian asked.

Natalie took a deep breath and said, "I don't like how my handwriting looks when I use those. I like these pens." She walked a few steps and picked up a pack of colorful felt-tips. She couldn't remember asking for Brian's opinion.

"You don't like how your handwriting looks?" Brian scowled.

"My handwriting is better suited to thicker ink. I don't have a delicate script." Natalie had always thought her handwriting could pass as a computer font when she used a felt-tip pen.

"You have too much time on your hands," he said as he furrowed his brows.

Natalie wondered why men felt this way. For some reason, they thought women couldn't be productive and make observations at the same time. "I do not. I am simply observant."

"I'm observant. You're obsessive." Brian took a step closer to her.

Natalie stood up straighter to stand her ground. "Just because I enjoy details doesn't make me obsessive. I won't be much longer. You can wait in the car."

Brian crossed his arms. "I don't know that for sure. If I leave you alone, you'll end up walking up and down every aisle, and I'll never get home tonight."

Her blood was really boiling now. "I didn't ask you to be here, and I don't appreciate your tone."

Brian took another step and leaned in. "I wouldn't have a tone if I'd been able to get anything done today. Instead, I had to answer seven thousand questions every five minutes."

Natalie mimicked his body language. "It was eighteen questions that could have been combined into three if you had bothered to elaborate on a single one of your answers."

Brian moved closer. She was tall, but he was taller. "I don't have time to write novels."

"I don't need novels." She poked his chest with her finger. "But if you'd use full fucking sentences, I wouldn't constantly have to ask for clarification." Natalie threw her pens in the cart and stormed off. She noticed out of the corner of her eye he was rubbing his chest. She hoped she left a bruise.

After hiding in the lightbulb section for a few minutes to regulate her breathing, she was finally ready to finish her list. She didn't want to seem ungrateful, but she found herself feeding off his crotchety attitude. After what her married ex-boyfriend had put her through, she wasn't the biggest fan of men, and Brian hadn't helped their cause today.

She made her way to the cleaning product aisle, and Brian remained out of sight. Natalie didn't know what all she might need, but getting a few of her favorite staples was a good start. She'd take stock tonight and have the rest delivered the next day.

Natalie jumped when she heard, "I'm sorry." She spun around, and there was Brian.

"I'm also sorry for scaring you just now," he said.

Natalie took a deep breath. "It's okay."

"Today was a rough day. Everything seemed to go wrong. Yes, you sent a lot of texts. And you are right. If I had taken a few extra seconds to answer them, there would've been fewer. I shouldn't have taken it out on you this evening." Brian took a hesitant step in her direction. He looked sincere, and Natalie believed he was sorry.

"I'm sorry too. You've been going above and beyond to help out a total stranger. A lot has happened in my life recently, and apparently, my fuse has shortened because of that. How about we start over?" She extended her hand. "Hi, I'm Natalie. I'm Lindy's great-niece."

Brian smiled and shook her hand. "Hi, my name's Brian, and I'm Charlotte's grandson."

"So, the Grand Dearies tell me you have an awesome apartment I'll be renting." Natalie pushed the cart slowly.

Brian followed along and chuckled. "I love that name for them, and I hope you like the apartment."

"I don't see how I couldn't. From what I can tell so far, it's going to be awesome when you are all done. You should be proud of yourself."

"Honestly, finishing your apartment has given us all a new sense of excitement about the project. It's giving us a glimpse of the completed product."

Natalie stopped the cart and looked at him. "See, one man's trash is another man's treasure. My life crumbling down around me turned into a blessing for you. Not only do you get to spend time with me, but you get a sneak peek into your future."

Brian rolled his eyes. "You're funny. But I am sorry to hear about what happened. Gigi filled me in a little bit. That sucks."

"It does, but it's getting better." Natalie commenced pushing the cart again. "I think I'll like my new job. And spending this much time with Aunt Lindy has been fantastic. I've missed having her nearby. So, you know, no rain, no rainbow."

"That's good, I guess. Hey, let me know if you want me to key his car for you. You don't even have to be there. I'll take Henry as my lookout."

"That's even nicer than redoing an apartment for me."

Instead of heading to self-checkout, Natalie went to the clothing section, and the first thing she saw was a display of sweatpants.

Brian's brow furrowed. "Oh god, what's going on here?"

"Don't worry." Natalie hurriedly picked out a pair of sweatpants in her size. "This is the last thing on my list. I need more elastic-waist pants in my life."

* * *

Even though Brian had insisted on paying for the cleaning products, Natalie didn't let him. He was already doing so much for her. Footing the bill seemed like the right thing to do.

"You can get this round of supplies, but the rest of them are on me," Brian said as he looked over his shoulder to back out of the parking space. "I'll need them eventually anyway. Give me the remainder of your list, and Henry will send a crew member out tomorrow to get everything."

Natalie reluctantly acquiesced. "Fine. I'm not going to quibble about who buys what. But I prefer certain scents."

"Of course you do. Send me the list, and I'll try to get your extra-smelly products," Brian said.

Natalie breathed through her nose loud enough that she was sure Brian noticed. "They are, in fact, the opposite. They do not have an astringent chemical smell. And I prefer citrus scents. I like lemon more than orange, but I'll settle for grapefruit. Most floral scents are overbearing and make my eyes water."

Brian gripped the steering wheel tighter. "You've over-thought this way too much."

"I like what I like, and there's nothing wrong with that," Natalie said, feeling assertive.

Brian stared at the road. Natalie crossed her arms and looked out the passenger window. She wondered where their goodwill from earlier had gone.

Not a word was spoken until they pulled up to the building and Natalie said, "If you don't mind coming in and telling me what's in all the boxes, I can take it from there."

Brian put the truck in park. "Fine."

A new notebook and pen were a great, if not better, combo than peanut butter and jelly. Simply holding both items made Natalie's heart skip a beat. Brian walked around the bar telling her what was in each of the boxes, and she wrote down everything he said. In the margins, she made little sketches of the boxes' layout, and if she needed to, she took pictures so she wouldn't forget what went together.

Thankfully, all the weighty items were already stacked neatly in the storeroom. Natalie looked around the room and saw several shelving units were underutilized. Everything from the bar could easily fit in the backroom. The problem was, no one had taken the time to put anything away efficiently.

"This isn't as bad as I thought," Natalie said as she made her final note of the night.

Brian looked at her in complete shock. "Did you just see what I saw?"

"All my attention to detail that you've scoffed at all evening makes me good at organizing things. I've already started figuring out a system. Tonight, I'll put together a spreadsheet and be ready to jump right in tomorrow," Natalie said. She pulled her phone out, called for a car, and packed her stuff up.

"If you're done for the night, I'll go ahead and take you on back," Brian said as he patted himself down, looking for his keys.

"No need, my ride will be here in a few minutes. I also can get myself here after work. Despite what Charlotte says, I'm fine." Natalie threw her bag over her shoulder. "What time do you normally leave in the evening? So I can figure out my schedule."

"Don't worry about that. Henry opens the building, and I close it. I like having the place to myself at night. It allows me to see what we got done and what needs to be completed the next day." Brian checked his watch. "If you don't need a ride, I'm gonna go start my rounds."

Brian turned and walked away. Natalie couldn't figure him out, and she didn't care to. Any pestering thoughts of what it would be like to have him as a landlord, she pushed aside. She'd save those thoughts for after Thanksgiving.

Chapter 7

22 Days till Thanksgiving

During her lunch break on Wednesday, Natalie gathered all her notes from the previous night, the spreadsheet she had created, and the Thanksgiving to-do list. As she lay all the elements out in a logical order, everything came together. Things would be slightly different than her family's traditional Thanksgiving, yet not too far off. To her surprise, it looked like Natalie had plenty of time to get everything done and could even add in some extra days, just in case she fell behind a bit.

Jenny would have to eat her words.

Her sister-in-law had been sending daily texts ever since Natalie decided to go ahead with hosting. Susan created a group chat between Jenny, Natalie, and herself. Having both Jenny and her mom continuously ask if she was sure she could handle everything fueled her fire to make it the biggest and best Thanksgiving her family had ever seen. Or at least make sure it was up to their normal, near-perfect family standard.

Natalie's grandmother had coined the phrase 'Berry Perfect'—Berry after her maiden name. When anyone used the phrase, everyone in the family knew what it meant. Whatever party you were hosting or holiday you were decorating for, if it was to be Berry Perfect, it needed to be as close to perfect as a human could get. The standard of perfection being, could what you were working on be showcased in a women's magazine? Natalie could see how to some people, maintaining this standard might be off-putting, but her family found it an enjoyable challenge.

After Natalie made the final tweaks to the official Thanksgiving Family Weekend Prep Calendar, she sent a screenshot to prove she had thought of everything.

Her mother replied, *This looks great, and so doable.*

Jenny's response was in line with her character: *Did you attach the menu?*

Natalie rolled her eyes so hard. Of course Jenny couldn't give a compliment. Natalie didn't bother responding right away; it could wait till after work. After glancing at the clock, she realized she had a meeting in a few minutes.

She noticed Lisa walking toward her office. Natalie hastily shoved the last two bites of her lunch in her mouth, stood up, and grabbed her notebook. As she opened her office door, she regretted her large mouthful.

Lisa looked at Natalie's notebook and said, "I've been meaning to ask if you want a laptop. IT can get you one."

Natalie continued to chew. She waved her hand, trying to indicate she was fine with her notebook. Then she tried to charade that she was chewing.

"I know, I saw you. Your walls are glass," Lisa responded.

A flush crept over Natalie's cheeks. Obviously, Lisa saw her take those last huge bites. She wondered who else had noticed.

When the last remnants of lunch were finally swallowed, she said, "I was so in the zone, I forgot everyone could see me. I'm going to have to remember that going forward."

"What were you working on?" Lisa asked as they headed to the meeting.

"Just planning out my Thanksgiving to-do list. For my family, it is *THE* holiday," Natalie said.

"That's cool. We always just head to my grandma's."

Natalie held the door to the conference room for Lisa. They were the first ones to arrive, and she scanned the room for where to sit. She didn't want to be in someone's usual spot by accident. "We used to go to my parents', then my parents sold their house. Now we all take turns hosting. I picked the first year because I wanted to continue with as many of the family traditions as possible. I know things are going to change, but I thought I could ease us into the change." After realizing she was overthinking the seating situation, she opted for a chair that gave her a view of the door. Lisa plopped down in the seat next to her.

"What kind of traditions are you wanting to hold onto?"

"We always have over-the-top elaborate centerpieces." Natalie swiveled around and admired how Lisa had gracefully tucked her feet up in her seat before continuing. "And my grandmother started making these activity packets for everyone. They are filled with holiday word searches and coloring pages. Everything that'd make your elementary school heart sing. Plus, there's a fun-facts sheet that is personalized for each person, with silly bits of trivia they might find interesting. Everything is handwritten, and we draw little pictures that go along with the theme of the fact sheet. The packets are always a big surprise, and no one knows what will be in them each year."

Lisa looked at Natalie with her mouth agape. "I wish my family did things like that. That sounds so nice."

"It's a lot of fun. The best part is watching the grown men of my family race through the word searches to see who can finish the fastest. Or the coloring. I really love seeing adults enthralled by a coloring page. The bags are one of my favorite family traditions," Natalie said and tilted her head. "That and the place cards. In case you can't tell, my family is super extra, and so we also do these handwritten place cards. Your name is in calligraphy at the top, and there are reasons why the family is thankful for you listed below. Things like that help make the holiday feel extra special. I want to keep them going; I want my mom to feel like she can pass the torch."

"All those things sound sweet," Lisa said.

"They are sweet. What about your family? Do you have traditions?" Natalie asked.

"Do football and naps count?"

"They absolutely do," Natalie said as others joined them in the room.

Donna led an efficient meeting. Each member of the team gave updates about the projects they were working on. When it was Natalie's turn to share, she filled them in on how she put together a posting schedule for each social media platform and what types of content they'd post on each. She mentioned how so far customer engagement over the holiday flavors seemed promising before proposing a new idea.

"I've found creating a persona for a brand has helped get followers. If people like the character, then they want updates on that person's journey," Natalie said.

"I felt that way about Sad Chicken," Donna said as she leaned back in her chair.

"Exactly. In this case, I'm thinking about doing something with Marv. I see him as a get-off-my-lawn kind of guy with a heart of gold. We know Marv likes his Marv's Choice. I think we could explore other things Marv would choose," Natalie said.

She looked around the room and received nothing but blank stares.

"You mean, he's going to be mean?" a teammate asked. Natalie had this person's name on the tip of her tongue and made a mental note to ask Lisa for it after the meeting.

"No. Well, kind of. More like grouchy. Marv is going to be aimed at a younger generation, Lisa's generation. Oddly, they appreciate the old-man aesthetic and lifestyle. Plus, they welcome a good-hearted roasting." Natalie hoped what she said made sense to the rest of the team. She hadn't worked with this many people before.

"It's true, we do." Lisa acknowledged.

"I'm intrigued," Donna said.

Natalie was relieved, because her opinion mattered the most.

Donna added, "If Marv becomes popular, that could drive sales to the soda merch shop. We have a backstock of Marv's Choice socks. Maybe this could help move some of that product."

"Great," Natalie said. "Is it all right if I snag Lisa to help me with this, since she is our target demographic for this campaign?"

"That works for me as long as it works for Lisa," Donna said.

Lisa replied without hesitation, "Works for me."

"Love it. Get the ball rolling on this and keep me posted," Donna said.

After the meeting adjourned, Natalie and Lisa went to the breakroom to try more soda. "Which one is your favorite?" Natalie asked as she looked at the different flavors.

"I used to be a Toffee-tastic girly, but now I think it's too sweet. Last fall, they had a cinnamon flavor that tasted just like Red Hots. It was amazing. I really want them to bring that one back someday. But on a day-to-day basis, I reach for Marv's Choice. It's refreshing."

"It is good. I'm interested in trying this year's peppermint cream soda. I love peppermint ice cream. I'm hoping the drink will be similar," Natalie said as she filled her cup with Lime Twister.

Earlier, she had sat in her office longing to be outside on such a picnic-perfect kind of day. Maybe she and Lisa could take advantage of the weather now. "Would you be interested in talking about the Marv's Choice stuff outside? It's so nice out, it's a shame to be inside."

"That sounds great. Let me get my jacket," Lisa said.

The two women reconvened at the elevator. Natalie had loaded her bag with all kinds of office supplies for their outdoor meeting. The courtyard in front of the building had several tables nestled in among the raised garden beds full of mums and pansies. Her favorite part about the courtyard was that while modern, it still reminded her of a garden from one of the many British period shows she loved to watch. Lisa picked a table in the sun, and Natalie unpacked her bag.

"You brought the whole office with you," Lisa mused.

"I like having options. Plus, it's better to have lots of things. You never know what you might need," Natalie said as she lined up a variety of pens next to a stack of Post-it notes and several highlighters.

She opened her notebook and said, "First things first. For this Marv idea to work, we need a Marv. Preferably someone who works for the company. This way, we have easy access to them when we want to take pictures. We need someone who can be available for content creation days."

Lisa put her elbows on the table and rested her chin in her hands. "You're talking an older guy."

"Yes. Everyone knows the soda is named after the owner's grandfather, so he needs to be a grandfather type." Natalie had met a lot of people at the company so far, but she couldn't see any of them as Marv.

"We could always ask the owner," Lisa said.

"I thought about that. But he's so bubbly. I don't think anyone will believe he's grumpy." Natalie picked up an orange leaf that had fallen on the table and spun the stem between her fingers. The first person to come to her mind was Brian. He was grouchy, but he wasn't a grandpa. Henry was a grandpa, but he didn't work for the company. However, Henry had the perfect look. Natalie paused on that idea.

Yes, in an ideal world, if the Marv model worked for Mom and Pop Soda Brewery, it would be convenient—but not necessary. If they could talk Henry into it, with enough preparation, they could get tons of content.

"Okay, I might know someone. He's nice and has the exact look I am thinking about. From what I can tell, he's a pretty outgoing guy, so he might be into this," Natalie said.

"Do you have a pic?" Lisa asked.

"No, but I can get one tonight. He's renovating the building I'm going to live in. And I'm headed there after work to start cleaning up the ground floor pub for my family's Thanksgiving." Natalie clicked her tongue a few times before saying, "I feel like I need a bribe. Do you have a favorite bakery or cookie shop? I think sweet treats will be needed for this ask." She unlocked her phone to look up any suggestions Lisa might have.

"I love Sugar and Spice Bakery. They have the best cupcakes, but their cookies are also good, and so are their doughnuts. And I really love their rolls. Basically, anything from there is a win," Lisa said.

As soon as Natalie pressed enter, the bakery popped up in her search. On every platform, this place had five stars. The address looked very familiar, and Natalie realized it was only a few doors down from her apartment building. This would be dangerous once she moved in, but would work out perfectly for tonight. She could easily pop in there on her way to clean up the bar.

"The bakery is insanely close to my new apartment," she said while reading reviews.

"For reals? You have to bring us baked goods from there when you move in. You're so lucky! That location is such a fun part of the city," Lisa said.

Hearing that, Natalie wondered if she had miscalculated her assessment of the apartment's worth. She wondered what Brian could have rented it for, if he hadn't given her a friends-and-family discount. "A grandson of a family friend is remodeling a building there, and I'm staying in one of the apartments. It's a construction zone right now, but at least it's an apartment and not a couch in a retirement home."

Lisa laughed. "I think I'd do well in a retirement home. I really love jigsaw puzzles."

"There is a lady who works on one every single day. Now, let's get back to business. We need to start brainstorming the Marv character and the different things he might like," Natalie said, uncapping her pen.

By the end of their meeting, they each had their marching orders. Lisa was going to scout out potential photoshoot locations, and Natalie would start drafting the different posts and create the logo they'd use.

* * *

That evening, getting from work to the apartment took no time at all. A tram stop stood directly in front of Sugar and Spice Bakery. Natalie could see herself going in there all the time if the bakery turned out to be as tasty as Lisa said it was.

She smelled the sugar in the air as soon as she got off the tram. The bakery had a warm, inviting glow about it. She loved the elaborate Thanksgiving scene painted on the front window. The display case that ran the length of the room had corresponding decorations on top of it, and there were pumpkin centerpieces on the few tables scattered here and there. She felt like was walking into a little autumn hug.

Natalie pulled a ticket from the number dispenser and waited her turn. There weren't many people in front of her, so she had a nice view of the display case. Everything looked so good. Once they called her number, she walked up to the counter.

A jovial young man with a notepad greeted her and asked, "What would you like?"

Now that she had a closer look, Natalie was even more confused as to what she should get. If the smells swirling around the room were any indication of what things tasted like, she knew there couldn't be a wrong answer.

"I can't decide. It's my first time here, and everything looks so good. I'm trying to bribe someone into helping me out with a project. If you were me, what would you buy to ensure a successful mission?"

The employee set his pen down and pursed his lips in thought. "How old is this person?"

"Older. I guess he is in his mid-sixties," Natalie said.

"Pumpkin bread. We have a group of older gentlemen who come in every morning for coffee, and they can't get enough of the pumpkin bread. It's seasonal, and they lose their minds when it first comes out," the employee said.

Natalie hadn't expected that response because the display case had so many beautifully decorated cookies and a variety of flaky pastries. But it was the simple pumpkin bread that had won those men over.

"I'll take eight slices of pumpkin bread. Can you box it up four and four?" she asked. Four slices for Henry and four for Lindy and Charlotte to share. "Oh, and can you throw in a lemon cupcake?" This she would give to Lisa in the morning. Natalie thought about getting something for herself but decided not to because she knew she'd be getting very dirty soon and didn't want to eat anything while organizing the bar.

The bakery employee tied Henry's bribe up in a ribbon. She sent Brian a text as she left the store to let him know she'd be there momentarily. As she got closer to the building, she looked through the front windows and saw Henry and Brian looking at something in the bar. She knocked on the door, and Brian walked over to open it for her.

"You brought us sweets?" Brian asked, looking at Natalie's bag of goodies.

Natalie blushed and wondered why she hadn't brought anything for Brian. Even though he had been a jerk last night at Target, he was still doing her a huge favor. She decided to sacrifice Lisa's cupcake. "I got a little something for you and Henry."

Henry's head shot up from whatever he was studying, and he looked at Natalie. "Really, you got something for me?"

"I did. I got Brian a lemon cupcake since he can be sweet and sour. And I got you pumpkin bread," Natalie replied as she set the bag on the bar.

"I'm not sour," Brian said.

"You were last night," Natalie said.

"Only because you were," Brian replied.

Natalie took the cupcake out of the bag and handed it to him. "It doesn't matter. I hope you enjoy it. I've been told they make amazing desserts."

Brian wiped his hands on his jeans and took the cupcake. "Thank you."

"Thank you for helping me with the apartment and letting me use the bar," Natalie said.

Henry walked over to her. "I love their pumpkin bread."

Natalie made a mental note to tell the employee how spot-on his recommendation had turned out to be. She carefully lifted a box out of the bag and gave it to Henry.

"This is so nice of you," Henry said.

"Well, it's also a bribe. I have a favor to ask of you. You are more than welcome to say no. It won't hurt my feelings in any way. You know the soda flavor, Marv's Choice? I'm doing a marketing campaign for it, and I could use your help. I need a Marv, and am wondering if you'd be interested. It's a very small time commitment. We'd take pictures of you holding things the character Marv might like," Natalie said.

A wide grin spread over Henry's face. "Marv's Choice is one of my favorite soda flavors. So it's just pictures? I don't have to say anything?" Henry asked.

"Yup, just pictures. We will work all this around your schedule. I don't have many details for you yet, because I wanted to talk to you first. You look kind of interested," Natalie said. She was hopeful he'd say yes.

"Count me in. I think I'd earn some cool points from my grandkids," he replied.

"That's great. I'll have more details for you tomorrow!" Natalie exclaimed.

"Speaking of tomorrow," Brian said. Natalie realized he had walked away from them and now stood at the piles of paper the men had been examining when she had first gotten there.

"We ran into an issue today. One of our guys discovered a leak that has to be addressed ASAP. Which means we had to turn the water to the whole building off," Brian said.

"How long will it be off?" Natalie asked.

"I think no more than a week," Henry said, walking over to Brian.

Natalie ran through the calendar in her head. A week with no water would cut into her cleaning time. Cleaning this bar definitely required hot, soapy water. But if she flipped cleaning time with her crafting time, everything might still stay on track. "I can rearrange my plans for getting the bar ready. This doesn't impact me much," Natalie said.

"And we'll have porta-johns brought in, so those'll be available to you," Henry added.

Without a shadow of a doubt, Natalie knew she would not set foot into a porta-potty. "I'll get everything organized and start the cleaning when the water is back on," she said.

Brian opened his cupcake box and took a huge bite. Mid-chew he said, "Great."

Natalie set her purse down on the bar and took out the leggings and shirt she had packed. "Before I change into grubbies, is there anything else I need to know?" She looked between the two men.

"Nope, that covers it," Brian said through a mouthful of cupcake.

She came out of the bathroom and saw a mask and gloves had been left for her by her purse. She took out her notebook and reviewed her game plan. Then she picked up her gifts left by the guys and got to work. When she placed the first box on an empty shelf in the storage room, it made a *thud* and sent a plume of dust into the air. Before she knew it, she was covered in dirt from head to toe. In that moment, she was grateful she'd been given an industrial mask. Before picking up the next box,

Natalie helped herself to a pair of safety glasses from a box of them she had found.

In two hours' time, she had made a major dent in what needed to be done. She left several notes around the storage room and pub so she'd remember the method to her madness the next time she came to organize. As she wrote her last Post-it note, Brian walked into the bar.

"Wow, you got a lot done tonight," he said, looking around the space.

Natalie walked over to a stack of boxes and placed her note on top of it. "Organizing can go quickly if you have a plan." She took her gloves off and set them on the counter.

"That's clear," Brian said.

Natalie removed her glasses and mask and reached for her hand sanitizer. "Do you want some?" she said, offering Brian the bottle.

He took one look at her and burst into laughter.

"What's so funny?" Natalie asked.

Brian took out his phone and took a picture of her. Then he turned his phone around to show her. Natalie had a perfect dirt outline on her face from where the mask and glasses had been. She wondered why she always had to look so bad in front of him.

"I am disgusting. I need a shower," she said.

"You're not disgusting ... just filthy. Let me lock up, and I'll take you home," Brian said, and headed toward the door.

"I can get a ride," Natalie insisted.

Brian stopped and looked back at her. "As soon as the car pulls up and the driver gets a look at you, they'll drive on by."

He was right. She was filthy.

"Gather up your stuff, and I will meet you out back," he said.

Natalie didn't bother arguing. The quicker she got into a shower, the better. Gingerly, with just the tips of her fingers because were the only clean part of her body, she loaded all her things into her purse. She followed him with her arm outstretched, holding her bag away from herself. She didn't want to risk her nice clean purse touching her gross body.

Brian stood at the door waiting for her. "What are you doing?"

"You have eyes. Would you want me touching your stuff?" Natalie asked. She sidestepped through the door so she wouldn't have to lower her arm. "Do you want me to sit on a towel?"

He rolled his eyes and made sure the building door locked behind him. "I've been dirtier in my truck. It'll be fine."

Natalie set her purse down on the backseat and got into the front. She hated even buckling her seat belt based on how dusty she was.

Brian noticed her hesitation as he fastened his. "You're fine, just buckle the damn thing."

Natalie glared at him and buckled her seatbelt. A dirty car would serve him right, she thought.

"Are you hungry? Do you want me to drive through somewhere for dinner?" Brian asked, driving away from the building.

It was kind of him to ask, but Natalie didn't want a single delay. She needed to bathe herself immediately. "No, thank you. They served meatloaf tonight, and Lindy saved me a plate."

Brian chuckled. "Sounds like you're enjoying retirement-home living."

"With the exception of sleeping on a couch and having zero privacy, it's a pretty great place to live. I have access to all the hard candy a person could want. And the water aerobics classes are invigorating, plus the food is pretty good," Natalie replied.

"You go to water aerobics?" Brian asked in a sarcastic tone.

Natalie rolled her eyes. "Obviously, someone hasn't ever taken a water aerobics class before."

"Be honest. Had you ever taken a water aerobics class before moving into Montrose?"

Natalie thought about lying but decided against it. "No, I didn't. But I never made fun of it like you just did."

Brian responded without hesitation. "I never made fun of the class. I asked a simple question, and you misinterpreted it as making fun."

Natalie faced him. "You think I misinterpreted your snide question? Nothing could be further from the truth."

"Many things could be further from the truth. For one, you thinking I was sour yesterday."

Natalie gasped. "You were sour yesterday!" she exclaimed. "You were all pissy about what pens I liked, and then after our truce, you got your panties in a twist about the cleaning products I wanted. How is that not sour?"

"That wasn't me being sour. I was simply stating facts."

He was getting her all riled up again and was enjoying himself. He liked seeing her lose her cool. Well, not this time, she thought. Natalie straightened up in the seat and looked out the windshield. She would not give him the satisfaction of ruffling her feathers.

A few times before they arrived at Montrose, Brian acted like he wanted to say something, but then he didn't. When they pulled up to the front door, Natalie hopped out to get her bag from the back seat.

As she was about to close the door, she heard Brian give her a jovial "Good night." Natalie looked at him and saw his sarcastic grin. She glared at him and slammed the door, walking to the entrance in a huff.

CHAPTER 8

21 Days till Thanksgiving

Charlotte came over to Lindy's for breakfast before Natalie left for work Thursday. "I started compiling a list of everything we'll need to look for at the church rummage sale," Aunt Lindy said as she broke off one of the corners from the last slice of pumpkin bread.

"Oh, good idea," said Charlotte. Lindy passed her the notepad.

Natalie hadn't had the time or brain space to think about everything she'd need for the new apartment and was glad Lindy had started making a list.

"Agreed," she said. "Since we don't know when we can go yet, I want to be ready in case it's tomorrow night." Natalie took a sip of her coffee. "I've decided I want to buy new bedding, and this weekend, I'll buy a mattress. I also want new towels."

Charlotte uncapped the pen and made notes of what Natalie had said.

"Tonight, when you get home, we can finalize the list, and when it's our time to shop, we can divide and conquer," Lindy said.

"I love that idea. During lunch today, I'll try and put together a mood board for my apartment, so you two have an idea of my style," Natalie said.

"Wonderful. And I'm going to put myself down for looking for kitchen stuff and apartment decorations. I have excellent taste," Charlotte bragged.

"Add Lisa into our shopping equation. She said she wanted to shop with us," Natalie added as Charlotte wrote.

Natalie took her last sip of pumpkin spice flavored coffee. "I've been thinking. Depending on the prices, if it's in my budget, it might be nice to serve Thanksgiving dinner on real dishes. None of them have to match. I like eclectic things, and having an eclectic Thanksgiving tablescape sounds cute."

Charlotte clapped her hands. "Oh my goodness yes, you could use similar but different tablecloths, and we could get an assortment of brass candle holders."

"Exactly. I thought for the place cards—now, this again is dependent on the price and how many they have—we could use picture frames. I could paint them all to match," Natalie said.

"I love that," Lindy said. "It will be like how Ruth used to do it."

"I've been tossing the idea around in my head of painting the frames fall colors," Natalie said.

Charlotte was so excited she could barely contain herself. She bounced up and down in her seat. "What are your thoughts on cloth napkins?"

"If we can find enough, I think they'd look so good. I'm calling florists today to price a long floral centerpiece. I have a budget in mind for all my apartment stuff. If I can stay within that, I'd love to have fresh flowers all along the table," Natalie said.

"Dried oranges!" Charlotte practically yelled. "We should do dried oranges."

Natalie chuckled and stood up to put her plate and mug in the dishwasher. "I love that idea. Tonight, when I get home, I want to put everything into categories. You know, the things I need to get versus I want to get."

"Don't forget we can use the craft room here. We have all kinds of craft supplies. You can paint the picture frames in there. There is even a sewing machine, in case we need to make our own napkins or tablecloths. I can sew," Lindy added as she took another corner of pumpkin bread.

"Perfect. I hope to have the bar mostly organized by tonight and done organizing on Saturday or Sunday. Then I'll be ready to clean as soon as the water gets turned back on. While I wait on the water, I can start making the crafts." She picked up her phone and requested a ride. Then looked at Lindy. "Do you mind putting together a head count for us? I think we are at twenty-six, but I don't know about the Iowa cousins," Natalie said.

"I will call them today. I love that job," Lindy said. "Tonight they're serving chicken-fried steak and chicken pot pie. Which of those would you like, dear?"

Natalie gathered her purse as she thought the choices over. "Chicken pot pie, and if they have cranberry marshmallow salad, I'd like some of that too, please." She leaned down and kissed her aunt on the head. "Thank you, Aunt Lindy."

Aunt Lindy reached up and patted Natalie on the shoulder. "I am so glad you are here. I love having you close by."

"I love being close by too. All right, see you two tonight," Natalie said, and headed out the door.

* * *

Once Natalie arrived at work, she sent Donna a quick email to update her about the campaign. With Henry on board, the social media drive for Marv's Choice was going full steam ahead. Natalie marveled at all the clever ideas Lisa had come up with for Marv's character. The only problem was Henry had a family obligation the upcoming week. The earliest he could meet them after work was ten days before launch, which was the day before Thanksgiving. Natalie normally liked to have more time for editing and tweaking, but she had worked within tighter constraints before.

Her holiday prep timeline also had to be adjusted. Everything had tightened up, but she'd already made accommodations for that. She had three full weekends before Thanksgiving, and that was plenty of time. Granted, those weekends also needed to include shopping for a mattress, moving into her apartment, and cleaning the whole pub. But she didn't have anyone to hang out with yet besides Lindy, so her evenings were free. Everything was still on track.

Natalie sent her mom a text about all the ideas they'd come up with. Her phone dinged, and she sighed when she realized her mother had replied back to her in the group chat with Jenny. She had included a screenshot of Natalie's idea text.

Mom: I love everything you've come up with. Thanksgiving is going to be beautiful.

Natalie: Thanks, Mom! I think so too.

Jenny: What kind of flowers are you thinking? Have you made a Pinterest board that we could see? No offense, but it sounds like it could be too hodgepodge.

Why did Jenny need to see a Pinterest board? This was Natalie's holiday function. Jenny could do whatever she wanted when it was her turn to host. Natalie wanted to write back *offense taken*, but she reminded herself she was an adult.

Natalie: I haven't put together a Pinterest board or really looked at Pinterest. I can, if you need help seeing the vision.

Mom: Inspo pictures could be nice. It will help everyone see your boho theme come to life.

Natalie: Sure, I'll put one together tonight.

Mom: I talked to Dad last night and we are planning on being there a few days early. I don't have an exact date yet, because he's still thinking about the detours he wants to take.

Natalie: That'd be great! Dad can help me cook and you can help with any last-minute finishing touches.

Mom: That's what I was thinking too.

Jenny: Susan, Kevin and I might come with you. He and I have vacation days we need to use. We could ride down with you and then fly back.

Natalie threw her head back and let out a silent scream. Then she remembered her walls were glass and abruptly looked around to see if anyone had seen her. Luckily, most people were at lunch, and the floor looked pretty empty.

Mom: Oh my goodness, we'd love that. When you two get home from work today, let's talk about the feasibility of this.

Natalie: Got to get back to work. You guys let me know what you decide.

Mom: Will do, love you oodles and noodles!

Natalie: Ditto

Natalie cringed at the idea of spending extra days with Jenny before Thanksgiving. But when they arrived, she'd have so much done Jenny would be hard-pressed to say anything negative. This text conversation made her want to double down on her holiday determination. She was absolutely going to make her Berry Perfect Thanksgiving happen, even with a tightened timeline.

After calling around to several florists, Natalie found one she fell in love with. The owner of Flowers, Flowers, Flowers totally saw her vision right away. The arrangement was going to be expensive, but so worth it. Before she replied back with a definite yes to the flower quote, Natalie looked at her savings account. She finalized her budget for apartment furnishings and for Thanksgiving. If she crossed her fingers and held her breath, everything might just come together.

Henry greeted her when she arrived at the apartment building and told her she was good to go for the Friday night shopping at the church rummage sale. He'd gotten permission for her to come before they closed up for the night. This was perfect because her odds of getting more things on her list were greater than if she didn't have to wait until Saturday. The downside was they'd only have a little over an hour to shop for everything. Obviously, she could go back the next day to pick up any remaining things she might need, but if she could get all the shopping done Friday night, her Saturday was freed up. And right now, she needed every spare minute she could get.

Henry even volunteered the use of his truck. Natalie felt relief at not having to ask Brian if she could use his. The less contact she had with him, the better.

CHAPTER 9

20 Days till Thanksgiving

On Friday morning, the ladies sat at Lindy's dining table to put together their shopping plan of attack.

"Aunt Lindy, you and Charlotte will take care of the kitchen, bathroom, and things for the Thanksgiving tablescape. Lisa and I will handle furniture and apartment decorations," Natalie said while looking over her list.

"What's Brian going to do? I already told him we need his truck," Charlotte said.

Natalie kicked herself for not telling Charlotte last night she had talked to Henry about using his. "Henry has graciously offered his. So you can tell Brian he doesn't need to come," she said, trying to sound nonchalant.

Lindy looked up from the list. "Dear, we will need two trucks. This is a lot of stuff, and if we're lucky enough to get it all, we'll need both."

Natalie dreaded the thought of Brian picking apart everything she bought. It'd be Target all over again, only worse. Unfortunately, Lindy was right though. If she wanted to cross most of the things off the list, she needed Brian's truck. Natalie internally rolled her eyes. "You're right. But I doubt he will want to shop for anything."

"We need all the hands we can get. We only have an hour. If we put Brian with you, Lisa can help me in the kitchen area, and Lindy can focus on Thanksgiving. That will free up a lot of time for Lindy and me," Charlotte said.

This was a nightmare. Natalie hated the idea of him going. He was an asshole, but Natalie couldn't tell his grandmother that. Then it dawned on her that his grandmother would be around, which would mean he had to be on his best behavior. Maybe this wouldn't be a disaster.

"Okay, that'll work." Natalie looked at her phone; her ride arrived in a few minutes. "Ladies, I have to run now. I'll see you two tonight at the church. I love you both oodles and noodles."

As Natalie closed the door, she heard Lindy say, "Love you noodles and oodles."

* * *

Natalie had been mentally preparing for a fast shopping spree her whole life. Ever since she was a child, she loved those shopping shows. She yelled at the contestants who missed their aisles or dropped something. She wondered if she had somehow manifested the church rummage sale.

Lisa appeared to be as giddy about this as Natalie. "My heart is racing, I am so excited," Lisa said.

"Me too," Natalie said, and looked at the map display on the dash of Lisa's car. They were moments away from arriving at the church.

They parked on the street and took the steps up to the church's circle drive. As they reached the top, they saw Lindy and Charlotte waiting on a bench under an awning. Natalie couldn't see Brian or his truck in the parking lot, but from her vantage point, half of the parking lot was obscured by the church itself. She wondered if he had decided not to show.

"Ladies, this is Lisa. We work together. Lisa, this is my Aunt Lindy and her best friend, Charlotte," Natalie said.

Lisa beamed as the two women gushed over her and showered her with compliments.

"You're just as cute as a button. Look at that adorable skirt you're wearing," Lindy said.

Charlotte waved at someone, and Natalie looked around to see who had caught her attention. Walking up the circle drive was Brian. Natalie wished every time he made an appearance, it didn't look like he had a wind machine pointed at him. It wasn't fair for him to have such luscious locks. His stupid, slow model walk didn't earn him any points either. In fact, it made Natalie dislike him more. No one should be that poised all the time. If Natalie almost tripped walking up the stairs, then the least Brian could do was stumble a little.

"This is my grandson, Brian. He was parking the truck. Brian, this is Natalie's friend, Lisa. They work together," Charlotte said.

Brian shook Lisa's hand, then walked over and stood next to Natalie. Last night at the apartment building, she had been able to avoid him completely, and now she was stuck shopping with him. Under her breath, she said, "I'd hoped maybe you wouldn't be here tonight."

Brian twisted around and acted like he was looking at something behind him. "I tried to get out of it. Twice. Gigi wouldn't let me. I don't want to be here as much as you don't want me here."

"Everyone is here now. What are we waiting on?" Lindy asked.

Natalie took a step toward Lindy and said, "Henry. I sent him a text as we were pulling up, and he said he'd come and get us as soon as they were ready."

She looked through the church doors for any signs of Henry.

Not a minute later, Henry walked out of the building and escorted them into the church foyer. There were a couple of other Friday-night shoppers, but not many. The pastor of the church gave everyone a tour of the different sales rooms and let them know the cashier's table was in the front entranceway. When it came to the furniture, he explained, if they saw something they liked, they were supposed to pull the tag.

Once the pastor explained everything, Natalie was ready to go.

She asked her group of shoppers, "Does anyone have any questions?"

They all shook their heads no.

"If we do, we will text you. We will also send you pictures. Charlotte and I studied the mood board you sent us," Lindy said.

Natalie beamed at her aunt. "Okay, then let's shop."

Aunt Lindy, Charlotte, and Lisa went down the long hallway toward the kitchen and decor area. Natalie and Brian headed in the opposite direction to the rec room, to check out the furniture.

"I didn't get a mood board," Brian said.

Natalie gave him a sideways glare before rolling her eyes. "I didn't know you'd be here until this morning. Plus, giving you more opportunities to tell me your opinions about my shopping choices was low on my priority list." She picked up her pace in hopes he wouldn't say anything else.

They hadn't seen inside the furniture room during the tour, only told where it was located. Natalie was blown away when she opened the door to a mammoth-sized gym that housed two basketball courts. Wall-to-wall furniture covered the whole space. As she scanned the room, her eyes stopped on a couch that needed to be hers.

Not fifteen feet from her stood a midcentury modern floral couch. It had clean lines and wooden legs. It looked like the perfect height, and it even had the original plastic cover on it. Natalie tried not to skip as she walked up to the sofa.

She handed Brian the end of her tape measure. "Hold this. I want to see how long it is," she said.

Brian reluctantly put the tape measure on the back of the sofa.

"It's the perfect size," Natalie exclaimed as she sat down. She was happy to discover it was as comfortable as she had expected.

"Seriously, this is the couch you want? This thing is at least sixty years old, if not older," Brian said. "Look at that one." He pointed to a gray couch sitting opposite the floral one. "That one looks like it was made in this century. I bet you it's only a few years old."

"I don't care. I want this one," Natalie said. She slid her hands along the plastic and admired the pattern on the fabric. She leaned over and looked at the price taped to one of the cushions. It was half of what she had budgeted for a couch. Without hesitation, she took the tag off. She stood up and took a picture of it to send to Lindy and Charlotte.

"You're really buying that? It's going to fall apart before you get it home," Brian said.

Natalie sent the text and turned to Brian. "That is where you are wrong. No one has sat on this couch. This couch has been babied for sixty years. The owner of this probably made their kids take their shoes off before entering the room where this lived. This is a living room couch only used by guests and for taking family photos."

"How do you know this?" Brian asked, crossing his arms.

"First, the plastic is a dead giveaway. I bet someone is downsizing to move into a nursing home. Perhaps even mine. Second, there are no stains, no fading, not a stitch out of place. The cushions still look brand new. I take the plastic off, and I basically have a new couch that was made during a time when they built furniture to last. That, on the other hand," Natalie said, and put her hand on the back of the grey sofa. "Who knows what they did on this couch? I bet they spilled drinks, cut their toenails, and let their dogs sleep on it. Trust me when I say no one cut their toenails on mine." Natalie walked to the next section of furniture, dining room furniture.

"You're insane."

As soon as the words came out of Brian's mouth, Natalie's phone rang. Lisa was Facetiming her.

Natalie answered and positioned the phone so the couch was visible in the background. The picture on Natalie's screen showed a pile of dishes.

Lisa said, "We picked these out for your everyday dishes. Charlotte is selecting the Thanksgiving plates as we speak. We like these flour and sugar canisters, too."

Natalie enjoyed having a plate for every occasion. Her grandmother had several sets of dishes, and Natalie liked that she'd continue this tradition.

She examined the pile. "They're perfect. I love the mix of modern and vintage that's happening there." The everyday dishes were simple, thin white plates and the canisters looked like mason jars. Next to them sat a smattering of odds and ends that she would have picked out if she were there. Charlotte and Lisa were doing a great job.

"We love the couch," Charlotte yelled from somewhere nearish Lisa.

The phone image changed to Lisa's face. "Yeah, we love the couch. Got to go. After we get the next pile together, I'll call you again. This really does feel like *The Boxcar Children*," Lisa said.

"I know, right?" Natalie gave Lisa an overexaggerated smile and hung up the phone.

"I don't get it," Brian said. Natalie turned and found him seated at one of the tables. "You're not moving into a boxcar. Why do you guys keep referencing those books?"

Natalie headed to a smaller round table that had four matching chairs. It looked like it could be the right size for her breakfast nook.

"The part of the books that resonated the most for me was when they decorated an uninviting boxcar and turned it into a home. They used found objects that didn't match and created a cozy environment. What we're doing now is my version of that. I'm moving into a construction zone with only three suitcases. I'm outfitting the apartment with things I can find at a rummage sale. Ten minutes ago, I barely had anything to my name. Now I have that couch, this table, and two canisters that look like mason jars. I'm finding random pieces and creating my home."

"Aren't you also buying a mattress and shopping this weekend for bedding at an actual store?" Brian said in an obnoxious tone. He was clearly trying to poke holes in her fantasy.

"Yes, but that's beside the point. Now get up. I need side tables and a headboard."

Brian followed her around. Once she got in her groove, she became a woman on a mission. Eight minutes later, she had tickets for a headboard, two tables to use as nightstands, a wingback chair, a slim bookcase, and a dresser. Brian carried two lamps and a mirror. The last section to hit was the coffee table area.

In no time flat, Natalie picked out a narrow table that could be used for a TV stand and a brass coffee table with a glass top.

"Seriously, that is the coffee table you're picking out?" Brian set one of the lamps down to adjust the mirror under his other arm.

"Yes, it's the right size, and five dollars is the right price," Natalie said as she snatched the tag.

"It's the ugliest thing I've ever seen," Brian said, gawking at the table.

"Well, good thing you aren't living in my apartment. I need a coffee table. This meets all my requirements, and I went way over budget on the dresser, so compromises have to be made." Natalie headed out of the room. She needed to catch up with the other ladies to finish shopping before their time was up.

Natalie didn't worry whether Brian kept pace. He was being a big ol' wet blanket on her joyful adventure. She dropped her tickets off at the cashier's table and told them she'd be back. She found two of the three women in the kitchen area.

Lisa stood in front of a long white table covered with stuff. "Are these all the things you guys picked out?" Natalie asked as she eyed a butter dish.

Charlotte came to stand next to her. "Yes, from the white stack of plates to the end of the table is all your stuff. I was able to find almost everything on your list. I didn't like the selection of mixing bowls they had, so you'll need to get those someplace else. But everything else was there."

"I love everything." Natalie didn't bother looking around the room; there wasn't time, and based on the things that were picked out, she knew they got the cream of the crop.

"Lisa, go get the thing," Charlotte said, and pointed to Lisa. "One of the other families picked this out, but then put it back. It wasn't on your list, but Lisa and I fell in love with it. We hid it in the back because it'd put us way over your budget. But it's just too neat not to show you."

Lisa came back rolling a brass bar cart with a leather ice bucket on top. It had two tiers of glass shelves.

"I love it so much," Natalie said as she approached the cart. She looked at the tag, and even with her savings on the coffee table, this would still be a stretch. "I want it, but I'm not going to say yes until we're done. I don't mind going over the budget, but I need to wait and see what everything comes to."

"It's so good," Lisa said, and took the cart back to its hidden location.

"I'll stay here with Lisa to start packing everything up. Lindy is in the conference room," Charlotte said, bending down to retrieve an empty box from under the table.

Lindy sat at a long conference table with several stacks of picture frames in front of her.

"Those look great," Natalie said.

"We almost have enough. There are these two bigger pic-ture frames that maybe could be for the ends of the tables. If you sit couples at the end, this won't be an issue," Lindy said, and looked up at Natalie.

"I think that's a great idea." Natalie examined a box of candlesticks in a variety of metals and heights. "These look perfect."

"I think so too. There are a couple of questionable ones in there, but they were a quarter, so I went ahead and got them. I also got you that bowl and vase. Don't bother looking at the price tags. They are my housewarming gifts to you." Natalie admired the large porcelain pasta bowl with delicate blue flowers and a cut crystal vase.

Natalie smiled at Lindy and said, "These are gorgeous. You don't have to get me anything. Taking care of me these past weeks is all the gift I need."

"You being here has been more of a gift for me, trust me. Now you get moving, because I haven't checked out the linens yet," Lindy said.

Natalie looked at her watch. Their shopping spree was almost over. She could probably go a little bit long, but she didn't want anyone to have to stay late because of her. "I'll head there now. Thank you so much, Aunt Lindy."

The linen section was near the front door. As she arrived, she saw Brian and Henry were already loading the trucks. An elderly woman with a kind smile sat behind a table of sheets, gently folding mismatched pillowcases.

Natalie looked around and heard the woman ask, "Are you Natalie?"

Natalie was caught off guard. "I am. And who might you be?"

"I'm Mildred," the woman said as she put her hand over her heart.

"It's nice to meet you," Natalie said, smiling at her.

"I believe you bought my couch," Mildred said.

"That stunning couch is yours?" Natalie asked. She was so excited to meet the woman who had taken such good care of her new couch.

"It was. When I picked it out, I thought it was the prettiest thing I had ever seen," Mildred answered.

Natalie sighed and smiled. "I couldn't agree more. It spoke to me. It's beautiful, and I feel honored to be its next owner."

Out of the corner of her eye, she saw Henry and Brian walking toward her. "I see you have met my mother," Henry said. "You know, you bought her couch."

"She just told me," Natalie said.

Henry went over and stood next to his mother. "When you move in," he said to Natalie, "my only request is that I can come sit on the couch without the plastic on it. In my sixty-four years of life, I have never done that. Nor have I sat on it for more than a few minutes at a time. No one did. We weren't allowed in the living room. It was for guests only."

Natalie stared at Brian and cocked her head. Brian shrugged his shoulders, and she mouthed, "I told you so."

"Natalie."

Hearing Mildred say her name brought her attention back to the older woman.

"If you like the upholstery of the couch, I have matching fabric here I wanted to use for curtains but never got around to making them."

Mildred pulled a paper sack out from under the table and handed it to Natalie. Inside were several yards of similar fabric. The couch had a large floral design, while the fabric in the bag had the same florals but in a smaller print and more spread out.

Natalie said, "My Aunt Lindy said she'd sew curtains for me. This fabric would be perfect."

"Will you send pictures to Henry when they are done? I've always wanted to see this fabric hanging next to the couch," Mildred said.

Natalie was touched she could do this for Mildred. "Of course I will, and if you are up to it, I'd love for you to come and see it in person."

"Mom, I bet we can make that happen," Henry said.

Mildred smiled, but Natalie could see her mind had gone a million miles away. Natalie hoped Mildred had gone back to happy memories.

"I'd love that," Mildred said.

Brian and Henry left to finish loading the trucks, and Natalie picked out curtains for her bedroom. Lindy joined her and found some white tablecloths and cloth napkins.

"These tablecloths have a few stains on them, but I might be able to get those out, and if not, the stains aren't that noticeable and will be covered up with the centerpiece anyway," Lindy said.

Natalie agreed and took the linen ticket to the checkout table in the foyer. Charlotte had already sent Lisa with theirs. While the woman at the cashier's box tallied up her purchases, Natalie let her mind wander to what her apartment would look like. She smiled, thinking about how fun it'd be to decorate and find a home for all her purchases. The idea that everything would feel settled soon was within her grasp.

The woman finished adding up Natalie's haul. She had gone over budget, but not by much. Natalie looked at Lisa and said, "Go get the bar cart. It's worth it."

Lisa clapped her hands. "Oh, I hoped you'd say that!" She ran down the hall to the kitchen area.

Chapter 10

Everyone at the church had been so kind and made quick work of getting all her new treasures packed and loaded. Natalie profusely thanked the parishioners as she left. There were still several people shopping, and Natalie was relieved to know she hadn't kept anyone there later than they were planning on staying.

She had thought about all the details of this excursion except how to unload everything and get everyone home. She got to the trucks and wasn't sure what to do next.

"I owe all of you so much. You guys have gone above and beyond. When I get into the apartment, I'm going to make dinner for you all."

"I'm always down for a home-cooked meal," Henry said.

"Let's focus on the here and now. Not weeks from now," Brian said.

Natalie hated how he sucked all the air out of the room, even when they were standing outside.

"Henry, I want you to take Gigi and Lindy home. We will unload your truck in the morning when the crew gets there. Natalie and I will head to the apartment to unload my truck. I have a dolly, and it won't take us long," Brian ordered.

Natalie was annoyed that Brian bossed everyone around and didn't ask her what she wanted to do. Granted, she didn't have a plan, and his plan sounded pretty good, but she still felt like he should have asked.

"What about me?" Lisa asked. "I don't mind helping unload, but only if I can stop and get a dozen cookies first."

"We could use an extra pair of hands. You head to Sugar and Spice, and I will take Natalie in my truck. We can start unloading while you buy your cookies," Brian said, and headed to Henry's truck.

Natalie watched as he helped his grandmother and her aunt into the cab and carefully closed the door behind them. She walked with Lisa to the top of the steps and waited there till Lisa got in her car. Once everyone was loaded safely in their assigned vehicles, Natalie and Brian got in his truck.

After buckling her seatbelt, Natalie took a deep breath and said the thing she didn't want to say. "Thank you for being here tonight. I don't know how we'd have gotten everything loaded if you weren't here."

Brian nodded. "You're welcome."

They sat in silence for the rest of the ride. Brian pulled up to the parking lot behind the apartment building and propped the back door open. Natalie went to unlock the front door, so when Lisa got there, she could let herself in.

The last time she had been up to see the apartment was on the day she visited it with Lindy and Charlotte. It had been full of tile and other supplies. Where were they going to unload all her stuff? Why hadn't she thought to ask where they could put everything?

Brian had loaded the dolly with a few boxes and pulled the end tables from the truck. They were stacked on top of each other. "Can you push the dolly?" he asked as Natalie approached the truck bed.

"I can do that," she said.

Brian picked up the end tables and started inside.

Natalie carefully tilted the dolly and followed behind. "Where are we going?" she asked.

Brian scoffed and said, "To your apartment. Is there somewhere else you'd prefer for all this to go?"

"No, I just didn't know if there was room for it in there, and I feel like that was a pretty obvious question to ask," she replied. His tone drove her nuts.

Brian held the elevator door open for her, and she attempted to navigate the threshold of the lift. The fact that it only took her four tries seemed like a real win. However, she couldn't help but notice his eye roll. What did he expect? She had probably pushed a dolly maybe three times in her life.

As she went around the corner to her apartment, one of the dolly's wheels got stuck on something and she couldn't move forward anymore. Brian briskly walked across the hall and into the apartment. The lights came on inside and Brian stood in the doorway, watching her struggle.

"Need any help?" he asked.

"No, I've got it." She tried pulling the dolly back, but it wouldn't move that direction either. She could not figure out what it had gotten caught on.

Natalie tried to fix the situation herself several more times before Brian finally walked over and told her to step aside. He pulled a piece of shipping plastic out from the axle of the left wheel.

Natalie walked past and said, "I was about to get that."

"Sure you were," Brian said, following her with the dolly.

Natalie looked around her apartment, stunned at the amount of progress that had been made. Everything was coming together. The kitchen had counters and a farmhouse sink. Boxes of tiles for the backsplash were neatly stacked, ready to be installed. Brian began unloading the boxes as Natalie explored the room.

"It looks so good in here. You've done such a nice job."

"Thank you. Like I said before, finishing this apartment reminds me why I do this. When you're gutting and fixing all the things no one will see, you can forget the reward of completing a project."

Natalie unloaded the last box and stacked it in the corner with the others.

Brian looked around the room and said, "When you get done with your shopping, tell me what color you want the walls painted. I have my painter lined up for Tuesday, and I'll need to tell him what colors to buy."

She looked at him with shock. "I didn't realize I got to pick the colors."

Brian shrugged.

Natalie followed him out of the apartment. He pressed the button to call the elevator and said, "You don't have to if you don't want to."

"No, it's fine. I want to do that. I'll just have to think about that for a little bit," she said, pulling the dolly behind her onto the lift.

As the doors shut, Brian said, "Good, because I don't know how anyone is going to find a color that will match that couch and those curtains."

"Don't make fun of my couch. When it's all said and done, it's going to look so cool. I have a vision."

Brian got out of the elevator, and Natalie tried to pull the dolly behind her. But it got stuck again.

"A vision of delusion," Brian said.

Natalie gave one last hard tug. The dolly stayed put, but she went flying right into Brian. He caught her before she fell onto the floor. Before she knew it, she was wrapped in his arms. She felt unstable on her feet and knew if she let go, she might still fall over. Instinctively, she draped her arm around Brian's neck to help steady her swirling brain. All the sudden motion had made her dizzy.

Once the room stopped spinning, she looked up, and her face was only inches from Brian's.

Without thinking, she leaned in and kissed him. His lips were soft; he drew her into a tighter embrace. Natalie parted her lips, and Brian kissed her deeper. She clutched the collar of his shirt as he ran his hand up and down her back. Together they stumbled into the wall but did not break their embrace. Natalie couldn't stop kissing this man. She slid her tongue into his mouth and pulled him closer. His hand had just reached her waistband when she heard Lisa calling out from the front door. Natalie and Brian jumped apart.

"Back here," Natalie yelled. She straightened her shirt and made sure to avoid Brian's gaze.

Lisa came skipping down the hall as Brian removed the dolly from the threshold of the elevator.

"How can I help?" Lisa asked.

"Perfect timing, we were about to get another load from the truck," Natalie said breathlessly.

"This way," Brian grumbled, and walked full speed toward the back door.

Brian loaded the dolly up again and handed Lisa two lamps to carry. Natalie opted to push the bar cart with the mirror propped on top.

"That pub looks cool. Is that where you're doing your Thanksgiving?" Lisa asked.

Natalie was annoyed at how smoothly Brian maneuvered the dolly. "It is."

"It's going to look so good when it's all cleaned up. If you need any help with the cleaning, let me know," Lisa said as she walked through the door.

"You don't have to do that," Natalie replied.

"I like cleaning. There is something so therapeutic about it. I used to stay home on the weekends and clean my parents' wood paneling instead of hanging out with my friends," Lisa said.

Natalie was thankful Lisa filled the air with her stories; they distracted her from thinking about touching tongues with Brian. Lisa didn't seem to notice Natalie was doing her best not to look at him.

"That's weird," Brian said as he pushed the call button.

As the door to the elevator opened, Natalie asked, "Since we're the only ones here, why don't we prop the door open and pack the elevator full? I think that'll make things go faster."

"That's a great idea," Lisa said.

Brian propped the doors open, and Natalie abandoned her cart to start bringing more things inside. She wanted to get away from this place as fast as possible. Kissing Brian was not on her bingo card right now.

It only took fifteen more minutes for the truck to be unloaded, and a few minutes after that for the apartment to be filled with boxes. Brian arranged everything away from the walls, so the painter had plenty of room to paint.

"Your apartment's so nice," Lisa said as she walked around the room.

Natalie was thankful Brian had gone back downstairs and wasn't in earshot to hear her. "Brian has done a fantastic job on remodeling this. I can't wait to see what he does with the rest of the building. Are you hungry? Can I buy you dinner? I owe you big time."

"Can I get a rain check? I'm kind of tired, and my bed is calling my name," Lisa said.

"Of course you can," Natalie said. She linked arms with her to walk toward the elevator. "Let's get you home."

"Can I give you a ride home?" Lisa asked.

"No, I'm way out of your way," Natalie said as she pushed the first-floor button.

"From here, you're on my way. From work, you aren't. Getting home from downtown takes me right past Montrose," Lisa said.

"Well, if you don't mind, that'd be great."

The elevator doors opened, and on her way out, Natalie almost ran straight into Brian again. She took a big step to the side. "Do you need help locking everything up?" she asked, trying not to blush when she looked at him.

"Nope, I'm going to lock the door behind Lisa, and then I'll take you home," he said with an unreadable face.

"Actually, Lisa is going to give me a ride home. I'm on her way. But thank you." Talking to him was so awkward now. Moments ago, she didn't want to stop kissing him, even though he happened to be someone she couldn't stand. Future Natalie had a lot to unwrap there. Present-day Natalie needed to try her hardest to pretend the kiss never happened.

"Great," Brian said.

Natalie grabbed Lisa's hand and practically dragged her to the front door. The sooner they were away from the apartment building and Brian, the better.

CHAPTER 11

19 DAYS TILL THANKSGIVING

Living with Aunt Lindy was easy. Now that Natalie wasn't crying on her couch for hours at a time, she enjoyed getting up early with her. And going to the Saturday morning water aerobics class was a no-brainer. Even though she had found her bathing suits, she still opted to wear Lindy's because of the full coverage of her butt. Lindy's suit didn't ride up anywhere. This time, however, she did opt to wear her own coverup.

Charlotte had brought them cinnamon toast and bananas for breakfast before class. After they ate, Natalie yawned as she reached for her towel.

Lindy instantly scolded her. "You better stop that right this minute."

"I'll do my best," Natalie said, and tried to stifle another yawn.

"I promise the coffee at the cute little coffee shop will be worth the wait. Also, who doesn't love carrying around a hot beverage on a crisp day while they shop? I know I do," Aunt Lindy said as she walked down the hall.

"I agree, and I love a fancy coffee," Natalie said while trying to push her brain fog away.

Water aerobics helped wake her up, but it did not improve her self-esteem. At the end of class, she still found herself holding her sides in exhaustion. Luckily, no one her age was there to see her struggle.

After they were both back in Lindy's room and dressed for the day, Natalie offered Lindy her arm and asked, "Shall we go?"

"We shall." The two walked arm in arm to the shuttle.

Natalie was surprised to see other people on the bus. She had gotten so used to it just being Lindy, Charlotte, and her. "This must be a popular shopping center," Natalie said as she took the seat next to Lindy.

"It's great shopping, even better food. Once word got out we were going, they sent out a sign-up sheet, and all the spots filled up in no time," Lindy replied in a low voice. "Coming home will be a little tricky with everyone's bags. I have a feeling the driver will have to take multiple trips."

"I didn't even think of that," Natalie said quietly.

"This morning, while you were getting ready, I mapped out our whole trip. Start with coffee and then shop based on the size of the item we need. That being said, we should start with bedding. Even though the comforter will be big, I know the Grey Goose will hold our purchases for us till we are ready to pick them up. As far as rugs go, if you find one you like at Secondhand Rose, I'm sure we can make arrangements for delivery," Lindy said.

"That all sounds great. I'll follow your lead," Natalie said.

As they made their way to the shopping center, Aunt Lindy filled Natalie in on their fellow shuttle riders.

* * *

"Unfortunately, she insists on bringing that terrible salad to every potluck," Lindy said as they pulled up to the plaza.

Once the bus came to a stop, Lindy shot out of her seat and headed to the door. Natalie hurried to follow her. Her great-aunt was a woman on a mission, and Natalie was just along for the ride.

The autumn breeze seemed to propel Lindy toward the coffee shop. Natalie adjusted her scarf as she chased after her great-aunt. She wanted to stop and take inspo pics of the different store displays, especially the ones that had hay bales stacked with pumpkins and mums. But that would have to wait until later because Natalie didn't want to lose sight of Lindy.

When they got inside the café, the line was relatively short. There were only four patrons in front of them. "We did good. We needed to get here quickly because everyone on the bus will want to start here too," Lindy said.

Natalie peered out the window, and sure enough, the shuttle passengers were making their way to the coffee shop. Out of the corner of her eye, she saw Lindy had taken a step closer to the counter. Natalie did the same and examined the menu.

"Is it too much pumpkin if I get a pumpkin spice latte and a pumpkin pie cookie?" Natalie asked.

"I don't think there's such a thing as too much pumpkin. You know, pumpkin has a lot of great properties. It's chock-full of vitamins and antioxidants. It even helps your eyes. You deserve to treat yourself. You've gone through a lot, and it's nice to see you coming out of the fog," Lindy said.

"The fog lifted so suddenly. I'm a little worried it might overtake me again," Natalie said.

"It's okay if it does. At least this way, you know clear skies aren't far away." Lindy's words touched Natalie, and she choked up. The tears weren't forming because she was sad, but because she was moved by all the love and kindness she had received lately. They stepped up to the counter to order. Lindy insisted on paying and pushed Natalie's wallet away.

When Lindy's name was called, they walked to the pickup window. Lindy handed Natalie her cookie. "Here. Pumpkin pie has a way of keeping the rain clouds away."

Natalie took the cookie and smiled.

"Good girl. So when the fog starts creeping in around the edges, remember this moment, this beautiful fall day, and pumpkin pie cookies, and how you have the strength and cour-age to overcome any obstacle," Lindy said as she patted Nattalie on the shoulder.

"We have to change subjects right now, or else I'm going to start crying happy tears," Natalie said.

"Well, we can't have that. There's a bench out there. Let's go drink our coffee, and you can show me what you envision for your bedding," Lindy said.

* * *

While in Secondhand Rose, Natalie found two antique postcards that had the sweetest matching brass frames. "I think you're right, Aunt Lindy. The light blue in the background should be the bedroom color, and this soft pale yellow should be the living room."

"I think it will be lovely. Do we need to make a stop at the hardware store for paint swatches?" Lindy asked.

"No, I'll give Brian the postcards; these will work as swatches. Whatever store he buys the paint from can scan the postcards, and boom, they'll have the color," Natalie responded.

"Technology is truly amazing," Lindy said.

The whole shopping trip was a success. Natalie bought the majority of the things on her list. It was a toss-up between the mattress and her new bedding for her favorite purchase of the day. She'd splurged and got the fluffiest mattress topper she had ever seen. Sleeping on it would be like sleeping on a cloud; plus, it was cooling. She imagined lying in her new bed cuddled up under her new whisper-blue damask comforter. It would be heaven.

The shuttle driver had to make a special extra trip just for Lindy and Natalie since her bags of pillows took up so much room in the van.

It took Natalie four trips to get their haul from the lobby to Lindy's apartment. She knew she should change and go over to the apartment building to finish organizing, but that'd require too much energy, and she was exhausted from a full day of shopping.

And she didn't want to see Brian yet. Anytime thoughts of their kiss floated through her head, she quickly pushed them aside. At some point, she would have to face him, but not today.

She texted him though, telling him she'd bring the swatches tomorrow when she came to organize. After she sent the message, she wondered if he'd even be there to let her in. But then she remembered the water leak and how they were working every day until they fixed it. That was why Henry's truck had gotten unloaded this morning instead of last night.

Guilty feelings lingered at the edges of her brain for not being there to help unload everything. But she figured she would have been in the way, and she desperately needed to do laundry.

She and Lindy decided to watch a movie and order a pizza that evening when Lindy got up from a much-needed nap.

While Lindy rested, Natalie started her laundry. She began with her bedding, and while it was in the washer, she did her best to organize her chaos. All the shopping bags and her stack of suitcases made the living room nearly impossible to navigate. She repositioned the couch a bit, and hid most of her purchases behind it. It wasn't the best solution, but at least it made Lindy's living room seem less cluttered for the time being.

Natalie borrowed one of Lindy's zipper-front robes so she could wash every single thing she had been wearing. She put her hands in the pockets while she inspected her tidying job and found a handful of Kleenex and a few peppermints. Lindy came out of her bedroom dressed in a similar robe.

"I love what you're wearing," Lindy said as she admired her niece.

"I can see the appeal. These are very comfortable," Natalie said, and then did a squat. "Plus, there's plenty of room for activities."

Lindy laughed and looked around the room. "Where on earth did you store all of your stuff?"

Natalie skipped over to the couch and presented the back of the sofa to Lindy. "I moved the couch out a bit and put everything behind there. Now it doesn't look like a store blew up in here."

"I didn't even notice you moved the couch. You did such a nice job of rearranging things." Lindy sat down in the overstuffed chair and crossed her legs. "I hope you don't mind, but I've invited Charlotte to join us."

"Not at all. I was about to walk down there and invite her myself," Natalie said as she took a seat on the couch.

"Excellent. I shall text her the attire for the evening." Lindy took her phone out of her pocket. She slowly typed out the text and reread it a few times before sending it.

Natalie marveled at that, because she hardly ever proofread a text before sending it, although she wished she did. It would save her a lot of embarrassment. "All right, Charlotte said she was already in said attire and is heading our way. She'd like a pizza with lots of vegetables on it."

"Got it!" Natalie exclaimed. She pulled out her phone and ordered two pizzas: a vegetarian pizza and a Canadian bacon and pineapple.

"I come bearing wine," Charlotte said while entering the apartment. She'd gotten there right in time to help pick the movie.

"Great, I'll take a glass right now. Which Hepburn are you in the mood for?" Aunt Lindy asked.

"Katharine, unless it's *Roman Holiday*, then Audrey," Charlotte said from the kitchen as she got two wine glasses from the cabinet.

"*Desk Set* it is," Lindy said. Natalie scrolled over to highlight *Desk Set* on the TV.

Charlotte walked into the living room and handed Lindy her wine. "Oh dear. Natalie, I completely forgot to ask you if you wanted a glass of wine. Darling, I can go get you a glass right now."

Natalie shook her head. "Wine makes me sleepy, and it's only four thirty. I am not ready to go to sleep just yet."

Charlotte sat on the couch next to Natalie. "Show me pictures of everything you got."

Natalie picked up her phone and showed Charlotte pictures from their shopping trip, then reached behind the couch to open one of the bags near the top so Charlotte could see her comforter.

"That's lovely," Charlotte said, and took a sip of wine.

"And it's reversible. It's pale blue stripes on the other side," Natalie said.

"I think the whole space is going to flow together so nicely," Lindy added.

As Natalie pulled up the picture of the rug she purchased, her phone dinged that the pizzas had arrived. "Let me put on my shoes, and I will go down to the front desk to pick up the pizzas."

In her haste to organize the living room, she didn't realize she had also put her shoes behind the couch. Natalie opted to borrow a pair of Lindy's slippers—a pair of fur-lined loafers. She marveled that with the right outfit, they could pass as shoes, but with the house dress on, they were clearly slippers. She had just put her phone in her pocket when there was a knock at the front door. Everyone who worked at Montrose was so kind. Natalie loved that someone was delivering their pizza, and she didn't have to go down to the front desk to pick it up.

Natalie opened the door, and Brian stood there holding the pizzas. "What are you doing here?" she asked.

Brian took sighed and said, "I sent you several texts about the paint samples. My guy wants to get the paint tomorrow, so I needed them tonight. You didn't respond, so I came over here."

"No, you didn't text me. I have had my phone on me the whole day, and I haven't gotten a single text from you," Natalie said. She clicked on the message icon on her phone. There were no new messages from Brian. She selected his name to show him he hadn't sent anything, and right then, the messages populated. She remembered her phone had updated when she first began the laundry, and she'd restarted it. He must have texted in that window.

"See, there they are," Brian said, pointing to her phone.

"Why do you have our pizza?" Natalie asked.

"I walked in with the pizza guy and told the desk clerk I'd take these up to you guys."

From inside the living room, Lindy hollered, "Who's at the door?"

Brian leaned past Natalie and said, "It's just me, Lindy."

"Is that Brian?" Charlotte sang out.

Brian was still leaning over Natalie. "Yes, Gigi."

"Get in here," Charlotte said.

Natalie moved aside and waved Brian in.

"And you brought up our pizzas. What a nice surprise," Lindy marveled.

"Have you had dinner yet?" Charlotte asked him.

Natalie knew the answer to that. It wasn't even five yet—of course he hadn't had dinner. "No, ma'am," Brian responded.

Lindy stood up and walked to the kitchen. "Well, you absolutely must join us. I am not taking no for an answer."

Brian set the pizzas down on the dining table and said, "You don't have to do that. I'm here to figure out the paint colors."

Charlotte got off the couch and walked to the dining area. "Let us feed you. I know I how much you love pizza."

"And I already have a plate for you, so the matter is settled," Lindy said while carrying four plates to the table.

Natalie knew there was no arguing with these two. Brian sat down at the table without another word; he had lost this battle like so many before then. Charlotte opened the pizza boxes and told them both to dig in.

"What are my options?" Brian asked.

Pineapple on a pizza was an annoyingly controversial topping. Natalie hated this debate. People liked sweet and salty things together in so many other forms, so when it was on a pizza, why was it such a big deal? She braced herself for him to become argumentative after he saw his options.

He inspected the two open boxes and said, "I'll take two slices of ham and pineapple."

"Really?" Natalie asked. She couldn't believe he didn't have anything else to say, since he had something to say about everything else in her life.

"I love pineapple on pizza. Wait, are you one of those people who hates it?" he asked.

"No, it's my favorite," she said as she put two pieces on his plate and then two on hers.

"How's the remodel coming along?" Lindy asked him.

While they ate, Brian told them all about the progress on the water leak and how they had started framing out the accessible bathrooms. Natalie listened and wondered what it'd be like to live in the building while they were working on it. Everything Brian said sounded like a foreign language.

"That's such a big project. When do you find time to sleep?" Lindy asked.

"What's sleep?" Brian responded.

"Brian, you have to take time for yourself," Charlotte demanded.

"I will Gigi, I promise." He looked at Natalie. "Can you get me the postcards?"

Natalie had forgotten why he was there. "Oh yeah. Of course." She hopped up and headed behind the couch. Luckily, she'd had the foresight of leaving them toward the top of one of the piles. She walked back to the table and handed them to Brian. "Here you go. I like the blue background color for the bedroom, and the yellow background color for the living room."

"Okay, but what about the kitchen, hallway, and bathroom?" Brian asked.

Natalie hadn't put any thought into what those should be. She glanced between Lindy and Charlotte. "I don't know. I haven't thought about any other colors."

Lindy and Charlotte both shrugged; they clearly hadn't either.

"Maybe a soft white. That could be nice," Natalie said.

Lindy and Charlotte nodded in agreement.

"What does a soft white look like?" Brian asked.

"It's not as harsh as a white white, but it's not as creamy as an eggshell," Natalie responded as she sat back down in her seat.

"Exactly. It's going to have cool undertones," Charlotte added.

Brian looked so confused. "We are talking about white paint. Correct?"

"Yes," Natalie said.

"Well, I need you to come with me to pick out the paints. I don't know what cool undertones mean," Brian said. He stood up.

"I can't come right now. We are just about to watch a movie," Natalie said.

"We can wait till you get back," Lindy suggested.

Brian looked at her with a smug grin, like her going with him was some kind of victory. Natalie started to glare at him, but her eyes landed on his lips. Images of their kiss flooded her memory. She felt her cheeks redden.

"They can wait till you get back. It won't take long. So why don't you change, and we will go," Brian said.

Natalie looked down at her outfit and forgot she had on a housecoat and slippers. At that same moment, she realized all her clothes that weren't packed away deep behind the couch were in the washing machine. Natalie took a deep breath and said, "I don't need to change. I am ready to go." She stood up and headed to the front door to get her purse.

"Will you bring back ice cream?" Lindy asked.

"Yes, cookies and cream for me. One scoop in a cup... no, two scoops," Charlotte added.

"I want two scoops of butter pecan in a cup," Lindy said.

Brian looked between his grandmother and Lindy. "Yes, we can bring back ice cream."

"Come on, let's go. I want ice cream too, and I'm ready to watch a movie," Natalie said impatiently.

When one finds themselves having to go out in public in a truly ridiculous outfit, there are only two options. One, try to cover oneself up to show the world you didn't plan on wearing it, or two, proudly wear the outfit like that had been the plan all along. Natalie chose option two. She threw her shoulders back and held her head high as she made her way to the front lobby. Having confidence wearing a housecoat and slippers was one thing at a retirement village, but something else entirely at a hardware store.

Brian already looked embarrassed to be seen with Natalie, and they were still surrounded by retirees. "Did you grab the postcards?" Natalie asked. In her haste to leave, she had forgotten to look behind her to see if he had picked them up.

"I did," Brian said coolly.

Brian wasn't bothering to initiate a conversation, and Natalie wasn't too keen on having one either. In fact, the less they talked, the easier it'd be for her to forget she knew he had soft lips.

After they arrived at the hardware store, they sat in the truck in silence for a while. Natalie stared at the door handle but couldn't bring herself to touch it.

"You ready to go in yet?" Brian asked.

"No. I think I should stay in the truck," Natalie answered.

"I need you to make sure the paint is correct."

"It's just that, now that we're here, I'm really regretting this outfit," Natalie said, looking down at the housecoat.

"I have a hoodie in the back seat," Brian said.

Natalie looked at him. "I am not wearing pants. I don't think adding a hoodie to this outfit will make me look any less crazy. In fact, I think adding a hoodie will only intensify the fact I'm in a glorified robe and slippers."

Brian tried and failed to stifle a laugh. "It's not that bad," he said as tears started to well up in his eyes.

Seeing the pleasure he received from her mortification fueled her to get out of the car. The only way to make this better was to get it over with as rapidly as possible. Natalie stormed into the store and headed directly to the paint section.

It ground her gears listening to Brian softly chuckle as they made their way to the swatches. Natalie slowly turned to him and smiled, because the only thing worse than being dressed in an embarrassing outfit was being with the person in an embarrassing outfit. Natalie refused to suffer alone. In a loud and clear voice, she said, "Honey, come look at all these different shades of white."

Brian stopped in his tracks, and his eyes opened wide. All pleasure derived from the ridiculousness of her attire drained from his face.

"Do you think this one would look good in the kitchen, dear?" Natalie asked as she pointed to the entire white section.

Brian stepped closer to her and sternly whispered, "What are you doing?"

"Picking out a soft white. What are you doing?" Natalie fiercely whispered back.

Brian breathed heavily through his nose. "This isn't funny."

"You thought it was a few moments ago. Now we both think it's funny. Besides, what are the odds you will ever see these people again?" Natalie asked.

"The guy at the counter's name is Rob. I see him all the time."

Natalie hadn't thought about that. Embarrassing him in front of strangers was one thing, but doing it in front of people he knew was different. She reached into her pocket and pulled out a peace offering. "Peppermint?"

The gesture made Brian laugh. He yanked the peppermint from her hand and unwrapped it. "You are too much. Pick out your damn paint. I'll take the postcards to Rob to get started on the blue and yellow."

Natalie looked at all the different whites and decided to pick one based on the name. Cloud White sounded like a good choice.

As she walked up to the paint counter, Brian introduced her to Rob. "Rob, this is my friend Natalie. She's slightly insane."

"Babes, we are more than friends," Natalie said, playfully touching his arm.

Brian rolled his eyes. "Don't listen to her, she's off her rocker. But really, can you match the colors?"

"Yup, easy peasy," Rob said. "I will have those ready for you in a few minutes."

Natalie put the white paint swatch on the counter. "Can I get two gallons of this also?" Brian asked.

"Same kind of paint?" Rob asked, and Brian nodded. "Give me about ten minutes."

"Great, I'm gonna get a few things, and we'll be back," Brian said. He tilted his head toward one of the aisles.

"That was easy," Natalie said as she looked at all the different paint brushes they were passing.

"Cloud White is going to be soft enough for you?" Brian asked.

"Just the right amount of softness," Natalie answered. "What are we looking for?"

"I was gonna snag some new drop cloths to lay over your stuff. Mine are dusty, and you have a seventy-year-old new couch to protect," Brian said as he stopped in front of the drop cloths.

"She's so pretty! I love her so much already," Natalie said, clutching her chest.

Brian rubbed the back of his neck and slowly turned to look at Natalie. "So are we going to talk about it, or are we going to pretend it didn't happen?" he asked.

Natalie suddenly became fascinated by all the varieties of painter's tape. "I think it's best to pretend it didn't happen."

"Agreed."

Her mind could pretend it didn't happen, but somebody needed to tell that to her heart. She wanted to talk about anything other than their kiss, but the only thing she thought about was how good it felt to be in his arms and have his hand exploring her back.

"Baseball," she said out of nowhere.

Brian looked at her with a quizzical gaze. "What?"

"Baseball. Have you heard of it?"

"Yes, I've heard of baseball," Brian said, furrowing his brow.

"Cool. Me too. What about nachos? Have you heard of nachos?" Natalie asked.

"Are you just saying random words?"

"Yes, until you come up with a different topic to talk about, I'm just going to say words that come into my head. What are your thoughts on stairs?"

Brian looked at her and smiled. "I like stairs. You can go both up and down them. That's pretty cool."

Natalie's brain had gone completely blank. No other words came to her mind. She stood there, not knowing what to say or do next.

Brian rocked back and forth on his feet a few times before saying, "Why don't we go check on the paint?"

"Great idea," Natalie said.

Rob had finished with the yellow and blue. Brian went ahead and checked out while they waited on the white. Natalie carried two gallons out to the truck, and Brian carried the other four.

"Where are we getting ice cream?" Natalie asked, loading the paint into the back of the truck.

"I thought Pretty Much Perfect Creamery. It's not too far from Montrose." Brian paused for a second. "Plus, they have a drive-through."

Natalie was grateful she wouldn't have to go into another store in her housecoat. "Good choice," she replied.

Chapter 12

18 Days till Thanksgiving

Sunday morning, Natalie went to the apartment building dressed in her own clothes. She found the dolly sitting by the elevator and borrowed it to help her finish moving all the remaining boxes to the back room. By the end of her time there, she felt confident she could navigate the dolly through an obstacle course. Once she had finally finished organizing the back room, she went poking around the building looking for either Henry or Brian to show them her work.

Natalie found Henry talking to one of his crew members. She waited for him to get done talking before asking, "If you're free, I wanted to show you the method to my madness downstairs."

"I'd love that. I'll meet you down there in five minutes or so," Henry replied.

Natalie made her way back to the pub. Now that it was all cleared out, she could picture how she wanted to set everything up for Thanksgiving. While she waited, she dragged a table into the main space. Then she got a chair to figure out the spacing between the bar, the tables, and the buffet. Natalie hated events where everything was so packed together you couldn't maneuver around the room. Initially, she considered serving off the bar, but she thought it might be too high, and she wanted the kids to be able to easily access the food.

The tables looked to be in great shape, even though the one she moved around the room was a little wobbly, but that'd be easy enough to fix once everything had been all arranged. The wooden chairs were the perfect aesthetic. They were similar to the chairs she had pinned on her Thanksgiving Pinterest board she'd reluctantly made for Jenny.

Natalie placed four chairs around the table so she could start to envision what the space would look like when set up for Thanksgiving. She pulled one of them out to take a seat and as soon as her butt made contact, one of the legs broke off, and she fell to the floor.

She lay on the hard tile, stunned. But at least she found out that chair was broken, and she'd been the one to fall, and not her mom or Lindy. After dusting herself off, Henry still hadn't joined her yet. So she decided to check out more of the chairs. She needed a total of twenty-seven. Of the eight she checked, six were usable. At this rate, no one would have anywhere to sit, or it would have to become BYOC—bring your own chair.

Henry walked into the bar as Natalie discovered a tenth unusable chair.

"Watcha doing?" he asked.

"I sat on a chair and one of the legs fell off. I thought I'd test the rest of them, and most of 'em are insanely wobbly, or the legs are loosey-goosey. I'm a little nervous about having enough for everyone to sit on," Natalie said.

"Well, if you need more chairs, there are a couple of dollies full of folding chairs on the fourth floor. You are welcome to use those," Henry offered.

Great, more dollies, Natalie thought. "Thank you. When I come back to clean, I will keep checking these, but it's nice to know we have some backups. I have a vision in my head, and these wooden ones fit it perfectly."

"I get it. In any case, the folding chairs are there if you need them. Now give me the tour of the back room," he said.

Natalie was so pleased to see his expression when he walked into the room. "I had no idea you could fit all these supplies in here. There is even extra space," Henry said.

"These shelves were my saving grace. Being able to go vertical made a big difference. I've labeled all the shelves and put labels on the walls with painter's tape, so it should be easy to find everything and easy to add more stuff in here," Natalie said.

"This is great. Has Brian been down here to see any of this?"

"I am not sure. I haven't shown it to him." Natalie wondered why she hadn't seen him yet that day. They had agreed not to talk about the kiss, but maybe it was still too awkward for him. Seeing him wouldn't have been weird for her; she had barely thought about the kiss today.

Natalie considered texting him that she'd finished organizing. She composed a message in her head when Henry interrupted her thought process.

"Well, when he gets back, I will send him down to check this out. It looks good," he said.

"Oh, he's not here?" Brian's absence explained why she couldn't find him when she'd gone looking for him—or Henry. Either one of them would've been fine, she reminded herself. But it still surprised Natalie how disappointed she was to hear he wasn't in the building.

"No, he had to go get supplies we desperately needed, and it's taken him hither and yon." Henry's phone rang. He looked at the screen and said, "Hey, I've got to take this. Be safe getting back to Lindy's." He walked out of the bar as he answered the phone.

Natalie decided she should head on home. With Brian not there to see her progress, she didn't have anything else to do. The chairs could wait until it was time to clean. At least there were backups. Just not backups that excited her. She sent a little prayer up into the universe that they wouldn't have to use the folding chairs.

* * *

The next few days went by so slowly. She couldn't clean because there was no water. She couldn't paint the picture frames because there was a class in the craft room that took up all the space with their projects, and she couldn't make the goodie bags because the supplies wouldn't arrive till the end of the week. With the help of Charlotte, she did manage to make some dried oranges to add to the centerpiece.

Every day, she adjusted her Thanksgiving calendar to make accommodations for all the delays. The wiggle room she had padded into the schedule slowly started to dwindle, and if things didn't get on track soon, she'd have to start making cuts. She already had to most likely sacrifice the chairs, and she didn't want to have to make any other changes to her vision.

Natalie didn't know what was going on in her apartment because Brian had gone radio silent since Sunday. Between their kiss and weird shopping trip, who could blame him? Anytime her mind began to think about what he might be doing, she tried to refocus. She had just gotten out of a disastrous relationship, and having any kind of thoughts about Brian other than him being her future landlord was out of the question. One man had easily left her homeless; she wasn't going to get involved with another who could do the same. And the kiss happened because she was caught up in him saving her from falling or hitting her head on the wall. It hadn't meant anything.

With Thanksgiving prep paused, Natalie decided to focus on work. She enjoyed everyone she worked with, especially Lisa, who turned out to be a fast study and full of ideas. Donna was encouraging and gave Natalie a lot of creative freedom. The ideas Donna didn't green-light weren't hard nos, just not right nows, due to budgetary constrictions.

During the Uber home from work on Tuesday, Natalie's mom called. "Hello, dear. I wanted to check in on you and see how the new job is going."

"It's actually going really well. Lisa is invaluable. We've got several fun things planned that I'm looking forward to. I'm still getting up to speed on everything, but so far, so good," Natalie replied.

"She's the one who helped you shop the other day, right?" Susan asked.

"Yes, and that sweet angel has volunteered to help me clean the bar when the water's back on. Which is going to be a huge help, because my to-do list is paused until I can get in there to clean."

"Is there anything I can do? You know Jenny keeps offering to help. We can make something here and bring it with us."

"I'd have you make something," Natalie lied, "but I have all the supplies ordered. They just haven't gotten here yet." At least the second part of her statement was true.

"Well, Dad and I will be there a few days before Thanksgiving, and I think it's going to work for Kevin and Jenny to come early too. Your brother is checking in with work to see if he can get the time off."

Natalie sighed. "Great." Her parents getting there early would be a huge help. Jenny, not so much. But Natalie wasn't going to say that to her mom.

She loved crafting with her mom; it was something they had done together for ages. Anytime Jenny joined them, all she did was point out how hers looked exactly like the picture, and Natalie's didn't. That was because Natalie added her personality to a project, and Jenny couldn't do that because she didn't have a personality.

"I'm serious about wanting to help out. I know asking for help is hard for you. But you've been through a lot, and hosting Thanksgiving on top of everything is extra stress," Mom said.

Natalie didn't like thinking about everything she had been through in the past few weeks. "I'm fine. I'm not thinking about any of that right now."

Natalie could hear her mom sigh over the phone. "I've been worried you were doing your Scarlett O'Hara thing again."

Natalie couldn't figure out what her mom was talking about. "What?"

"You know, in *Gone with the Wind*, when Scarlett says, 'I won't think about that now, I'll think about that tomorrow.' You've done that since you were little."

Her statement caught Natalie off guard. She did, in fact, have a nervous breakdown scheduled in her planner for the weekend after Thanksgiving. Everyone would be gone, and that seemed like a good time to cry for forty-eight hours. "Is that really so bad? It has worked for me in the past."

"When has it ever worked for you?"

Natalie was at a loss for words. An example didn't rush to the forefront of her mind, but it obviously had worked at some point. Otherwise, why else would she still do it?

The car pulled up to Montrose Retirement Village, and Natalie decided to walk out to the gazebo instead of heading directly up to Lindy's apartment. "All I know is, I can't break down right now. I'm afraid if I do, I won't ever stop crying. Everything is so different here, and I thought I was good with change. So for now, I'm just pretending. I'm going to fake it till I make it." Natalie settled onto a bench in the gazebo, looking out over the fountain.

"So, you're throwing yourself into Thanksgiving instead," Mom said.

"Exactly. When my scheduled breakdown comes around, more time will have passed, and by then, everything won't be that bad. Because currently, being homeless and living on a couch in a retirement home is kind of bleak," Natalie said as she wiped a tear from her eye. "Plus, I can't think about how dumb I was to move out here. I need to wait until later because then I will have a place to live and be settled in my job and have friends, albeit in different generations. Hopefully, then the math will make sense, because right now it's not mathing."

"Oh, sweet girl, this move, while not how you were expecting it to turn out, was not the wrong decision. You were slowly drowning back home because you were stuck."

"I don't know about that. A month ago, I felt so close to the finish line of my happy ending, and now I'm starting over." More tears appeared in Natalie's eyes.

"He wasn't your finish line, he was a false start. The race had already been disqualified and wouldn't have counted."

Natalie laughed at the direction their conversation had taken. "All those years of watching the Olympics are paying off."

"I do love track and field. But I'm serious, Natalie. I know you. I know he wasn't your person. Good things are coming your way, and after your predetermined cry time, they will be waiting for you with open arms if you just let them in. Embrace all the change. Don't try to control everything. Let the chaos take you wherever it's supposed to take you."

"I'll try to lean into the chaos, because I'm flying by the seat of my pants and don't feel like I have control over anything." A chill ran up Natalie's spine, and she realized her arms were covered in goosebumps. "Hey, Mom, I'm outside and it's getting cold, and my sweater isn't cutting it anymore. I'm going to head up to Lindy's apartment. I'll talk to you tomorrow."

"Sounds good. I love you oodles and noodles," Mom said.

"I love you noodles and oodles," Natalie replied.

Natalie sat in the cold for a few more minutes to collect herself before heading inside.

* * *

Brian texted Natalie Wednesday night as she got ready for bed to tell her that the water had been turned back on and she could move into her apartment on Saturday. On one hand, she was excited to move in, but on the other, she had been enjoying all the time she spent with Lindy.

Natalie walked over to Lindy's room. Her great-aunt was tucked in bed, reading a book. Natalie gently knocked on the doorframe to get her Lindy's attention. "Brian texted the water is back on, and I can move into the apartment on Saturday."

"Oh, that's exciting news," Lindy exclaimed, looking up at Natalie and taking her reading glasses off.

"You get your couch back."

"You could stay here forever, as far as I'm concerned," Lindy said.

"I know. Thank you for that," Natalie said as she leaned against the doorframe.

"No thanks needed. I'd like to come and help you clean the bar. I know your checklist is getting a little behind," Lindy said sweetly, and laid her book on her lap.

Her aunt was in her eighties, and Natalie wouldn't let Lindy help her clean while everything still had a thick layer of dust. Natalie didn't want Lindy to help her clean at all, but she knew better than to try and stop her.

"It's so dusty down there right now. Tomorrow my main goal is to just vacuum all the dust up. I have a shop vacuum that I used in the storage room and on all the boxes I moved. It helped a lot. Once the dust layer is gone, you're more than welcome to help me clean."

"It's such a big project. Doing it by yourself is going to be near impossible," Lindy said.

"I know. But Lisa will be there tomorrow. We talked about it today at work," Natalie said.

"Oh good. Lisa seems like a nice girl. It's so important to make younger friends. When you get to be my age and your friends start to die off, your younger friends are still around," Lindy said. She adjusted her glasses and picked up her book.

Natalie had heard that statement from both her grandmother and Aunt Lindy her whole life. Their mother had said it to them.

"Enjoy your book. I will see you in the morning bright and early for water aerobics," Natalie said as she walked back into the living room. Natalie would miss so many things about Montrose Retirement Village, like Aunt Lindy and water aerobics. But she wouldn't miss sleeping on a couch.

CHAPTER 13

14 Days till Thanksgiving

Thursday after work, Lisa went with Natalie to clean the bar. Lisa turned out to be a whiz at removing dust, which Natalie appreciated. With every section of the bar Lisa tackled, Natalie noticed her friend seemed to get more energized. By the end of the night, Natalie was exhausted, and Lisa acted like she was just warming up.

Lisa finished vacuuming and wrapped the cord around the handle. "I was thinking of ideas for the Marv's Choice photo shoot."

Natalie shook her head. "Lisa, I'm going to share some wisdom with you that was given to me. We're not getting paid right now to talk about our job. Only think about work during the hours in which you're being paid. If you can't bill those hours, don't work for free. But I do look forward to hearing all your ideas tomorrow."

"Oh, that makes sense," Lisa said.

"I was given this advice early on in my career, and it's served me well," Natalie said as she grabbed a broom.

Lisa stood on the brass foot-rail and leaned on the bar. "Okay, no work talk. Getting rid of the dust has helped a lot. This room is already looking better."

Natalie swept up the pile of dirt left from emptying the shop vacuum. "We still have so much to do in here."

"While I was in the manager's bathroom, I realized we should add that to your list of things to clean. And probably do the hallway too. As much of the first floor as we can."

Natalie dumped the contents of the dustpan into the trash can. "I hadn't even thought about the bathroom. But we totally need to do that, and good idea about the hallway. The notebook is on the table over there. Can you write those things down, so we don't forget?"

Lisa went to the table, sat in one of the few non-broken chairs, and started to read out the to-do list. "Have you given Henry your cleaning supply list?"

"Yes, I sent it to him today. Everything will be here tomorrow," Natalie said from behind the bar.

"Great. What about the folding chairs?" Lisa asked. "Have you checked them out yet?"

"No, but from what Henry said, there are a lot of them, and we should be able to find enough that'll work. I'm not worried about the folding chairs right now," Natalie said as she leaned against the bar.

"I'm going to put an asterisk by that, so we know it's one of the last things we do then," Lisa said while annotating the list.

Natalie nodded. "I'm thinking tomorrow, I'm going to start top to bottom. Really dust the walls, the top of the counter, and move my way down toward the ground. That way as dirt falls, it'll simply be taken care of when I clean the floors."

"I like that. I've been dying to crawl up on the bar top and dust the upper shelves. What about the brass footrail? Are we polishing that?" Lisa asked as she stared at it.

"I vote we leave it. I like the patina it has, and I don't know Brian's plans for it." Natalie propped the broom against the wall.

"You're probably right."

Natalie leaned on the counter. "You've done so much tonight. You don't have to come back here and help me clean anymore."

Lisa gave her an astonished look. "Don't rain on my rainbow. I love to clean. Seeing this place and what it can become makes my heart skip a beat."

Natalie held her hands up. "Okay, but know if you ever change your mind, you won't hurt my feelings." She looked around at how dirty everything still was. "Lindy and Charlotte want to come and help clean too, but I think it's still too dirty."

"It's not as bad as it was. The more hands we can get, the better," Lisa said.

"If we start on the walls, they could do the front window and the door. We could set two chairs over there, so if they wanted to sit down, they could," Natalie suggested.

"I can't help with anything this weekend because I promised my dad I'd come home and set up his new router. He wants it up and running before Thanksgiving. The thought of not being able to watch football on Turkey Day is more than he can handle," Lisa said as she stood up.

Natalie had two weeks till Thanksgiving. Everything was carefully scheduled. "Well, I wouldn't have even known when to tell you to come over anyway." Natalie stretched her back. "We finally get access to the craft room this weekend. I will be over there painting picture frames and bouncing back over here to move in. Then, cleaning at some point."

"We have plenty of time to clean the bar before Thanksgiving," Lisa said.

"Not really. The rest of my crafting stuff arrives on Monday. I figure I'll hit this place hard Monday and Tuesday and then spend the rest of the week finishing all the Thanksgiving projects I have," Natalie said as she threw away the last of the dirt-stained paper towel wads.

"Aren't we doing the photo shoot with Henry on Monday and Tuesday?" Lisa asked.

Natalie stopped and looked at Lisa. "I totally forgot about that." She scratched her head and started to talk to herself. "I'll be living here by then, so I can clean at night till I have to go to bed. Crap, the photo shoot throws a wrench in my plans. But I still have all next weekend. I can still get everything done."

She was so lost in thought that when Brian walked in the room, she jumped and yelled, "Holy shit!" at the top of her lungs.

Brian remained unfazed by her outburst. "Hey guys."

These were the first words he had spoken to her in person in close to a week. She felt like he had been avoiding her hard. In the evenings, instead of meeting Natalie at the door to let her in, she found it propped open when she got there, and received a text from him instructing her to close it behind her once she was in.

Natalie clutched her chest and tried to catch her breath. "You scared the crap out of me."

"That's obvious," Brian responded, giving her one of his signature smirks. Those smirks were annoying and made her want to smack them off his face.

"A normal human being would have knocked to make their presence known instead of jumping out of nowhere to scare a person half to death," Natalie said as she put her hands on her hips.

Brian tilted his head. "By jumping out of nowhere, do you mean walk into a room?"

"Yes. Jesus, who does that?" Natalie knew this was a lame reply, but it came out of her mouth before she could stop it.

"Who walks into a room? I believe everyone walks into a room," Brian said and mimicked a person walking.

Natalie threw her hands up in exasperation. "Not like you did. You silently walked in, and clearly intended to scare me. I do not appreciate your malicious tone of walking."

"Are you stringing random words together again and hoping something makes sense? Because if so, you're failing miserably," Brian said and took a step toward her.

"Your face is failing miserably," Natalie said.

Brian stared at her with a questioning look. He finally took a deep breath. "The Grand Dearies want to know if you have had dinner. If not, they wanted to know if you're in the mood for Thai food."

"Why'd they ask you and not reach out to me?" Natalie said as she walked to her purse.

"The queen of missed text messages wonders how she missed more text messages. When you didn't answer, Gigi called me."

Natalie pulled her phone out of her purse and was annoyed to discover she had accidentally put it on silent. She had missed several texts and a phone call from both Lindy and Charlotte.

"Well, crap." Natalie glanced at Lisa, who had her purse on her shoulder. "I'll tell them we are going to dinner."

Lisa shook her head. "No, don't. Go eat with them. I don't really want to sit in a restaurant right now. I'd rather wait until we're both in clean clothes."

"True, we are kind of gross," Natalie responded.

"So, is that a yes?" Brian said from behind her.

Natalie nodded. "It's a yes to Thai. I'll text Lindy," Natalie said as she typed on her phone.

"Fine, let's wrap it up here because the order will be ready soon," Brian said.

Natalie was so confused. "Wait, the order has already been placed?" Natalie asked, still looking at her phone.

"Yes, other people have to eat too," Brian said.

Natalie spun around to look at him. "We're picking it up?"

"Who did you think was going to get it?" He asked her like she was being dumb.

"I don't know. Stop acting like I had all the information," Natalie said, and shrugged. "I came into this conversation at the midway point. My plans for the night just completely changed, so excuse me for taking a second to get caught up. And a certain jerk-face gave me a heart attack seven seconds before all of this," Natalie said.

Brian looked at Lisa. "Are you two done for the night?"

Lisa nodded.

"Great," he said. "I'm gonna lock up. Lisa, it was nice seeing you again."

Brian walked out of the bar without saying another word.

"I'll see you tomorrow," Lisa quickly said to Natalie, and headed for the front door.

Everything happened so fast, and Brian was being so rude. Natalie watched from the window to make sure Lisa got in her car without issue, then switched off the lights to the pub. Brian stood by the exit impatiently tapping his foot. Natalie walked by him without saying anything.

Brian got in the truck and unlocked Natalie's door. She hopped in and slammed the door shut as she glared at him. Her gaze dared him to speak. With Brian, she never knew which person she'd encounter. Sometimes, he was so sweet, and others, he was the most annoying human she had ever met. He pushed all her buttons.

Brian unclenched his hands to turn the car on. Natalie knew she had touched a nerve of his too, and that made her smile.

She wasn't going to break their silent stand-off, even though she longed to ask where they were going and if he knew what they had ordered. Pulling out her phone to ask Lindy would require her to uncross her arms, and that wasn't going to happen.

Tension filled the cab of the truck as they made their way down the highway. The silent treatment had become a game of chicken, and Natalie refused to crack first. Brian slumped in his seat a little and let out a small sigh before saying, "The storage room looks good."

Pleased with her victory and a little taken aback by the compliment, she said, "Thank you."

"You're welcome."

Since he had spoken first, she felt free to ask her questions. "So where are we going?"

"I'm not sure. Gigi sent me an address. I haven't heard of this place before. But apparently some lady at Montrose swears by it," Brian said as he stared straight ahead.

It drove her crazy how she hated him one moment, and then he'd be all nice, and that made her want to be nice. Natalie rolled her eyes and said, "I'm sorry for being a jerk earlier. I know you didn't mean to scare me."

"I will walk louder next time I come into the room," he said, and gave her a quick glance.

Natalie unfolded her arms and said, "Or you could walk into the room singing. That'd be a pleasant way to announce your presence."

Brian chuckled. "What should I sing?"

"Whatever song's in your heart. That's between you and your inner child," Natalie said, shifting to look at him.

"How do you know if I can sing?" Brian asked.

"It doesn't matter if you can or can't. Singing is not exclusive to those who can," Natalie answered.

"I will remember that."

Natalie made circles on the seat with her finger. "So, move-in day is Saturday."

"Yup, everything is almost done. I've got a guy cleaning it tomorrow while I do the last-minute finishes, like hanging your curtain rods, so it'll be all ready for you."

"You didn't have to do that."

"Don't worry about it. Are you ready to leave the retirement village?"

Natalie shrugged. "Yes and no. It'll be nice to have my own place again. Even though all of this still feels like a dream, and I'm living someone else's life."

Brian flipped on his blinker to change lanes and exit the highway. "Why do you say that?"

"Three weeks ago, I got off a plane to be with a person I thought I knew. Then my world came crashing down when I found out he wasn't that person. Looking back, there were all kinds of flashing-neon red flags I totally missed."

"We all miss red flags. Don't beat yourself up over them," Brian said.

"True, but most people don't completely uproot their world for someone who..." Natalie stopped midsentence and choked up. She hadn't thought about her married ex-boyfriend in a while, and talking about him now made her feel stupid for believing all the lies he'd told her.

Brian reached out and took her hand. "This isn't your fault. This is on him."

Natalie clutched his hand and wiped a tear from her eye. "My parents had sold their house, and my friends had moved away. I felt so alone. I wanted to go somewhere I felt like I belonged. If I'm being honest with myself, I knew he wasn't the one, but I thought if we were in the same place, he could become the one. Plus, he made me feel like I belonged with him. And now I don't belong anywhere."

"He's an asshole. But maybe you were meant to move. And you do belong here. You belong with Lindy and Gigi. Henry loves having you around, and you seem to like your job. You're already making friends at work. I even like having you around, even though most of the time you make me want to pull my hair out." Brian smiled and squeezed her hand.

"Brian!" Natalie sang as she squeezed his hand as hard as she could. "Are we friends again?"

"No. I can never be friends with someone as weak as you. You have the strength of a toddler. And now that I'm saying that, that's an unfair statement about toddlers. They are much stronger than you." A grin spread across his face.

Natalie took her hand back and punched him in the arm. "Oh, shush. You like having me around. You said it, and you can't unsay it."

"I needed you to stop crying," Brian said.

Natalie placed her hand on his forearm. "Thank you." Touching him sent chills up her spine.

Brian breathed in through his nose, and Natalie felt like he wanted to say something but had stopped himself. She didn't know if she should pry or not. They were having such a sweet moment, and she didn't want to ruin it by saying the wrong thing. Natalie folded her arms against her chest and looked at the road because looking at him made the butterflies in her stomach flutter.

After they pulled up to the restaurant, Brian parked the truck, undid his seatbelt, and said, "I'll be right back." He got out and went inside to get their food.

She felt his presence missing from the truck. Not seeing him this week made her realize she enjoyed his company, even though he was the most annoying man on the planet at times. She liked fighting with him.

Brian came out of the restaurant doors carefully carrying two very full bags of food. Natalie wondered if Lindy and Charlotte had ordered the whole menu. Brian opened the door to the back seat, and the aroma that wafted in made her stomach start to growl.

"That smells so insanely good," Natalie said as she watched Brian put the food in the back seat.

"I wasn't planning on staying for dinner, but there is no way I'm passing this up," Brian said while climbing into the cab.

"What all did they order?" Natalie asked.

"No idea, but whatever this restaurant is doing, they're doing it well."

Curry, lemongrass, and coconut scents filled the air. "You better hurry up, or else I'm going to have to break into those bags before we arrive."

"We're minutes away," Brian said, and drove a little faster.

When the truck was officially in park, Brian and Natalie jumped out and made their way to the main entrance of Montrose.

"Hurry up," Natalie said as she ran to the door.

Brian closed the back door with his hip. "I had to get the food."

Inside the building, they walked as fast as they could without running. While waiting for the elevator, Brian gently hip-checked Natalie. She retaliated by playfully elbowing him in his side.

The elevator doors were almost closed when Natalie heard Janet ask them to hold the door. Natalie pressed the open button and watched painfully as Janet slowly drove her scooter to the elevator. Natalie had seen this woman zip around Montrose with a surprising amount of precision, yet now Janet couldn't seem to be bothered to go faster than a snail. Brian tapped his foot; he was clearly as frustrated as Natalie.

Once Janet had finally entered the elevator, Natalie pressed their floor number and Janet's.

"That smells terrible," Janet commented.

Under his breath so only Natalie could hear, Brian said, "You smell terrible."

Natalie stifled a laugh.

"What did he say?" Janet asked, whipping her head toward Natalie.

"Nothing," Natalie said as the elevator doors opened to Lindy's floor. She and Brian shimmied past Janet and headed down the hall to Lindy's apartment. Once Natalie was sure the elevator had closed, she said to Brian as they walked, "You are awful."

"Well, she has an awful sense of smell," Brian said.

Natalie laughed and opened the door to Lindy's apartment, singing, "Soup's on!"

Chapter 14

13 Days till Thanksgiving

Natalie was about to close her computer down and start her weekend when she remembered she hadn't responded to Donna's email yet. Donna had sent out a reminder that everyone needed to RSVP to the company holiday party if they hadn't already. Natalie wanted to take Lindy as her plus-one, but she wasn't available that night. She briefly thought about inviting Brian and then immediately shook the idea from her head. That was a terrible idea, and she shouldn't have even thought it.

So instead, she RSVP'd for one and officially signed off for the day. She walked over to Lisa's desk, and the two of them headed to the apartment so they'd be there before the Grand Dearies arrived to help them clean.

Lindy and Charlotte had Natalie and Lisa in stitches while they scrubbed the walls of the bar.

"You two know all the gossip about everyone," Natalie said as she climbed down from a stepladder to rinse her rag.

"I wish. Our biggest source left Montrose earlier this year to be closer to her kids. Since she's gone, it's been a lot harder getting the intel. But we're up for the challenge," Charlotte said, looking at Lindy.

"Beverly had an in with everyone," Lindy said.

Everyone's heads swiveled when they heard Brian knock on the doorframe leading to the bar. "Wow, you guys have done a lot in here."

"We haven't done anything," Lindy said as she pointed to herself and Charlotte. "Natalie and Lisa have done the work of ten men tonight."

Charlotte clutched her invisible pearls and said, "Speak for yourself. I cleaned part of that window, and my stories gave them the energy they needed to complete the job."

Brian rolled his eyes. "I'm sure you did, Gigi." He walked over to Natalie and said, "I've got a surprise for you."

"What?" Natalie asked excitedly.

Brian held up a key. "Are you ready to see your apartment?"

"Oh my god, yes," Natalie said, hopping back and forth.

"Come on, guys, let's go," Brian said.

The apartment dazzled like something out of a magazine. The kitchen backsplash turned out to be more intricate than she'd anticipated; instead of the white tiles she thought were going up, Brian had installed hexagonal tiles in varying shades of dark blue. It popped, and made the apartment look so expensive. The space had a perfect balance of both old and new.

The brass light fixtures mixed with the stone countertop took her breath away. The wood floors looked like they were coated with honey.

Natalie couldn't believe her luck that this was her apartment. She walked over to the kitchen and ran her hand across the counter. "The backsplash is amazing," she cooed.

Brian joined her and examined the tile guy's work. "I had a pile of that tile in my garage. After I saw your insanely floral couch, I thought it'd look good and I had just enough for the project."

Natalie looked over at her furniture piled in the living room, and the mattress and rugs leaning up against the wall. In her mind, she saw everything in place. The thought made her warm and tingly. Her previous apartments had been so sterile, but this space already felt like a home.

"Oh my gosh, I love everything so much," Natalie said, and hugged Brian. She couldn't help herself.

"I'm glad," he said into her ear, and gave her a squeeze before letting her go.

"I can't believe I get to live here." Natalie looked up at Brian. "Thank you so much for making this happen."

Lindy joined Natalie in the kitchen. "It's really lovely, Brian," she said, and patted Brian on the back. "And Natalie, the things you picked out are going to look so good in this space."

"I know, right?" Natalie said. She walked to the couch. "All I want to do right now is start arranging the furniture and put the bedframe together."

"Why don't you two do that?" Charlotte pointed to Brian and Natalie. "The bar is at a good stopping point. Lisa can help us close it down. And the shuttle will be here before too long. Getting everything in its place tonight will help tomorrow's unpacking go by so fast. Then we can hang the curtains. Once those are hung, everything will be done, and you can focus on Thanksgiving."

Charlotte had a point. If she got the apartment arranged tonight, that'd free up all kinds of time this weekend. She looked at Brian. "Do you mind?"

Brian shook his head.

"Okay, great," she said. She gave Lisa a hug. "I'll see you Monday, and thank you so much for helping me tonight."

"My pleasure! I can't wait to see this all done," Lisa said, walking out of the room with Lindy and Charlotte.

"Take pictures," Lindy said, and closed the door behind her.

Natalie looked at Brian. "I am so excited right now."

"Well, I'm about to burst a little bit of your bubble," Brian said. "One of my guys broke the glass on your coffee table. We tried to replace it with an old windowpane we had, but that didn't work. So you don't have a coffee table anymore. I'm sorry."

"I was worried it was something really bad," Natalie said with relief. "And we both know you had them break the table on purpose."

Brian smiled. "I plead the fifth. That thing was so ugly. I still can't believe you picked it out."

"Shut up and help me move these boxes." Natalie walked to the piles of boxes that blocked the couch. She couldn't wait to unpack them and examine what all Charlotte and Lisa had picked out for her at the rummage sale. That night had gone by in a blur, and she only got a quick glance before everything got packed up. "I think if we move all the boxes to the kitchen area, we can start playing around with the rug."

Brian could carry three boxes to Natalie's one. She knew they weren't super heavy, but she was still impressed by his strength. With the boxes out of the way, Natalie could envision the space better. "I want to walk in and see the couch and not the TV," she said as she looked around the room.

After rearranging the furniture a couple of times, Natalie was pleased with the rug and furniture placement. The dinette only had one real place to go, and the bar cart fit perfectly next to the front door. She could see herself placing her keys there every day when she came home.

"Let's put the bedroom together now," she said, and clapped her hands.

As they opened the bedframe box and unloaded the pieces, Natalie insisted on reading the directions.

"Why are you reading the directions?" Brian asked. "This is a standard bed frame. Putting it together is common sense."

"To you, maybe. But I don't think I've put a bedframe together before. And I didn't know I was talking to an expert bed assembler," Natalie retorted.

Brian shook his head. "I have skills you don't even know about."

Natalie blushed. She knew he didn't mean for the statement to have sexual undertones, but being in a bedroom with him made her mind go places. She also had eyes and couldn't help but notice how handsome he was when he smiled. Or scowled, for that matter.

"Shut up, perv," she said.

"What? I didn't take it there. You did. So who's the perv?" Brian said, acting appalled.

"I only speak the truth. Now, get back to work and build my bed," Natalie insisted.

While centering the bedframe on the rug, Natalie's arm accidentally brushed up against Brian's. Touching him made her breath quicken. Brian took her hand and led her to the doorway. He stood behind her and put his hands on her shoulders to move her around till she had a perfect view of the room. He didn't drop his hands once he had her in place. Instead, he leaned in and softly said in her ear, "Is this where you want everything?"

Between the heat of his hands and his breath on her ear, Natalie couldn't tell which was more distracting. Her whole body vibrated. She choked down the knot forming in her throat. "This is good," she said.

As he removed his hands, she felt cold. She couldn't believe his touch affected her so much. This whole night so far had been very confusing. She hadn't gotten mad at him once. In fact, she liked that he flirted with her.

She reminded herself that flirting with Brian was bad, except she couldn't remember why it was bad. But it needed to stop. She was going to put a stop to it. They were landlord and tenant, friends at best. All she needed from him was his strength to help her assemble her bed; that was it.

She stood on the opposite side from Brian to place the box spring and mattress on the frame. Once everything was together, she crawled onto the mattress to try it out.

Brian stood next to the bed, and before she had time to think, she patted the place next to her. He lay down next to her with his hand resting near hers and said, "This is a good bed." He moved his arm so their hands were slightly touching. His pinky slowly started to glide back and forth along her pinky. This modest touch sent shock waves to her heart, and she no longer remembered what she was supposed to put a stop to. She bit her lip and tried not to think of how it'd feel if he made that movement on more sensitive places on her body.

She took a big swallow and said, "Yup."

Neither one of them moved until Brian took her hand in his and brought it to his mouth to kiss. This sweet, simple gesture made her want to mount and ravish him.

He suddenly threw her hand down. "We have to get out of bed."

Natalie couldn't have agreed more. They both jumped to their feet.

Her head spun, and she didn't know what to do or say. He'd just kissed her hand. That tender feeling still lingered. Brian adjusted his shirt and then inspected the window frame. Seeing him at odds made Natalie feel better; at least they both were lost in this moment.

"So, what now?" she asked.

Brian looked over at her. "I don't know."

"Food?" Natalie suggested.

Brian smiled and said, "Food. Have you heard of tacos?"

"I think so, but tell me more," she said as she made her way to the living room.

"There is a place not too far from here that has the best tacos on the planet," Brian said. He opened the front door for Natalie.

"That's high praise. How many tacos have you eaten, where you feel confident saying they are the best on the planet?"

Brian switched the lights off behind them. "You'll just have to find out."

* * *

The spell that had taken control of them in the bedroom had broken, and they were back to their witty banter as they made their way to the restaurant. Natalie sent Lindy a text telling her they were stopping for dinner before heading back to Montrose. Lindy let Natalie know she was heading to bed so she would be ready for move-in day.

Natalie didn't even bother looking at the menu; she let Brian order everything. After all, she didn't want to miss out on the infamous tacos. "Are you excited to see your family for Thanksgiving?" Natalie asked.

"I'm not this year," Brian responded.

"You're not excited?" Natalie was shocked. Charlotte always talked about how close they were as a family.

"No, I'm always excited to see my family. I'm not going to our family Thanksgiving this year," Brian said as he scooped some salsa onto his tortilla chip.

How did she not know this information? Natalie wondered. Charlotte had gone into great detail about all the fun family activities that were planned. "I didn't know that," Natalie said, still wracking her brain to see how she could have missed this key detail.

"You wouldn't know. I haven't built up the courage to tell Gigi yet. We have a walk-through with one of the inspectors for a city permit on the Friday after Thanksgiving. I know Henry can take care of this, but I want to be there too. Any big delays will cause havoc on my timetable," he said.

"On a very small scale, I completely get that. My Thanksgiving schedule is basically now a wish and a prayer," Natalie said. Her whole Thanksgiving extravaganza was built on a house of cards.

"I'm sure you'll get it all done. If everything is gonna fall apart, at least it's with your family. They'll just be excited to see you and your new apartment."

Natalie wished that were true. "For most of them, that'll be the case. But not for all. I don't see eye to eye with my sister-in-law. She and I have very different personalities. Jenny has a way of making me feel like I am the biggest loser, and my ideas and sense of style are ridiculous."

"So, she's not into flower couches?"

Natalie shook her head. "No, not at all. If it wasn't present-ed to her in a store showroom, it doesn't belong in her home. She plays this one-up game I don't understand. If I make a pie, she makes a pie from an award-winning recipe. If I find a shoe sale, she finds the same shoe sale and has coupons. There's al-ways a one-up. If this Thanksgiving fails, then I will hear about it forever. I can hear her now: 'Natalie, is this another one of your Thanksgivings?' or 'Remember when Natalie ruined the place cards?'"

Brian looked at Natalie with a concerned face. "It can't be that bad." His tone of voice wasn't condescending. He seemed to be taking in everything she said.

Natalie took a sip of her water. "Okay, well, maybe ruined place cards are an exaggeration. But the holidays will be littered with passive-aggressive jabs from here out."

"I wonder why she's like that?" Brian pondered.

"I don't know. But you can see her in all her glory at Thanksgiving. Since you can't go to yours, you'll be coming to mine," Natalie stated.

Brian raised an eyebrow. "Is that so?"

"Yes, and if you fight me on this, I will simply have to go to Gigi."

Brian threw his hands up in the air. "You play dirty. And I'd be happy to have Thanksgiving with your family. Do I need to bring anything?"

"You can if you want. But we will have so much food, it isn't necessary." Natalie reached for another chip.

"Are you and Lindy making everything?" Brian asked.

"I make most of it. My mom's side of the family was not blessed with a lot of culinary genes. My dad is a great cook, and his sister, who is coming, will be making a few of the pies. I have a cousin who will bring her corn casserole—it's good."

Brian had such a confused look on his face. "Where do they cook?"

"At the KOA. Most of my family have RVs, and they pile in and drive to wherever. That's why having a rotating holiday isn't a big deal. They were already traveling to go to my parents'. Normally, we'd spend Thanksgiving Day at my parents' house, and then the rest of the time, we all hang out at the RV park playing games and roasting marshmallows. If it rains, we just run back and forth between RVs."

"That sounds like a blast," Brian said.

"It is, and it's a big reason my parents downsized. All my mom's siblings travel around together in their RVs and have the best time. My parents wanted to travel more and join in the fun. Eventually, my parents will get an apartment somewhere, but right now, they're excited to be on the open road."

"Nice. So everybody has an RV?"

"The ones who don't have an RV will stay at the same hotel or rent a big house. I love that my parents are able to do the things they want to do, and the family tradition can still live on. Now we get to spread the fun around."

"I'm glad the tradition continues."

"Thank you again for letting me use the bar and for my apartment. You've helped turn my situation around," Natalie said.

Brian blushed. "It was Gigi's doing."

Natalie smiled. "Most of it was, but it means a lot that you'd go so far to help a stranger."

Brian stared at her. "We aren't strangers anymore."

"No, I guess we aren't," Natalie said, looking down at the table.

Just then, their server arrived with the food. Brian watched as Natalie took her first bite of taco. "It's good!" she exclaimed. "Like, really good."

"Good. I brought my red-flag ex here once, and she ordered chicken fingers off the kid's menu," Brian shared.

"I don't know this woman, but she's clearly an idiot. Did you break up with her during dinner?" Natalie asked.

"Nope, my love goggles were so intense it wasn't until I caught her with someone in my bed that I ended it," Brian said.

Natalie put her taco down. "Oh damn, I am so sorry."

"All the signs were there. I didn't put two and two together, and when it was over and done with, I felt so stupid," Brian said.

Natalie reached over and held his hand. "When did you guys break up?"

"Two years ago. I threw myself into work and have been doing that ever since."

"I get that. That's what I'm doing right now. I've been so busy I haven't had time to think about anything. I don't want to think about anything. I'm worried if I do, I'll have another meltdown and be stuck on Aunt Lindy's couch again," Natalie said.

Brian squeezed Natalie's hand once and let go to take a bite of food. "Well, if you do have another one, you have more of a support system around you now than you did a few weeks ago."

Natalie felt his words deeply. It had been a long time since she had felt this kind of support. Her old friends were great, but they were busy with their own lives. Her parents were always there for her, but they were finally fulfilling a dream of theirs. Maybe it was fate she found herself starting over from scratch.

"We need to change subjects now because you are going to make me cry, and I don't want to get my tacos all soggy."

Brian talked about the building and all the changes he wanted to make to it. He talked about restoring the bar and all the details he planned on bringing back to life. Now that Natalie was familiar with the building, she was able to understand his vision more fully. She also liked that Brian seemed receptive to her ideas.

"I never thought about tying the whole downstairs together. It'd give it more of a rich feeling when residents came into the building. What do you think about hunter-green walls?" Brian asked.

"I like that. With the dark trim, it'd give the place vintage-men's-lounge vibes.

Brian smiled. "Cool."

The check arrived, and Brian swatted Natalie's hand away, saying, "This one is on me."

Thinking there could be another dinner with Brian in the future made the butterflies in her stomach wake up. She checked the time on her phone, and it was still relatively early.

Not in terms of Montrose Retirement Village, but in terms of her old life.

"If you aren't in a rush to get back to Lindy's, I'd like to show you something," Brian said as they walked back to the truck.

"Lindy's in bed, so no one is waiting up for me. Show away," Natalie said. It took all her willpower to control her excitement about spending more time with him. She didn't want to come off as overly eager.

Once they were in the truck, it started raining. "So where are we going?"

"It's a surprise. I wanna get your true first impression when we get there," Brian said.

"Are you taking me to your murder cabin?"

"You're so dumb. My murder cabin is reserved for second dates, not first," Brian said as he merged onto the highway.

Natalie didn't know dinner had been a date. She wasn't upset it was a date. In fact, thinking of it as a date gave her the warm fuzzies. But they were talking about a murder cabin, so maybe he was just joking.

"Note to self, never go on a second date with Brian," Natalie said as she pretended to type on her phone. Keeping the mood light seemed like the right move.

"It's better to be safe than sorry," Brian joked. His response left Natalie even more confused. She decided not to think about it, even though he had kissed her hand and bought her dinner.

The mystery location turned out to be only a few minutes from the restaurant. Visiting an abandoned drive-in movie theater was not what Natalie expected.

"Henry and I are talking about buying this place and re-modeling it," Brian said as he parked in the middle of the drive-in lot.

"I used to love going to the drive-in. I personally am pro-drive-in."

Brian nodded. "I wish it wasn't raining. I'd show you the concession stand. It has some cool details."

"Do you want to run a drive-in?" Natalie asked.

"No, we will flip it. I think it could be a nice palate cleanser after the apartment building," Brian replied. He leaned forward and looked up at the sky. "The rain doesn't seem to be letting up."

"Let's give it a few more minutes," Natalie said, and unbuckled her seatbelt. "I want to see the concession stand."

Brian nodded and unbuckled his seatbelt as well. "Okay. When was the last time you went to a drive-in?"

"Man, it's been years. I always thought it'd be like in the movies, and I'd make out with my boyfriend, but I only ever went with girlfriends. Don't get me wrong, we had the best time, but there was never any hanky-panky. Also, there were kids everywhere. I don't know how a make-out session could happen anyway. I feel like you'd get caught," Natalie said.

"I've experienced hanky-panky at a drive-in without getting caught."

"You dirty bird. It must not have been in this truck because this center console looks like it'd make hanky-panky near impossible," Natalie said.

"It wasn't in this truck; it was when I was in high school. But this console lifts up." Brian lifted the console. Nothing sat between them now. "See, now hanky-panky can proceed." Brian stammered, "Not that I am saying it will right now. I was just showing you it's a possibility."

Natalie enjoyed watching him squirm. "I get what you are saying. But I still don't understand the mechanics of actually kissing without people noticing. Do teenagers forget there are people all over the place? When we used to go to the drive-in, people were constantly walking about or sitting outside watching the movie."

"Scoot over here and I'll show you," Brian said. Natalie gave him a look. "Not like that. Stop it. I'm going to give you a PG tutorial on how to make out on the sly at the drive-in."

Natalie gave him another look and, feigning reluctance, scooted over to him.

"Now, I always went to places that had two-sided screens. One side showed kids' movies, and the other side showed PG-13 and above." Brian put his arm around Natalie and rested his hand on her shoulder.

As Natalie settled in next to Brian, she said, "Oh, that makes sense. Ours only had one screen, and it only showed cartoons and family movies."

"If you would've had two screens, fewer kids would have been on the grown-up-movie side. I always tried to be sly, but I had a lot of friends who didn't care about getting caught," Brian said.

"I bet you weren't as sneaky as you thought," Natalie said.

"I absolutely was."

Natalie bit her lip and said, "Prove it."

"What do you think I am doing? I'd put my arm around my date and have her lean in like this." Brian pulled Natalie in so her shoulder rested on his chest. "You lean your head back and look at me, and I lean in." He put his hand on Natalie's chin and tilted her face up while he moved closer.

As he spoke, their lips were almost touching, and she felt the gentle breath of his words on her mouth.

"The headrest blocks the back view, and it simply looks like we are cuddling."

"I don't think you were fooling anybody," Natalie said, frozen in place. "I think they knew exactly what was going on." Neither one moved an inch. "You might have been able to get away with it if you were just talking, but there is more movement with kissing."

Brian squeezed her shoulder and let out a deep sigh. "I don't think you know what you're talking about."

Natalie bit her lip again. "To prove it would require a demonstration."

"This is basically science now. I think a kiss is required to complete the experiment," Brian said as his breathing grew heavier.

"Agreed," Natalie whispered.

Brian's lips met hers as soon as the words were out of her mouth. They started off with soft, gentle kisses. Natalie placed her hand on his face and slowly parted her lips. Brian gently caressed her tongue with his. Each kiss got deeper and deeper.

Natalie didn't want the kisses to stop, but her neck ached from the odd position she was in.

"Hold on." She pulled away and stretched her neck from side to side.

"I'm so sorry. I didn't mean to—" Brian began.

Natalie put her hand on his thigh and interrupted him while she rubbed her neck. "The last time I made out in a car, I had a much younger body." She scooted away from him, over to the middle of the seat, and twisted toward him. "Okay, now you twist toward me maybe?"

Brian followed her directions. She took his head in her hands, and they began kissing again.

Brian slid his hand behind her back. He tugged at her ponytail and tried to lift his hip off the seat to pull her into an embrace.

"Wait." He stopped and sat back down in the seat. "I'm getting caught on the steering wheel. Maybe we need to treat this like we are on a couch. Let's move to your side."

"Good idea," Natalie said as she moved to her door. "If I angle toward you, then you can kind of lean over me." She adjusted and then paused. "But now you are battling the middle humpy thing on the floor."

"What if I put my knee on the seat and lean over you like this?" Brian awkwardly moved about the cabin. Eventually, he ended up with one knee on the seat and the other leg between Natalie's.

He leaned over her, and she slid down a bit so he wouldn't hit his head on the roof. Natalie put her hand on his shoulder as they began kissing again. Since she had slid down, her back was scrunched, and moments away from starting to ache.

Natalie stopped kissing Brian and patted his cheek. "If we continue kissing like this, our old bodies will start to hurt again. I think it's obvious we are going to have more success in the murder cabin."

Brian snorted with laughter. "Shut up. I need to get several good kisses in before my forty-year-old back gives out."

Natalie moved her hand to the back of his neck and pulled him to her. She loved how soft his lips were and how well their mouths fit together. Kissing him felt like second nature. The only thing awkward was how they'd positioned their bodies.

She was so absorbed in the moment that she jumped a little when Brian pulled away. "I have to call it. My back and my knee can't stay like this any longer." He slowly returned to his spot behind the steering wheel. While he repositioned himself, Natalie wondered what he was thinking. Tonight's hanky-panky had been far from sexy.

"I don't want to take you to the murder cabin just yet. But would you like to join me for dinner one night this weekend?" Brian asked as he looked at her and ran his hands through his hair.

Natalie beamed. "I'd like that. Tomorrow night is best for me."

"Works for me too. It's a date. Let's see how your move goes in the morning, and we will figure out a time after that. I think a good-night kiss in front of your door will be much more successful," Brian said.

Natalie went to buckle her seatbelt. "Only time will tell."

Chapter 15

12 Days till Thanksgiving

On Saturday morning, Natalie, Lindy, and Charlotte had all the boxes unpacked, the bed made, and all the clothes hung in the closet by ten a.m. It had been a productive morning. Lindy sat at the kitchen table making a list of a few last-minute odds and ends Natalie needed.

"Add dishtowels," Charlotte said as she shut the silverware drawer.

"Good idea," said Natalie from the bedroom.

Lindy looked up from her list. "We got some the other day. I bet they got put away with her bathroom towels."

Before Charlotte could make her way to the linen closet to check, there was a knock at the door. Lindy leaned over and opened it from where she sat.

Natalie came around the corner into the kitchen and said, "Toilet bowl cleaner and a toilet brush." She stopped in her tracks when she saw Brian standing at the door holding a bouquet of flowers. She smiled shyly. "Hi."

Brian locked eyes with her. "Hi."

"Those are beautiful," Charlotte exclaimed.

While still looking at Natalie and slightly blushing, he said, "Thanks, Gigi. They are a housewarming gift for Natalie."

Charlotte looked between Natalie and Brian, who were still frozen in place. "Lindy, won't these look perfect in the vase you got for Natalie?" she asked and headed to the kitchen to get the vase out of the cabinet.

Lindy stood up and joined Charlotte in the kitchen. "They will. Brian, you did such a good job picking out flowers."

They kept eye contact for a few more seconds before he looked away. "I thought I'd come and do a trash run for you. Are any of these boxes ready to go?"

"That'd be such a help," Lindy chimed in. "I can condense some of these to make them easier to carry." She headed to a pile of boxes and started to break them down, placing the smaller ones into the large TV box.

Charlotte stood in the kitchen filling the vase. "We should get the flowers in water."

Natalie hadn't moved or stopped looking at Brian. Hearing about the flowers again broke the spell she was under, and she came to her senses. "Oh my gosh, those are so pretty." She looked back at Brian. "Thank you so much."

"Charlotte, bring me the boxes from the bedroom," Lindy instructed. She was already through most of the kitchen boxes.

Charlotte went into the bedroom. Natalie walked over to the vase and Brian joined her in the kitchen. "This was so nice of you," Natalie said as she gently bumped him with her shoulder.

"I wanted to welcome you to the building and give you your keys."

Natalie took the arrangement and placed them in the vase. She looked around the room and decided to set them on a side table in the living room. "So what do you think, now that it's all accessorized?"

"It looks good. Your couch is even growing on me," Brian said.

"Her bedroom is adorable," Charlotte said, coming out of the bedroom carrying a box of boxes.

Brian quickly walked to her and took the box out of her hands. "Let me take those. I'll take them to the dumpster real quick."

"No, give me that one," Natalie said. She took the smaller box from him. "And you take the big one."

"We will be back," Brian said as he picked up Lindy's box.

On the way to the dumpster, it dawned on Natalie she'd be sleeping in her apartment that night. "I don't know why I didn't think to ask this sooner, but I'll be here in this building at night by myself, correct?" She felt like she had just moved into her very own murder cabin.

"No, we have a security company who sends someone out every night to watch the building. I usually don't leave here till about ten at night, and someone from Henry's crew gets here about four a.m.," Brian said as he threw his boxes in the dumpster.

Natalie handed Brian hers. "I don't know if that makes me feel better."

He took a step closer to her and put a hand on her shoulder. "Henry also insisted we use a steel door for your front door, and we installed a camera in the hallway you'll be able to access. You can add a security system if you like, and a doorbell camera if you want to. I can help you install everything."

Everything Brian said sounded good, but it was still weird to think about being alone in a giant building. "I'll make sure I am home every night before you leave," Natalie said.

"And if you're not, the security guard can walk you up to your door if that makes you feel better."

Knowing Brian and Henry had already thought about her living there alone did help. They'd come up with ways to make her feel safe. She'd definitely get a security system and a new can of mace, just to be sure.

"As a woman, I have to think about these things." Natalie tried to keep her tone light so he wouldn't think she was overreacting.

"I know, and I hate you have to do that. It's awful. I'll show you how to work the cameras, so you can see everything. I'm only ten minutes away. If you need anything, you call me." Brian finally tossed the boxes he was holding in the trash. "Tonight, when I bring you home, I will introduce you to whoever is on duty. It rotates between three guys. I like all three of 'em, and it makes me feel better knowing they'll be here with you."

His reference to their date and the fact he wanted to keep her safe made her shiver all over. Natalie wanted to close the gap between them and kiss him. But she didn't want their next kiss after the disastrous car make-out session to be in front of a dumpster.

"I'd like that," Natalie finally said. "Let's head back upstairs. I think we are almost done."

"Do you guys need a ride back to Montrose?" Brian asked as they headed into the building.

"No, Aunt Lindy wants to go get lunch before we start sewing. I might need your help tonight hanging the curtains, if you don't mind."

"I don't mind at all."

Natalie looked down at her shirt so he wouldn't see her blush. She noticed there were little Styrofoam balls from one of the boxes stuck to her. She did her best to wipe them off, but they kept jumping back onto her. What she needed to do was take her shirt off and whip it in the air a couple of times.

When she had finally conceded defeat, she looked up and Brian stood in the elevator waiting on her. "Tricky little buggers," Natalie said.

"Happens all the time," Brian responded.

* * *

After getting back from lunch, the ladies made their way to Montrose's craft room, which was huge and had everything a person would need to get down to crafting business. The sewing area was in the back of the room, and deep base cabinets with a stainless-steel countertop wrapped around most of the wall space. There was even a loom stored against the wall near the utility sink. Tables were scattered around, and the cabinets were full of art supplies. It was a one-stop shop. Natalie had ordered fall-colored paints, but had forgotten to buy paintbrushes. Luckily, she found a whole basket full of them.

Lindy and Charlotte sat in the sewing area measuring and pinning the flower material that matched Natalie's couch, and Natalie painted the picture frames at one of the tables.

"How long do we soak the tablecloths for, to get the stains out?" Natalie asked as she started on her first frame.

Lindy looked at the clock on the wall. "I'd say for another thirty minutes or so. Then we'll give them a good rinse. The stains weren't bad at all. One soak should do the trick. But we can always do two."

"Sounds good to me," Natalie said, and set a timer on her phone.

The women worked in silence and were each engrossed in what they were doing. Charlotte pinned the panels and Lindy sewed them. Natalie had just settled into her groove of painting frames when the timer for the tablecloths went off.

While looking for paintbrushes, Natalie had found a collapsible drying rack and set it up in the corner of the room. Lindy gave clear directions on how to rinse the tablecloths, and Natalie followed them to a T.

"Now, hang each one carefully on the drying rack. In a few hours, I'll inspect them, and hopefully they will be done, and we won't have to do another round of bleaching."

Carefully, Natalie hung each tablecloth, making sure they were evenly spaced and not touching the ground.

"I know I'm not close to the tablecloths, but they look pretty good to me. I don't notice any stains," Charlotte said, looking up from her pinning.

Natalie inspected the last piece she hung up. "I don't either. Once they dry, if we do see anything, it'll be barely noticeable. I don't think we'll have to resoak anything."

Charlotte went back to pinning. "What's your plan for cooking? You have a lot of people coming and just one oven."

"I know. I've been brainstorming this with my mom. Every RV has an oven, so the plan is that I will make up all the casseroles and side dishes that need to be heated beforehand, and send them back to the KOA with my parents. On Thanksgiving, everyone will bring them hot and ready. True potluck style," Natalie said as she resumed painting.

"If it's okay with you, I'll send my macaroni and cheese with Brian. I only make it at Thanksgiving anymore, and since he won't be at ours, he can at least eat it at yours," Charlotte said.

Lindy stopped sewing and looked at Charlotte. "I didn't know Brian was coming to our Thanksgiving."

"He told me this morning before we left the building. He said he couldn't get away. Natalie was sweet enough to invite him to yours," Charlotte said, smiling at Natalie.

"We will be delighted to have him join our ranks," Lindy said. She was just about to resume her sewing when she said, "Oh no, we don't have a picture frame for him."

Natalie hadn't thought about a place card for Brian. "I'll add buying another frame to my list." The frame was the least of her worries about putting together a place card for Brian. The thing that made the cards keepsakes was that every year, each card listed all the reasons that person was special. Writing one for Brian seemed incredibly intimate. Maybe too intimate.

"How's your Thanksgiving to-do list coming?" Charlotte asked Natalie.

"Well, I'm not where I'd like to be. I have all the supplies for the goodie bags and a spreadsheet put together of what needs to go in them. I had visions of getting out my calligraphy pens and taking my time on each. But I don't know if I have time for that now. I think I might have to scale the bags back a little bit." Natalie opened a new paint bottle.

"You take after your grandmother so much. She loved going above and beyond. But it's okay to not go over the top," Lindy said.

"I know, but she always made me feel so special, and she did everything so perfectly. Continuing her traditions keeps her memory alive." Natalie started to tear up.

Lindy stopped sewing and looked at her niece. "My sweet Natalie, she's all around us. Trust me, she'd understand about this year being different. You've had a lot of roadblocks thrown your way. You're handling them beautifully, but no one is going to be bothered if everything isn't 'Berry Perfect.'"

But Natalie would know it wasn't perfect, and Jenny would be delighted to point out all the areas where Natalie failed. Her family was known for perfect parties, perfect weddings, and perfect holidays. Natalie would not be the one to let everyone down.

Thinking about compromising on Thanksgiving made Natalie want to throw up. But compromise wasn't an option yet, so she wasn't going to think about it. There was still time, and she could still make this all happen. She channeled all her energy into getting the frames painted.

Two hours later, Natalie had them neatly laid out on the counter, drying next to the rack of tablecloths, and Lindy and Charlotte were putting the finishing touches on the curtains.

Natalie was in total awe of their skills. "I can't wait to hang those in my living room."

"Are you sure you don't want to stay for dinner?" Lindy asked as she neatly folded the curtains and placed them in a bag.

Natalie and Brian had agreed to keep their date between the two of them. Until there was news to share, it wasn't worth talking about. "I'm sure. I'm really looking forward to spending the evening in my apartment. And I need to start on the place cards and goodie bags." This wasn't a complete lie. She was looking forward to spending most of the evening in her apartment. Just some of it would be spent away from the building while at dinner. At some point, she'd also continue working on her to-do list.

"Send pictures once they are up," Lindy said.

"I will." Natalie took the bag from Lindy and gave her a hug. "I'll see you two tomorrow for breakfast at my apartment. That sounds so nice say."

"I can't wait. I'll bring the picture frames and tablecloths with me," Lindy said.

"Perfect," Natalie replied, waving goodbye as she walked out of the room.

CHAPTER 16

It had been years since she'd gone on a real date. Yes, she had gone to dinner with Brian and attempted to make out with him in his truck, but that hadn't been planned. Tonight was a date date. And best of all, she was getting ready in her own space. Tonight, she was no longer a resident of a retirement home, but living in her own adorable apartment.

Even though most of the items in the apartment had been purchased in under an hour, her place felt more like her than any of her previous homes. Surprisingly, she didn't miss any of the things she'd sold before moving here. Looking around at her new possessions, everything represented a new beginning. At some point, her parents would make their way to their storage unit and send Natalie her boxes of sentimental items. Once those arrived, her apartment would be complete.

Natalie took her time getting ready. Having a bed to lay her clothes on seemed like such a luxury. And she could walk around her room in her underwear instead of battling to get dressed in Lindy's half bath. She could not wait to go to bed and sleep with her arms and legs completely outstretched.

Brian arrived right on time. She opened the door and was surprised to see him wearing a shirt that wasn't flannel. He'd donned his signature jeans, of course, and added a blue cotton button-down shirt, a brown leather belt, and matching brown leather shoes.

"You look very handsome," Natalie said, and stepped aside for Brian to walk into the apartment.

"Thank you, but it's clear who the pretty one is between the two of us. You look beautiful," Brian said as he looked Natalie up and down.

She knew she looked good. The black dress she wore was one of her favorites—a short-sleeve jersey dress with a circle skirt. It could easily go from casual to dressy. Tonight she'd paired it with black tights, flats, and a jean jacket.

"Thank you," she said while twirling, because who could resist twirling when wearing a circle skirt? "I'm starving. Where are we going for dinner?"

"I have a few places in mind. But if there is something else you're in the mood for, let me know," Brian said. Natalie nodded for him to continue so he began to list off the options. "I thought I'd show you the restaurants within walking distance. There's a great burger place down the street, an Italian restaurant's a few doors away, and a new gastropub I've heard good things about is a couple blocks over."

"Burgers. A hamburger and onion rings sound so good right now," Natalie said without hesitation.

"Burgers it is." Brian held his arm out for Natalie. She looped hers through his.

Natalie liked that he gave a little tour of her new neighborhood on the way to Ron's Burgers.

"That place has a very cool rooftop bar during the summer," he said, pointing to another art-deco building they passed. "In my opinion, they have the best spicy margarita in town."

Natalie looked toward the top of the building. "That's a pretty big statement."

"I said what I said." Brian smiled.

The restaurant was hopping, and Natalie had trouble hearing Brian talk as they waited for a table. When they were seated, they decided to sit on the same side of the booth so they wouldn't have to yell at each other.

"This is weird," Brian said as he read the menu.

"What's weird?" Natalie asked.

"Sitting right next to you, instead of across from you. This feels weird."

"I'm not the one who has old-man ears and couldn't hear a single word of our conversation. Get hearing aids and you can sit across from me next time." She elbowed Brian in the side.

"Me? I was the one who couldn't hear anything? You were the one sounding like an owl by asking 'who' over and over."

He was right; Natalie had been straining to hear him, but only because he wasn't speaking up.

"I don't know what you are referencing. I think you might have memory issues. Have you thought about getting tested for early-onset dementia?" Natalie asked, trying not to smile.

"Listen, whippersnapper. I may be a few years older than you, but I'm not ancient by any means." Brian nudged her leg with his.

"The jury is still out. I was in the truck when you failed to make out with me."

"It was your neck that got sore," Brian exclaimed.

"And your back couldn't hack it."

"You try staying in that position for an extended period of time and see how long you can last." Brian looked at Natalie.

Natalie placed her hand on her chest, "I am basically a young, nubile maiden. I bet I could hold that position all day. Unfortunately, it's not a very flattering pose, and I'm nothing if not a lady, so it's not in the cards for me."

Brian shook his head. "What am I going to do with you?"

Natalie blushed and shrugged as their waiter approached the table.

* * *

Brian was right—the burgers were fantastic. Having so many tasty spots close to her place excited Natalie. As they walked back to her apartment, she liked that there were so many people out and about. She particularly enjoyed all the Thanksgiving window displays they passed.

It was a chilly night, but not cold enough she wished she had put on a heavier coat. The cooler weather gave her an excellent excuse to walk closer to Brian. She liked how easy it was to talk to him; the banter between them felt effortless. They passed an ice cream shop, and she insisted they go in.

Natalie licked the last remaining evidence of her pecan pie ice cream from her finger. "I don't know why, but I love cold things when it's cold, and hot things when it's hot. Ice cream in the winter and soup in the summer."

Brian scoffed. "Ice cream is great all year long, but soup in the summer? That's not natural."

"You're not natural," Natalie replied.

Brian sighed. "You are the weirdest woman I have ever been on a date with."

Natalie acted offended. "Me? That seems unlikely. I'm a sane, normal human person who sold all their worldly possessions to move in with a married man and then moved into a retirement home instead. That's a perfectly rational story. It's basically every woman's story."

"You forgot about shopping for your whole apartment in under an hour and moving into a construction zone. Plus, hosting Thanksgiving for your entire family in a dirty bar that only has broken chairs," Brian added.

"See, that's the part that makes it different. The rest of it is pretty average. But my flower couch and cleaning up the bar take me over the edge. So maybe I'm the most ... *exciting* woman you have ever dated," Natalie corrected.

"I see what you did there. I stand by weird," Brian said.

"Looks like someone doesn't want a goodnight kiss," Natalie said while pulling out her key and opening the front door of the building.

"My bad, let me change that. Most intriguing woman. Is that better?" Brian followed her to the elevator.

"No, too little too late," Natalie said. "I guess the only way to make it up to me now is to help me hang my curtains."

They got in the elevator and Brian pushed the button for her floor.

"If I must," he said.

With Brian's help, the curtains went up in no time. He stood back and said, "This damn pattern is growing on me."

"You aren't just saying that because you want to put your tongue in my mouth?" Natalie smiled and gave Brian some side-eye.

"I do want to do that, but this all looks pretty good together. It feels right in this apartment. Your unit is the only one that will have this much of a vintage feel. The molding is original, and so are the wood floors. I wanted to modernize a little bit, but not too much. All the other apartments will be almost completely uniform," Brian said.

Natalie sat cross-legged on her couch. "I've been meaning to ask, what's the deal with you and this apartment building? This is a huge job. Do you always do projects this big?"

Brian sat on the other end of the couch. "I didn't at first. I took over my family's construction firm from my dad. I started off doing my own thing, because I wanted to prove I could make it on my own before getting into the family business. A couple of years ago, we merged my company with my family's. Buying this building was the last thing my dad did before he retired."

"Aren't you nervous doing this all by yourself?" Natalie asked.

"No, I've been helping him with projects like this for ages. And whenever I need to brainstorm or problem-solve, he's only a phone call away," Brian said. "What makes this project different is the bar. One of my passions is restoration, and restoring the bar to its original glory is exciting to me."

"It's going to be a big project," Natalie said.

"I know, I can't wait. We probably can't even think about starting on it until next summer. But seeing the space cleared out and all the progress you've made with cleaning it makes my brain have rapid-fire ideas." Brian's eyes twinkled with excitement.

"I am happy to play a small part in your idea generation."

Brian looked at his watch. "Terry should be here now. I want to take you down to meet him. He's the security guard who's here the most."

"Sounds good," Natalie said as she stood up and adjusted her dress.

They arrived downstairs, where a stout, bald man sat on a folding chair in the front entryway. He had a tablet set up on a second chair in front of him, playing a football game. A small cooler sat on the floor next to him.

"Evening, Terry," Brian said as he walked toward him.

Terry didn't bother to look up from his tablet and nodded at Brian. "Evening, Brian," he said curtly.

"I need to introduce you to someone," Brian said.

Terry looked over at Brian and stood up when he noticed Natalie. Terry's tone changed from gruff to nurturing. "Who do we have here?"

"Terry, this is Natalie, our one and only tenant so far," Brian said.

"Well, this is a pleasant surprise." He reminded Natalie of her vice principal in junior high, who had been stern with the boys and a pushover with the girls. "Nice to meet you, Natalie. You let me know if I can help you in any way."

"I will, thank you, Terry. It's nice to meet you too. I promise not to be any trouble." Natalie extended her hand.

Terry took her hand and gave it a gentle squeeze. "I don't think that's possible."

"I was a little nervous about being here overnight by myself, but it makes me feel a lot better knowing you are so close by," Natalie said.

"I've got a good crew here. You're in good hands," Terry said. He put his hands in his pockets and rocked back and forth on his feet.

"He really does. Everyone's been great to work with," Brian said.

"I look forward to meeting them," Natalie said.

"Terry, gonna let you get back to your game. You have a good night," Brian said.

Terry tipped an imaginary hat to them. "You too."

Brian put his hand on the small of Natalie's back and guided her to the elevator. Her heart did a little summersault from his touch.

"He seems nice," Natalie said quietly.

"He's good people. They all are," Brian said. "Do you feel better about staying here by yourself?"

Brian led Natalie onto the elevator, and she said, "For sure, but it's going to take a minute to get used to. I still have new-apartment jitters. But those will pass quickly."

"If you need anything at all, you call me. I'm not far from here," Brian said.

Natalie hadn't even thought about where Brian might live till right now. As a kid, she was always weirded out seeing teachers outside of the school. Teachers belonged in a school, just like Brian only existed in this building and his truck. But he obviously had to live somewhere. She made a mental note to ask him about his place sometime.

"Why do we never take the stairs?" Natalie asked as the doors opened.

"We can take them. I am so used to constantly using the elevator. I'm all over this place. I go up to seven, down to three, back up to nine. It's a habit now." Brian said as they got off the elevator.

"I don't mind. I was just curious. I don't think I have ever seen the stairs here," Natalie said, walking to her door.

"You're a woman on a mission, and I support your dreams," Brian said.

Natalie started to open her front door and Brian put his hand on her arm and spun her around. "I believe this is a front door, and I am pretty sure I promised you a kiss by your door."

Natalie's pulse quickened. "This door?" She pointed to the door behind her. "Are you sure it was this door?"

"I can't think of any other door it could be," Brian said as he slid his arm around Natalie and brought her closer to him.

"There are so many doors in this place. Hundreds of doors, in fact. I can think of twenty off the top of my head." Natalie draped her arms around his neck. She licked her lips in anticipation.

"But this is the kissing door," Brian said, wrapping his other arm around her and drawing her in tighter so there was barely any space left between them. He nudged her nose with his.

"Well, if this is the kissing door..." Natalie didn't finish her sentence before his lips were on hers. His soft, gentle kisses made her knees weak. She had always been a fan of little kisses. She appreciated how tender his were as she ran her hands through his hair.

Brian moved his head back and smiled at her. "Okay, well, that was fun. I think I should go."

"Shut up," Natalie said, and pulled his head toward hers. She parted her lips and kissed him deeper. Her tongue found his, and she savored the sweetness of their touch. Still embracing her, Brian walked them so her back pressed against the wall next to her front door. Natalie was grateful for the added support because he made her want to melt into a puddle right there in the hallway.

The electricity between them pulsed through her body. His hands hadn't traveled an inch, yet her body longed for him to explore her. Natalie's mind started to race. She wanted this man desperately, but it also felt like it was too soon, and she had already complicated her life enough by kissing her landlord. But she was not conflicted enough to stop kissing him.

After her brain had finally quieted and focused on his mouth, Brian pulled away slightly.

"I think I should go," he said and gave her a little kiss. "If I stay any longer, I'm not going to have any control over myself." He gave her another little kiss.

"Are you sure?" Natalie asked breathlessly.

"Yes," Brian responded, adding several more little kisses.

Natalie tugged him to her and his lips met hers. He held her tight and kissed her deeply. He pulled her hair back and kissed her neck. All at once, he jumped away.

"I should go," Brian said.

Natalie opened her mouth to speak, and Brian held his hand up to silence her. "I need to go, or else I'll never leave. I'll check in with you tomorrow. Please call or text me if you need anything tonight." Brian walked away, and Natalie stood stunned against the wall.

Brian took two steps and then said, "Just one more small kiss."

Natalie stepped toward him, and he drew her into an embrace. He gave her one soft little kiss.

"Okay, just one more," he said.

Five little kisses later, Brian walked to the elevator, and Natalie opened her door. Brian waited to get in the car until Natalie was safely inside her apartment.

Natalie felt torn about wanting things to go farther. But it was refreshing that she didn't have to put a stop to things for a change. She liked that he had left her wanting more. He hadn't made her feel in any way like the only thing he wanted from her was sex.

She got ready for bed and dug out the vibrator she had hidden in her dresser drawer.

CHAPTER 17

11 DAYS TILL THANKSGIVING

The next morning, Natalie gathered all her trash to make a stop at the dumpster before heading to the bakery to pick up pumpkin spice bread and coffee for the three of them. Getting groceries was high on her priority list today.

The wind rushed into the building as she opened the back door, and the brisk air hit her in the face. It was so strong it took her breath away. Once she got outside, she did her best to block her face with her arm. After she tossed the trash in the dumpster, the wind calmed down. Natalie took a minute to adjust her coat and tried to get several strands of hair unstuck from her lip gloss. She did one final hair toss and out of the corner of her eye, she saw Brian's truck. He hadn't told her he planned on being at the building this morning.

Natalie was about to walk back inside to look for him when she noticed Brian sitting in his truck. Upon further investigation, she realized he was asleep in the cab, still wearing the same clothes as last night. A ton of questions swirled in her head. Had he gone to a bar last night and couldn't drive home? Was he dead? Did he have car troubles? Once she got closer to his truck, she knew he wasn't dead because saw him breathing. Natalie gently knocked on the driver's side window and hoped she wouldn't startle him too much.

Brian slowly opened his eyes and then tried to shield them from the light. He looked over and smiled when he realized Natalie was standing there. He turned the truck on and rolled the window down.

"What are you doing here? Why are you sleeping in your truck?" Natalie asked.

Brian rubbed his eyes. "I didn't mean to fall asleep. I wanted to be close in case you needed me last night. It was your first night here by yourself, and I wanted to make sure it went okay."

Natalie's heart exploded. That was one of the sweetest things anyone had ever done for her. "Aren't you freezing?"

Brian shook his head. "Honestly, the cold didn't bother me a bit. I turned the truck on and off throughout the night. I don't know when I fell asleep. The last thing I remember was turning the truck off at about three." He sat forward and stretched his back. "Did you have a good night?"

"I did have a good night. Meeting Terry helped. Do you want to come up? Lindy and Charlotte are coming over for breakfast in a little bit," Natalie said.

Brian yawned. "Good deal. If it's okay with you, I think I'm gonna go home and try to get a little more sleep."

Natalie wanted to laugh. He'd spent the whole night in his truck making sure he'd be nearby in case she needed him, and he was asking her if it was okay if he went home. Natalie wondered if this was what people meant by the phrase, 'If he wanted to, he would.'

"Please go home and get some sleep," Natalie insisted. "It was so kind of you to do this for me, but I absolutely want you to get some sleep now."

Brian nodded and put his seatbelt on. "Have fun with the Grand Dearies. I'll text you later?"

"Please do," Natalie replied. She stepped away from his truck so he could back out of the parking space. She waved goodbye and waited until he had left before walking back inside. Never before had a man done something like that for her. It almost made her feel uncomfortable, like she wasn't worthy of someone going above and beyond for her. She was so used to being the one who went out of her way for the guy she dated, she didn't know how to feel about someone reciprocated that.

Natalie checked her watch. Lindy and Charlotte would be there soon; she needed to hurry up and get to the bakery. Even with the lengthy line, she didn't have to wait long for her number to be called. When she got back up to her apartment, there was just enough time for her to get the pumpkin bread neatly arranged on a plate before she went back downstairs to meet the shuttle bus.

Natalie waved as the bus pulled up to the sidewalk. As soon as the doors opened, she could tell something was wrong.

Both Charlotte and Lindy had somber looks on their faces as they stepped onto the sidewalk.

"Is everything okay? What's happened?" Natalie asked as she walked over to her aunt.

Lindy looked down at the bags she carried. "The frames and tablecloths didn't turn out like we thought they would."

Relief washed over her. Everyone was okay; they were just upset about the frames. Natalie nodded to the building. "Show me inside. It's cold out here."

As they made their way to her apartment, Natalie told them about her trip to the bakery. She thought about telling them about her date with Brian but decided against it. That was her and Brian's secret to keep.

Lindy wasn't saying a word and looked like she could cry. Natalie knew how the frames turned out. Sure, they needed a second coat of paint, and if she had time, she'd do that, but they would still be fine if she didn't get around to it. If the stains were still visible on the tablecloths, that also wasn't a big deal because once the centerpiece was in place and the table all set, they wouldn't be noticeable.

Natalie opened the door to her apartment and motioned for them to go in.

"Those curtains make this room feel complete," Charlotte said, and set her purse down on the bar cart.

Natalie looked at Lindy and said, "I know. Thank you guys so much for making them for me."

Lindy pulled one of the dining chairs out and set the bag down. She took a big breath before looking at Natalie. "So you know how the craft room had been booked all last week for that art class?"

"Yes," Natalie answered as she went to the microwave to warm up their coffee.

"Well, apparently, the cleaning crew wasn't able to get in there and clean last week. So they did a deep clean of the room yesterday," Lindy said.

Natalie nodded and pushed the start button on the microwave.

Lindy sighed and continued her story. "Well, right after we left the room, one of the young gals that cleans went into the room and moved all your picture frames so she could clean the counter."

"That's fine. They needed a second coat anyway. I can easily take care of fingerprints," Natalie said.

Lindy shook her head and paused before she said, "She stacked them on the drying rack. And they're now all stuck together, and they were stuck to the tablecloths as well. I don't think any of it is useable."

Natalie felt like the wind had taken her breath away again. She wasn't expecting this news.

Lindy hastily added, "I'm so sorry. I didn't think to check on the frames until this morning. I was going to go in last night to see if the tablecloths needed another soak, but I was tired. If I had, maybe I could have saved the frames."

Natalie needed a moment to process this information. She took the coffee out of the microwave and put both of her hands on the counter. After taking a deep breath, she carefully brought the three cups of coffee to the table. "How did you know it was the cleaning crew?" she asked.

Lindy looked at Charlotte, who had taken a seat at the table.

Charlotte said, "That was me. Lindy called me from the art room, and I immediately went into investigation mode. I had seen the young woman walk in there not long after we had left. I went down to the front desk to ask where she'd gone. I planned on asking her if she saw any residents go in the room after she finished cleaning." Charlotte pointed to the bag of stuck-together frames. "This is the kind of thing our brains come up with as solutions sometimes. But she told me she was the one who had moved them to clean the counters. She said she thought she put the driest ones down first on the drying rack."

Natalie's jaw gaped. "What? I don't even understand that thought process."

Charlotte reached out and patted her hand. "I know. It's not for us to understand. She is very young. I bet she isn't even twenty yet. Her hippocampus hasn't fully developed. It wasn't Alzheimer's that did us in, it was the logic of a young person."

Natalie sat with her arms folded tightly across her chest. "Do I dare look in the bag?" she asked Lindy.

Lindy looked at the bag and shook her head. "I tried taking them apart, but some of them are fused together now, and I didn't pull too hard because I was worried the frames would break," she said. "Perhaps we could sand down the picture frames. Maybe we can save a few."

If this had happened earlier in the month when Natalie had been twiddling her thumbs, she could have, but now there was no time in her schedule to add fixing frames to her list. Thanksgiving was only eleven days away; there was no way.

"I don't think so. I haven't touched the goodie bags, the bar isn't clean yet, and I've got a ton of extra work stuff planned for this week. Plus cooking for Thanksgiving. I wasn't sure I had time to give the frames one more coat, let alone sand them down." Natalie leaned over and peeked into the bag. "I don't have time to squeeze in a miracle." She did her best to ignore the tightening feeling in her chest.

Lindy gazed at Natalie with sad eyes. "I am so sorry. I'd offer to do that for you, but I didn't get the craft genes. Your grandmother was the one who could fix anything, not me."

Charlotte took a sip of her coffee and said, "You know, a bare table can be very chic. And a beautifully written place card is still personalized and special."

Natalie looked between Lindy and Charlotte. "Logically, I know that. And Aunt Lindy, you didn't do anything wrong. This was an accident." She took a deep breath and continued. "I'm just bummed I keep getting farther and farther from my vision. I had this idea of what a Berry Perfect Thanksgiving would look like here in the city, and the reality is nowhere near what I had originally wanted. Instead of being in a new modern apartment building with stunning views of downtown, dinner is going to be in a dusty bar with missing ceiling tiles. It's just another reminder of the epic fail that is my move here. If I had stayed home, I wouldn't be dealing with all of this."

"Your move has not been an epic fail. It simply hasn't turned out like you originally thought it would. If you'd stayed home, you'd have been alone and still seeing a married man. Now you have us nearby, are free of your terrible married ex-boyfriend, have a job that excites you, and live in this beautiful apartment," Lindy said encouragingly.

Natalie knew everything Lindy said was correct. But there were just too many changes taking place all the time. Nothing had gone according to plan, and that was all she'd wanted. Then her mind added Brian into the mix, and everything seemed too much. The idea of starting a new relationship right now added an extra layer of uncertainty she wasn't sure she could handle. "Can we eat pumpkin bread now?" she asked.

"Of course we can," Lindy said.

Natalie quietly ate her breakfast and did her best to hold back tears. She wanted to fast-forward a few months to when things would feel settled.

Once everyone finished eating, Charlotte gathered the plates and took them to the kitchen sink. Natalie stared out the window and tried hard not to think about anything.

She jumped a little when Charlotte started talking. "Okay, you two humdrums, we're going to start our day. First things first, we need to go to the grocery store. Then when we come back here, Natalie gets to decide what we do next. We either head down to the bar to continue cleaning it, or we start on the goodie bags."

Both tasks needed to be done, but one was a need, and one a want. "We should probably clean. We won't have anywhere to eat if the bar isn't clean," Natalie said, still staring out the window.

Lindy nodded. "Sounds good to me. I'm not artistic, but I'm good at an assembly line. I'm happy to come over in the evenings and help you put together the bags."

Natalie calmed herself down by reminding herself all was not lost. "That'd be nice. And Mom gets here Saturday, so she can help put them together too. At least those will get done. I know the table will still be beautiful. The flower centerpiece, which I've spent a fortune on, is going to be stunning. The plates you two picked out are lovely, and when you add in the candlesticks and dried oranges, it's going to be beautiful."

Saying all the reasons why Thanksgiving could still be Berry Perfect made the knot in her chest start to unwind. Natalie paused while her brain started to problem-solve. "The magical thing about the place cards is reading why someone thinks you are special. I can still do that and lay them on everyone's place setting."

"There you go," Lindy said as she stood up. "You know your grandmother added to and changed some of the things our mother did for Thanksgiving. This could be your interpretation of our Thanksgiving tradition. She only used picture frames because she had an excessive amount of them. You're putting place cards on the place settings. I think this is a lovely progression."

"I guess I thought they were always in picture frames since that's how it's been my whole life," Natalie said as she threw her paper coffee cup in the trash.

Lindy walked over and hugged Natalie. "She'd been doing it that way since your mom was little."

Natalie hugged her back and rested her head against Lindy's.

"Your grandmother wasn't big on keeping a lot of pictures out because when the kids played, the frames got knocked over. That's why she always had photo baskets around—no worry of any glass breaking with those. Whenever someone gave her a picture frame, she took the picture out and put the frame in a box in the attic. One day she went into the attic to add a frame to the box, and it was overflowing. That's when she decided to put the place cards in frames and let people take everything home with them. It was a way to get the unused frames out of her house. It was such a hit, she kept doing it."

Natalie gave her aunt one last squeeze and then let her go. "Thank you for sharing that with me. That makes me feel better."

"Good," Lindy said. "Now, open your app and get us a car while I run to the bathroom."

"I think I'm going to have the groceries delivered. It'll be one less thing we have to do today. It'll take a couple of hours for the groceries to get here, and we could work on the bar in the meantime."

"I think that sounds like a fine idea. Technology is a wonder," Lindy said as she made her way down the hall.

Natalie pulled her phone out to place her order.

* * *

Natalie had forgotten how expensive it was to start a pantry from scratch. She thanked her past self for having the where-withal to not move to another city without having a job. This move had been expensive and was seriously cutting into her savings, but her first paycheck would be deposited soon, and that'd be a step in the right direction.

While cleaning the bar, Lindy and Natalie brainstormed about what to write for their family's personalized fun-fact sheets. Natalie got in the zone and deep-cleaned all the counters and tabletops in the room. She felt totally comfortable eating at the tables and bar now. The floor would be a huge undertaking though, and no one had touched the hallway, bathroom, or elevator area. But there was still time, and Lisa had already said she wanted to help, so Natalie didn't panic too much.

Charlotte insisted on putting all the groceries away while Natalie and Lindy worked on the goodie bags. Natalie wished the oversized coffee table she had bought still existed, but she'd make do with what she had. They laid all the bag items out on the dinette table and kitchen counters and took stock of what was there. Lindy made a list of what bags got what items and stuffed them while Natalie personalized them. She drew intricate doo-dles and carefully wrote out facts with her new calligraphy pens.

"Albert sold his boat this year and bought a sports car, so maybe say something about that," Lindy said as she stuffed one of the goodie bags.

Natalie rested her head on her hand and thought about what to say. "I could look up facts about highways, since he'll be cruising down highways now."

Charlotte stopped adding sugar to the canister. "You can find all kinds of interesting things about Route 66. People go nuts for that road."

Natalie grabbed her phone to do some research. "Good idea."

By the time Lindy and Charlotte left, most of the bags were stuffed. Between looking up facts, drawing little pictures related to the facts, and then meticulously writing everything out, it was a time-consuming process. It took about two hours to personalize each bag and its contents. But Natalie enjoyed doing it. She enjoyed taking her time with them. It was the one thing that had gone to plan. And with her mom arriving on Saturday, she really didn't have to rush the project, because she and her mom had several days to work on them together. She had twenty-four left to do. During breaks at work, she'd research facts for each person, and it would all be okay.

Natalie had been secretly texting with Brian throughout the day. He had offered to bring over dinner, but she didn't want to slow down her momentum. Thanksgiving was only eleven days away, and she needed to get serious.

Chapter 18

10 Days till Thanksgiving

Monday morning, Natalie checked the weather forecast to confirm only light morning showers were expected. She and Lisa went about their day prepping for their afternoon outdoor photoshoot with Henry in the company courtyard. But dark rain clouds rolled in that afternoon, and Natalie couldn't believe it. She checked her weather app again, only to find that it now said a torrential thunderstorm was expected to last until midnight. Henry was due in ten minutes.

Lisa ran into Natalie's office. "Do you see those clouds?"

Wide-eyed, Natalie put her phone down. A crack of thunder made her jump. She turned to the window to see a downpour of rain. She swiveled in her chair to look at Lisa. "We move on to plan B."

Lisa, still looking at the storm outside, asked, "What's plan B?"

"I've no idea," Natalie said, taking a notebook out of her desk to start devising a new game plan.

Lisa took a seat across from her. "Okay, so we'll swap today's photo shoot with tomorrow. Most of tomorrow is indoors."

"Maybe. Most of the businesses we're partnered with aren't even open on Mondays." Natalie stared out her office's glass walls and willed herself to come up with alternative ideas. She looked toward the main entrance; Henry had just walked off of the elevator. He was completely soaked from head to toe and left little puddles behind as he walked.

Lisa followed Natalie's line of sight and said, "Oh no."

"We will figure this out," Natalie said, and pushed a lock of her hair behind her ear. She stood up, waved at Henry, and headed his way.

"You must be freezing," Natalie said, reaching for his arm.

"I've been warmer," Henry replied, trying to wipe some water off his coat.

"Come into my office. I have a space heater in there and can get it toasty in a flash." Natalie led him to her office.

Lisa had read Natalie's mind, and the space heater was already set to full blast when they walked in.

"Let me take your coat," Lisa said.

Henry handed it to her, and she hung it up on Natalie's coat rack. "That rain really came out of nowhere. I had just locked the car when the skies opened up and started dumping buckets," he said.

"I'm so sorry you got caught in that. Lisa, can you look to see if we have a sweatshirt Henry can put on?" Natalie instructed.

"Oh, don't bother about that. My coat got the brunt of it. My sweater is fine, but my socks weren't so lucky. I stepped in a puddle," Henry said.

"Well, socks we for sure can handle," Natalie said.

"You have an extra pair of socks lying around?" he asked.

"That and more. We have all kinds of stuff in our promotional closet, from sweatshirts to pool floaties. We have everything on the website, plus specialty stuff that is for promotional use only," Natalie said.

Lisa left the office, and a few minutes later came back with three pairs of brightly colored soda-themed socks for Henry to choose from. "I've got this year's winter flavors," Lisa said as she set a pair of socks down that featured cans of soda surrounded by mistletoe. "And here's a pair of our green Sour Candy Apple socks. This last pair is my favorite—the Zazzle Berry socks."

"I am a Zazzle Berry fan myself. I think I will go for those." Henry reached for the cranberry-colored socks with *Zazzle Berry* in block lettering around the top. Natalie approved of his choice; those would have been the ones she'd have picked too.

She sat down at her desk while Henry went about changing his socks. "Our plans for today have drastically changed. Unless the rain suddenly stops, and the radar isn't indicating it will, we have to think on our feet."

"Yeah, this rain doesn't look like it's going to let up anytime soon," Henry said as he placed his wet shoes near the space heater.

"The goal is to get lots of shots our product and other business' products because cross-promotional opportunities are beneficial to everyone, especially while we're still working on growing our social media presence. However, most of those shots will have to wait until tomorrow when it's not raining."

Natalie rested her chin on her hands and closed her eyes. The rain had thrown a wrench into her plan. Rescheduling the photo shoot wasn't an option. Not only would it interfere with her work schedule, but her Thanksgiving timeline as well.

She brainstormed ways to fix today's photoshoot. "Okay, so if we aren't outside today, then we are inside. Marv isn't enjoying his time at a park today—instead, he is enjoying his time in an office building." Natalie drummed her fingers on her cheeks. She looked to Lisa for inspiration, and Lisa shrugged in return.

"All right, so Marv obviously isn't hanging out in an office building. Marv would be hanging out at his house." Natalie put her hands down and sat up straighter. "We need to turn the office building into a house," she stated.

Lisa raised her hand and said, "Patty has a blanket in her office. Could we throw that over a chair to make it look homier?"

Natalie scrunched her face up in skepticism and said, "Maybe."

Lisa proclaimed, "Our break room kitchen looks kind of like a normal kitchen."

"Yes!" Natalie pointed at Lisa. "We can totally use the kitchen. The lobby of the building has some cozy-looking living room-type spots. The only problem is, we can't control who is coming and going from those areas. That's why the park setting was so perfect, because people are supposed to be at parks."

Lisa pressed her lips together and tilted her head. "Hear me out. What about your apartment building? We could use your apartment for homey shots. You showed me pics, and it's great. I don't think Marv would have a flower couch, but we can put him in the chair and throw a blanket over the couch. Then we also have the bar, which is mostly done. No one will see the floors. There's a kitchen, living room, dining area, bedroom, bathroom, and bar. And think of how cute we could make the bar cart look filled up with our products."

This was a great idea and could be the answer to their problem. And she could run out, pick up some things from the bakery, and buy burgers for them for dinner. They could get so much content, more than they ever could staying at the office.

She looked to Henry. "I hate that you came all the way down here, just to turn around and head back to the building, but Lisa's right, that could save us today."

Henry shook his head. "Don't worry about it at all. I'm enjoying seeing how the doughnuts are made."

Natalie gave Henry a weary smile and clicked her teeth a few times before saying, "Lisa's got my brain going a million miles an hour, and I have a ton of ideas. A new location changes everything, and we will be working on the fly. I think this'll go later than we planned. On the bright side, you'll finally be able to sit on your mom's couch without the plastic."

"A lifelong goal is being fulfilled today," Henry said.

"Great. If it gets too late and you need to leave, don't worry about it. Oh, and I am still feeding both of you," Natalie said.

Henry held up his hands. "Whatever you need. I told my granddaughter I was doing this, and she got so excited. I gained so many cool points. However, I have thought of one thing I would like in return."

Natalie was so thankful he agreed to the location change, she didn't care what he asked for. "You name it."

"Can I get two more pairs of these socks so my wife, granddaughter, and I can all match?" he asked. "I think they'd get a real kick out of them."

"We'll give you three pairs of each sock design. I'll even throw in sweatshirts if we've got them. You sit here and warm up while Lisa and I raid the promotional closet." Natalie rushed out the door before Henry could protest. She needed to work fast to get everything she might need to turn her apartment into a giant ad.

The rain had slowed down by the time they were ready to load up and head out. Henry had parked close to the building, so they loaded the cab of his truck with all the photo shoot supplies. Natalie heard Lisa's stomach rumble, and they decided to have an early dinner. Natalie got Henry's burger order before hopping in Lisa's car.

Once they pulled up to the apartment building, she sent Lisa inside with the keys to her apartment and the burgers. Natalie popped into the bakery to buy a few extra goodies.

She opened the door to her apartment and saw stacks of soda cases in her kitchen next to her boxes of Thanksgiving dishes. Lisa had already placed promotional products all around her apartment. There was a Soday Pop blanket on her couch and branded coffee cups on her counter.

"Let's do the burger shots while the food is still warm. Then we can start with the rest of it," Natalie said. She cleared off the Thanksgiving goodie bags and arranged the table with Marv's Choice soda, Henry's burger and fries, and a menu from the restaurant.

Any doubts she might have had about the new location working out washed away as soon as she started getting the scene set. This was what she did best. While most of her Sad Chicken content were solo missions, she did a lot in the restaurant with employees and the owners of the company. Natalie easily stepped into the role of creative director and gave directions with confidence.

"I want you to start by eating some fries, and then eat on the burger. I'm going to take several pictures from different angles. For some of them, you'll smile, and on some, you won't," Natalie instructed as she pulled a chair out for Henry.

"Sounds easy enough," he said, taking a seat.

Henry turned out to be a natural model. Right off the bat, she got a ton of great shots. There'd be so many pictures to choose from, just from their first setup.

Ten minutes later, Natalie put her phone down. "Okay, now you can eat for real."

Natalie took her bag of food and sat down at the table. Lisa had already begun eating hers as she watched the photo shoot from the kitchen. She brought her dinner over to join them.

"I think that while I get the kitchen set up, you can style the bar cart," Natalie said to Lisa as she dipped a fry in ketchup.

"I can do that. I have an idea already in my head that will look so cute," Lisa said.

Henry looked between the two of them. "What do you want me to do?"

Natalie had no idea. Lisa could already read her mind; she didn't know what to assign to Henry. "You can help me in the kitchen. If you unbox the soda, I'll place it where it needs to go. Also, can you make coffee? We'll need a pot of coffee for the morning shots."

"I can definitely make coffee, and I can unbox soda," Henry answered.

"Where's Brian? Is he joining us tonight?" Lisa asked.

Both Natalie and Henry started to respond, but Natalie motioned for Henry to fill Lisa in. "He's at dinner with a couple of our suppliers. He comes by the building most evenings, so he might pop in."

"He likes to see the day's progress and walk the building while it's quiet," Natalie added.

Lisa's ears perked up, and she gave Natalie a sly gaze. "Interesting."

Natalie caught Lisa's glance, blushed, and abruptly stood up. "I think I am going to start on the kitchen."

Henry crumpled up his burger wrapper. "I'm done. I'll make a pot of coffee."

Natalie purposely kept her back to Lisa while she arranged soda cans to avoid her gaze.

In no time, the three of them had Natalie's apartment looking like a Mom and Pop Soda Brewery showroom. After getting some shots of Marv eating pumpkin bread and drinking coffee, they had Marv pour a soda, then wash some dishes. Marv read a book and snuggled up in a blanket to watch a movie while drinking a soda. The ideas flowed easily, and the three of them worked in perfect harmony.

After the apartment shots were done, they packed everything back up and took it all down to the bar. They stocked the shelves behind the counter with soda and even threw Lisa into some of the shots as the bartender.

Lisa had poured her fourth glass of Marv's Choice when a voice from the doorway said, "I'll take what he's having." Natalie spun her head around to see Brian leaning against the doorframe to the bar.

"Brian, come help us out. We're having a great time. You can be my buddy I'm sharing a drink with," Henry said.

"That's a great idea," Lisa added.

Brian looked at Natalie and she smiled before saying, "I think so too. If you want to. You don't have to, though."

"Henry texted me and said you guys were having fun, so how could I resist?" He gave Natalie a little wink, and she wondered if anyone else had seen it.

Brian took a seat next to Henry, and Lisa handed him a can of Marv's Choice. "Tell us what you ate for dinner," Natalie said.

Brian looked at her and said, "I had a pork chop and—"

Natalie interrupted him. "No, tell Henry. It's easier to hold a conversation than to pretend to be holding a conversation."

Brian nodded and looked to Henry and Lisa. "I had a pork chop." While he talked about the rest of his meal, Natalie moved about the room to take pictures. Suddenly, she became very aware of her body. Before Brian arrived, she bent and twisted in all sorts of weird angles to get the shots she wanted. Now that he was there, she felt self-conscious about some of her picture-taking positions.

"What about standing by the window? I think Marv would enjoy looking out at a rainy downtown," Lisa said, starting to clean up the counter.

"I like that idea. Hand me a book, because I reckon Marv would also like reading while it's raining," Henry said to Lisa.

Lisa walked to the stack of props. "I'll get the logo throw blanket too. I bet we can make one of those chairs look like an armchair."

Natalie went behind the counter and continued the clean-up. Brian walked over to her and stood close enough for his arm to graze hers. "Looks like you guys have been productive."

The nearness of Brian ignited the butterflies in her stomach. "The rain threw me off at first, but I think what we've done tonight is even better than what I originally planned." She let her hand dangle by her side so more of her arm could be touching him. When this happened, his pinky finger started to caress hers. She blushed, and her heart raced. Natalie willed herself not to move because she didn't want this moment to stop.

However, Lisa hollered for Natalie's opinion on something, and she reluctantly walked to the front of the room.

"If we take the picture from this angle, then you can see the blanket, the book, and the rain," Lisa said, looking at the composition on the phone's screen.

"I like that," Natalie said from behind Lisa.

Lisa took several photos and put her phone down. "I can't think of any other pictures we could take."

"I can't either. I think that's the last shot of the night," Natalie said as Lisa handed back her cell phone.

Henry stood up and folded the blanket. "This has been fun. Do you guys need help loading Lisa's car?"

"No, we can manage. Everything is pretty much still bagged up from when we brought it downstairs," Natalie said.

"Don't be dumb. I'm gonna help you load the car," Brian said, and picked up one of the bags of promotional materials.

Natalie thought the quicker they got the car loaded, the quicker Brian could walk her up to her apartment and she could get another good-night kiss. "You three start loading what's ready to go. I'll bag up these last few things and meet you out there."

"Okay then," Henry said. He handed Natalie the blanket. "Brian, before I forget, I want to go over the invoices I received today with you. They're in my truck, and I can show them to you on our way out."

Natalie looked at Brian while Henry talked and tilted her head. He shrugged back. Natalie nodded and put the blanket in a bag. But Henry had messed up her plan for a goodnight kiss.

"Text me when you get home," Natalie said to Lisa, and closed the car's passenger door.

Natalie, Brian, and Henry stood on the street and waited till Lisa had started her car before heading back in. Henry led the way, with Natalie and Brian following behind. Natalie had been standing close to Brian on the sidewalk, and heat had radiated between them. He placed his hand on her lower back to guide her into the building, and shivers ran up and down her spine. His hand only left her back for a moment as he locked the main door.

Natalie wished Henry would yawn and say they'd look at the invoices tomorrow. But he hadn't done that yet. Brian and Natalie walked to the elevator bay and waited a few more seconds for Henry to change the plan, but he just stood there texting on his phone, waiting for Brian.

Reluctantly, Brian sighed. "Well, I guess this is where we leave you."

"I guess it is." Natalie turned to Henry. "Thank you so much for today. You make an amazing Marv."

Henry beamed. "It's been my pleasure. I'll see you tomorrow afternoon."

Natalie called for the elevator. "See you tomorrow."

Brian mouthed to her, "I'll text you."

Natalie nodded and went up to her apartment alone.

She double-checked the time on the microwave against the one on her phone because she was shocked by how late it had gotten. It was almost eleven. She washed her face and put her pajamas on. She lay in bed with her laptop, updating the Thanksgiving calendar and to-do list, when Brian texted her.

Brian: Henry and I left at the same time. I've pulled over in case you want me to come back.

As much as she wanted a goodnight kiss from Brian, she also wanted to stay in bed. She had lost all her steam for the night.

Natalie: Rain check? It's getting late, and I'm ready to spend some quality time with my pillow.

Brian: Do you have dinner plans tomorrow night?

Natalie punched the air with both fists in excitement before answering.

Natalie: Only with you.

She mentally patted herself on the back for her quick response.

Brian: Excellent. I know you are doing stuff with Henry again. Let me know when you're free.

Natalie: Absolutely! I'm thinking we will be done no later than 7, but I will keep you posted.

Brian: Sounds good. Also, Larry arrived right as Henry and I were wrapping up.

Natalie: Thank you. See you tomorrow, and drive safe.

Brian: Sweet dreams, Natalie.

Natalie threw her phone down, smiled, and then screamed into her pillow.

CHAPTER 19

9 DAYS TILL THANKSGIVING

The next morning, Lisa walked into Natalie's office with determination. "When I got home last night, I put together a list of everything left to clean and the order in which I think we should clean tomorrow."

Natalie clutched her chest in mock surprise. "You're speaking my love language. I think what you just said is one of the sexiest things anyone has ever said to me."

Lisa blushed. "It gets me going too."

"Pull up a chair, and we'll talk cleaning while we review last night's pictures," Natalie said.

Lisa dragged a chair behind the desk and sat next to Natalie.

"As we're looking through these, we need to weed out the ones that don't have the Marv vibe we're going for. We only want pictures that depict an older gentleman who is kind of cranky but really into the things he likes."

Lisa tucked her feet under her and said, "I totally agree."

They had picked out about fifteen pictures when Natalie's phone rang. She dug her phone out of her purse. "One second," she said to Lisa. She looked at the screen—it was her mom. She stepped out of her office and answered. "Hey Mom. You guys on the road yet?"

"Hi honey, that's why I'm calling. Dad went out this morning to start the RV, and it made a noise. He and Kevin took it to a repair place to get it checked out. I don't think we will be leaving until this afternoon."

"I'm glad you are getting it looked at before you head this way. Keep me updated," Natalie said.

"I will, sweetheart. You are having a good day?" Susan asked.

Natalie smiled and rolled her eyes. It was eight thirty in the morning; she hadn't had time yet to have a bad day. "Yes, Mom. I am having a good day. But I need to get back to work."

"Of course. I love you," Susan said.

"Love you too, Mom." Natalie hung up the phone.

If the RV was going to make a noise, she was glad it happened before they had left Kevin's house. When her parents first floated the idea of downsizing to an RV, one of her biggest objections had been that they could get stranded on the side of the road someplace inconvenient, but her parents assured her they had signed up for all kinds of roadside assistance programs.

* * *

The weather radar promised clear skies for the afternoon. Natalie had made sure to keep an eye on it just in case. Thankfully, when Henry arrived at her office the second time, the sun was out, with nary a cloud in the sky. It didn't take them long to get the outdoor shots they needed. Because of the previous night's photo shoot, Henry had already become an old pro at being Marv.

The businesses they planned to partner with were all within walking distance. Natalie decided to send Lisa and Henry ahead to get started.

"You two head over to McNeely's. I'll pack up here and meet you there," Natalie said as she bagged up some cans of soda.

"Are you sure?" Lisa asked.

"Positive. I'll be five minutes behind you. By the time you two are done getting the exterior restaurant shots, I'll be there, ready to do the inside stuff. This will shave a few minutes off our schedule," Natalie assured her.

Lisa and Henry agreed and headed to the next location. Natalie's phone rang as she bagged up the last of the soda swag. She wondered what Lisa had forgotten and was pleasantly surprised to see her mom calling. She had gotten so wrapped up in the campaign she forgot to check back in with her. "Hey, Mom. What's the update?"

There was silence on the other end of the call. Natalie questioned if she'd accidentally rejected the call instead of answering it, but before she could check, her mom finally spoke. "Well, it's not great."

"Oh no, what's going on?" Natalie took a seat on a nearby bench.

"The RV has a belt that needs to be replaced," Mom said.

"That's good news. Belts are easy to replace," Natalie replied.

"Yes, but they don't have the size we need in stock. Apparently, we need a unique size. They called around to a few different places, and nobody seems to have it. They've ordered it, but it's going to take a few days to come in."

Natalie pulled her Thanksgiving calendar up in her head. "What do you mean by a few days?"

Natalie heard Susan let out a big sigh. "The RV won't be ready until Friday."

"What? They can't get the belt in until Friday?"

"Well, no, the belt's coming in on Thursday. But the whole shop is going to a funeral that day, so they won't be able to work on it until Friday."

"Why aren't you going to a different shop?" Natalie asked. She felt her frustration starting to bubble up.

"I suggested that, but you know how Dad is. He's already made friends with everyone there, and we're getting a big discount. And they're going to rotate the tires for free. Don't be mad at us," Mom said sheepishly.

Natalie took a second to collect herself before responding. "I'm not mad. I am irritated by the situation. I had planned on you guys being here early, but I'd rather you arrive safely. Since you aren't leaving until Friday now, when do you think you'll be here?"

"I'm thinking Tuesday."

Natalie began to sweat. Tuesday was ages away. She had been counting on her parents being there to help her this weekend. Logically, she knew none of the delay was her mom's fault, but her anxiety wasn't listening to logic. Natalie didn't want to think about this too much because that could activate tears, and she needed to finish the photo shoot today and have dinner with Brian. Tonight, when she sat down to figure out yet another new plan, she could cry, but not now.

"Well, I just want you guys to get here safely, Mom. I'll text you later. Thank you for keeping me updated, but I need to get off the phone and get back to work."

"Of course. Bye, sweetie," Mom said.

"Bye, Mom," Natalie said and hung up the phone.

Natalie took some deep cleansing breaths to push away the bad energy that had floated around her. Before she put her phone away, she sent Brian a text confirming their date time. She wondered where she could get a slice of pumpkin pie, because now seemed like the perfect time to activate its healing properties.

* * *

As soon as the photo shoot wrapped, Natalie insisted both Lisa and Henry go home. She headed back to the office to drop off the bags of soda swag they'd used as props. The conversation with her mom had created a rain cloud above her she couldn't shake. She decided she'd update the Thanksgiving calendar, feel her feelings for five minutes, and then push that all aside to focus on her date with Brian. None of what was going on with her parents was within her control, so she needed to focus on what she could take hold of.

Natalie was in the middle of piling the photo shoot bags in the corner of her office when Brian texted to say he'd left the apartment building on his way to pick her up. This was ideal timing. She'd have enough time to adjust the calendar for the seventeen-thousandth time and send out a quiet prayer to the universe for everything else to go according to plan. Because maybe, just maybe, she could still pull off her picture-perfect Thanksgiving.

With the list done, Natalie was determined not to think about anything other than enjoying her time with Brian. She walked out of the building and saw him waiting, just like he had been the last time he picked her up from work.

"Did you remember to bring me a snack?" Natalie asked.

Brian shook his head as he opened her door. "I'm taking you to dinner. Isn't that snack enough?"

She hopped in the cab and said, "I guess it's going to have to be."

Watching Brian walk to his door gave Natalie a little thrill. She had been looking forward to spending more time with him. It wasn't just the making out that excited her. While his kissing skills were top-notch, she also simply enjoyed hanging out with him. Being around him was easy. Even when he got under her skin, she didn't want him to go away. Which was a nice development, since she had secretly hoped, when they first met, that he'd get a paper cut under his fingernail.

She even considered inviting him to her company's Thanksgiving party, but then remembered the deadline to RSVP had been yesterday. Natalie wasn't sure if he'd even be interested in going to a big function with her. And she didn't know if her heart could handle him saying no.

As Brian closed his door, he said, "Since you don't have a car, is there anywhere you need to go? I thought before we got dinner we could run any errands you might have. I'm happy to act as your taxi tonight."

If she had been next to a river, Natalie would have washed away. It took all her self-control to not lean over and attempt to make out with him in his truck again. "Are you serious?"

"Why wouldn't I be?" Brian asked while he started the truck.

"Can we go to either Costco or Sam's Club? I have been wanting to get some of those buffet serving pieces where you put the dish on top, and the little Bunsen burner candle thing underneath keeps everything warm."

"Let's do it," Brian said as he pulled away from her building.

"Thank you," Natalie said. She had wanted to go buy a few of these buffet serving sets but didn't know when she'd have the time. She had thought about asking Lindy and Charlotte to pick them up, but they had done enough already.

"It's not an issue. I can only imagine how frustrating it has been not having a car," Brian said.

Natalie coughed out a laugh. "It's wild being carless. I don't know what I was thinking when I thought I could adapt to public transportation. Taking the tram to work has been so convenient, and I'll probably still do that once I get a car again, but shopping is awful. The few times I've gone to the store without using the Montrose shuttle have been so annoying. So much waiting around. All the delivery fees are starting to add up too. I don't know how Europeans do it."

"I couldn't live without my truck. Even if I wasn't constantly picking up supplies, I don't think I could," Brian said.

"My car was on its last leg and needed to be replaced. There is no way it would've made the trip here. But I can't wait to have the brain space to start car shopping," Natalie said as she watched the streetlights pass by.

"Well, in the meantime, if you ever need a ride, just holler," Brian said.

"Thank you." Natalie felt comfortable with Brian but not comfortable enough to ask him to take her to the grocery store. They had shopped together before, but that was different. Then, she didn't like him. In Natalie's opinion, shopping with a suitor was like going to the bathroom in front of someone. It was too intimate of an experience to do with someone you hardly knew. No one wanted to reveal all their guilty pleasures right up front.

Brian flipped his blinker on. "Do you care if we go to Sam's Club instead of Costco?"

"Nope, I have membership cards to both. My parents love buying in bulk."

"That's interesting since they live in an RV now," Brian said.

Natalie didn't want to go into the fact that these big bulk stores sold more than huge cases of toilet paper. And how most of her parents' clothes came from them. "Bulk habits are hard to break," she said.

It had been months since Natalie had been under the blazing florescent lights of Sam's Club, but she loved it—the overbearing shelves equaled quality savings in her mind.

"I can't even tell you the last time I was in one of these stores," Brian said as he admired the electronics section.

"Well, the world is our oyster, friend. Be careful, because before you know it, you are spending four hundred dollars on deals that can't be beat," Natalie said as she slowly pushed the cart.

Brian picked up a pair of headphones. "These are a great deal. I've been needing a pair of noise-canceling headphones."

"Buy them without guilt. You're saving so much money getting them here. Look around." She motioned to the rest of the store. "The whole place is filled with—oh my god." She stopped in her tracks.

Brian looked at Natalie with concern. "Are you okay?"

She slowly pulled her eyes away from the food section of the store back to Brian. "Brian, they have samples out."

"Don't they always have samples?" Brian asked.

Natalie scoffed at his dumb question. "No, normally, they are reserved for the weekends. Sometimes you can find them on a Thursday or Friday. But a Tuesday night is unheard of." She put her palms together and tapped her index fingers against her lips. "I don't think you understand how special it is to come across a rogue sample day. And my money is on those being holiday samples."

Brian stammered a little bit. "Umm, okay."

"Sir, you are in for a real treat. Because this is now dinner. A whole dinner of amuse-bouches." Natalie threw her hands into the air. "I love nothing more in life than trying all the foods!"

"What the hell is an amuse-booche?" Brian asked, following Natalie to the first sample display.

"It's one bite of amazingness. It's not a whole appetizer, just a bite. Obviously, you don't watch *Top Chef.*"

As Natalie and Brian soon discovered, they had unknowingly stumbled into a Taste of the Holidays sample night. "My heart is racing, I'm so excited right now," Natalie said as they waited in a small line for their first sample.

"We're waiting for some kind of dip. Are you really that excited for dip?" Brian asked.

Natalie glared at him. "Brian, this is free delicious food. What is not exciting about that? Plus, there's a surprise around every corner. We don't know what splendors are coming our way. Tonight even has a theme. It's Taste of the Holidays. Let your imagination go on what wonders we are in for. I need you to put aside your cynical hat for a little bit and be open to this experience."

"Fine." Brian took a step toward the sample cart. "How often do you come to sample days?"

"I don't plan my trips around sample days, but if I catch one, I'm excited. The trick is to hit the produce section last. Because there they have fresh squeezed orange juice."

"Really?"

"At least at my Sam's they did. After all your samples, it's like a refreshing digestif."

Brian rolled his eyes. "You and your words. Did you learn that from *Top Chef* too?"

"Probably. That or Martha Stewart," Natalie replied.

When it was their turn to get a sample, the employee asked if they'd like to try the featured hot corn dip.

"Yes, we both love corn," Natalie said as she reached for her sample.

"Great. This corn dip is easy to prepare," the employee said, handing Brian his sample. "All the ingredients simply go in a Crock-Pot. You set it and forget it. Tonight, I'm using a two cans of fiesta corn, cream cheese, and Dr. Smokey's Signature Seasoning Rub, which is only $6.99 right now."

"Thank you so much," Natalie said before she took a bite.

She and Brian then stepped out of the way so the next customer could get their sample.

Brian took a bite of the corn dip. "That's actually pretty good."

"It is, and I really do love corn," Natalie as she tossed her empty cup into the trash.

Brian followed Natalie to the next display. "Do we have to buy a jar of rub now?"

"No, that's the magic of a Sam's sample," Natalie said.

Brian stopped walking. "I think I might go get a jar. The flavors in that dip were pretty good."

Natalie nodded and said, "Tonight we feast. Sometimes we buy and sometimes we don't."

Brian jogged back and picked up a jar of the spice rub and tossed it in the cart when he got back.

"Do you cook a lot?" Natalie asked while they waited for the next sample.

"Grilling yes, cooking no. But you like to cook," Brian said.

Natalie nodded. "I do love to cook. Even though I have a kitchen now, I haven't done much yet. Haven't had the time. But I'm looking forward to cooking for Thanksgiving because I've missed being in the kitchen."

"I'm looking forward to trying your food." Brian craned his head toward the display. "I think this is a stuffing sample."

"We're getting little bits and pieces to wet our whistles for the upcoming holiday," Natalie said as she took a step forward.

Only after they had tried all the samples did Natalie and Brian make their way to find the buffet serving sets. "How am I full after only eating samples?" Brian asked as he loaded a box into the cart.

"It's because Sam's isn't stingy. They offer high-quality, high-quantity samples," Natalie said, moving a container of chicken salad and a box of Everything Bagel seasoned crackers in the cart to make room for another buffet serving set. "But if you were still hungry, I was going to suggest their hot dogs, which are a ten out of ten."

"Maybe next time," Brian said.

On the way home, Natalie wondered where she'd store everything she bought. Brian answered her question before she could say it out loud. "If you don't have room for all these boxes in your apartment, you can keep them in the storage room."

"You read my mind. I'm going to take you up on that," Natalie said.

"Yeah, not a problem," Brian said.

Natalie opened her mouth to say thank you and a huge yawn came out instead.

"Was that a yawn?" Brian asked.

"It was," Natalie said, and then yawned again. "I guess our late night last night and the thrill of Sam's Club are catching up to me."

"Stop that. Because if you keep yawning, then I am going to yawn," Brian said as he yawned.

Natalie laughed. "I have always thought it funny how contagious yawns are. I can read about a person yawning and want to yawn."

"Well, we'll get your stuff unloaded and then you can go straight to bed," Brian said.

Natalie looked at him. "Not straight to bed."

Brian smiled and turned into the back parking lot of the building. He parked the truck and walked around to open Natalie's door. As he did so, Natalie yawned again and rubbed her eyes.

"You are officially going straight to bed," Brian said while helping her out from the truck.

"We'll see about that," Natalie said, unloading a box of toilet paper.

Brian walked to the door and propped it open with a brick. It didn't take them long to have Natalie's purchases shelved in the storage room. After everything was arranged, Brian ran a hand through his hair. "I'm going to go now."

Natalie stepped in front of the storage room door and blocked the exit. "You aren't going to walk me to my door?"

Brian shook his head. "I don't think it's safe. If I go up there, we both know I'll be there for ages, and you're clearly very tired. We'll rain check our good night kiss."

Natalie put her hands on her hips. "I think we can keep it quick."

Brian tilted his head and peered at her. "Really? Honestly, you think we could have a quick good night kiss?"

"I do."

"I don't. I know me," Brian said as he looked her up and down.

Natalie took a step toward him. "I think we could keep it to ten minutes, easy."

"Ten minutes is too long. Two minutes is all I'm willing to give."

Natalie raised an eyebrow. "Two minutes? No. How about eight?"

Brian took a step closer to Natalie. "I'll give you four."

"I'll take six," she countered.

"Deal. Now, how do I know you won't take advantage of me and try for seven?"

Natalie placed her hand on her chest. "I can control myself."

Brian scoffed. "I highly doubt that."

Natalie pulled her phone out of her purse. "I'll set a timer for six minutes. Once the timer goes off, I'm going to bed."

As Natalie set the timer, Brian said, "Sure you are."

Natalie placed her phone on a shelf and walked up to Brian, pulling him to her. She rested her hands on his waist and kissed him. She started off softly and then quickly parted his lips with her tongue. Brian wrapped his arms around her and held her in a tight embrace.

Slowly, she untucked his shirt. She let her fingers explore his bare back. As her hand made contact with his skin, she liked how it made him release a small groan of pleasure. He felt warm to her touch. Natalie then let her fingernails slowly scratch up and down his spine. Brian brought her in closer, and Natalie felt how aroused he was.

Just as her right hand cupped his left butt cheek, the timer on her phone went off. Natalie instantly pulled back, and said, "Okay, well, I'm going to bed."

Brian shook his head, trying to get his bearings. "What?"

"Hey, listen. I'm doing exactly what you said, because I have control," Natalie stated. She picked up her phone, purse, and chicken salad, then left the storage room. She got a case of the shivers while in the elevator. Brian was different from any guy she had ever met. She liked him more than a little. In fact, maybe more like a lot. A lot a lot. Once she was almost to her door, her phone dinged with a text message.

Brian: I think you might be the most fascinating woman I've ever met.

Without hesitation, Natalie replied.

Natalie: Obviously.

Chapter 20

8 Days till Thanksgiving

Wednesday night, when Lisa, Charlotte, Lindy, and Natalie arrived at the bar to clean, Natalie could finally see the light at the end of the tunnel. The whole endeavor had seemed like a never-ending project, but now she felt like she'd made progress.

While Natalie and Lisa mopped the bar floor, Charlotte and Lindy began to clean the hallway. Natalie set up a speaker in the doorway of the bar and put on a Supremes playlist. Every once in a while, she glimpsed Lindy and Charlotte singing while they cleaned. Watching the two of them together always made her heart happy.

After the first round of mopping was completed, Natalie sent Lisa to clean the elevator lobby area. Then she went to the storeroom to fill her caddy with bathroom cleaning supplies. When she grabbed the toilet bowl cleaner, images of kissing

Brian there the night before made her blush. She took what she needed and left in a hurry, because fantasizing about Brian with Lindy and Charlotte close by felt weird.

Over the past few weeks, Natalie had learned Lenny was the only one who used the bathroom off the manager's office, and luckily, he had turned out to be a tidy gentleman who kept it in relatively good shape. However, it did need a good cleaning before her family arrived.

The bathroom was a decent size, and she made a mental note to call the florist to see if they could deliver a plant she could put in it. Greenery always spruced up any space. She put some toilet bowl cleaner into the bowl and as it soaked, she ran up to her apartment. She'd ended up with an extra basket she didn't have a place for, so she filled it with a box of tissues, room spray, and extra rolls of toilet paper and took it downstairs. On her way down, she found a chair with the back completely broken off and decided to use it as a table. There was room on the counter for the basket, but the plant would look better there instead of the basket. She finished cleaning the bathroom, stood back, and mentally patted herself on the back for a job well done. The room felt very inviting.

Lindy and Charlotte had already joined Lisa in the elevator area when Natalie arrived.

"This looks so much better," Natalie said, admiring their cleaning job.

"I stacked the boxes over there and straightened up those big tubs. Just doing that made a huge difference," Lisa said as she dusted the walls.

"You can actually walk around in this area now," Natalie said.

"Lindy and I have rested long enough. What do you need us to do?" Charlotte asked Lisa from the folding chair she sat on. Lindy nodded from her chair too.

Lisa looked down at them from the step stool. "If you can wipe down the elevator doors, then we just have to sweep and mop. After that, I think we're all done."

"I'm so indebted to all of you. I truly could not have done this in time without you three," Natalie said with sincerity.

Lindy stood up and said, "Charlotte and I have been happy to help. We enjoy spending time with you girls."

Lisa waved her hand to brush Natalie off and turned back to the wall. "You'd have figured it out. But I've enjoyed helping. I like cleaning."

When Lisa had first said she liked to clean, Natalie thought she might have been lying and had just said it to make Natalie feel better about asking for help. But over the course of the week, she realized Lisa did love cleaning and she was good at it. Cleaning had never been Natalie's strong suit, but Lisa had a gift.

Relief washed over Natalie as she plugged in the steam mop. Everything was about to sparkle. She steam-mopped the bar floor while the other three did some spot-cleaning.

After everyone agreed they had scrubbed everything as best they could, the four of them crammed into the doorway leading to the bar to admire their handywork.

"I can't believe it's done," Natalie said, looking at the bar. "This was the biggest task on my list, and it's done."

"I know, and it looks so good. Do you want to move the tables into place?" Lisa asked as she held onto the doorframe.

Natalie shook her head. "No, I want everything to dry really well first. Plus, I'm enjoying simply looking at the clean, open space. I can barely remember how terrible this looked two weeks ago."

"It was so bad, and now it's amazing. Imagine how nice it's going to look once they get in there to fix the ceiling and change out all the broken floor tiles," Lisa said as they stepped away from the doorway.

Lindy took a big breath. "I can see our family sitting in there, and it's going to be such a fabulous night."

"Agreed. I owe you three dinner now. Let's head upstairs. I got us some tasty chicken salad last night at Sam's Club, and the biggest grapes you've ever seen," she said while ushered the women to the elevator.

Natalie opened one of her industrial-size bags of crackers and set it on the counter. She let them serve themselves while she made drinks. Once everyone had what they wanted, Natalie joined them at the table. It felt good to sit down.

"So, what's the plan for the rest of the week?" Lindy asked as she placed her napkin in her lap.

"Well, tomorrow, Lisa and I have our company Thanksgiving party. After that, I'm just here making goodie bags and place cards," Natalie said before she took a bite of chicken salad.

"I wish we could come over and help you this weekend with the goodie bags, but we've got Hazel's grandson's wedding this weekend," Lindy said.

"I know. I think I can get it all done," Natalie assured her. Sleep was overrated anyway.

Lisa looked at Natalie. "You know I'd be here to help, but right after work on Friday I'm heading to my parent's house for the holiday." Lisa said to Lindy and Charlotte, "They give us the week of Thanksgiving off and the week between Christmas and New Year's. They whole company closes for those two weeks."

"Oh, that's nice!" Charlotte exclaimed.

"It's a real perk, and one of the reasons I picked Mom and Pop Soda to work for," Natalie said.

"I'm looking forward to tomorrow's dinner," Lisa said as she picked up the pepper shaker. "I love Thanksgiving food, so the more of it I get to eat, the happier I am. My mom has been watching all these cooking channel shows and wants to serve duck this year instead of turkey. So I'm glad I'll be getting my turkey fix beforehand. I mean, they call it Turkey Day, not Duck Day."

"Do you want me to save you some turkey from ours?" Natalie asked.

"Oh, my god, are you sure?" Lisa said.

"Of course," Lindy said. "Darling, you've been such a help getting the bar cleaned up, I feel you should get first dibs. I'll happily pack up some turkey for you."

"Exactly. And let me know if there is anything else you want," Natalie said as she picked up one of the grapes and popped it in her mouth.

Charlotte examined a grape. "These are some of the biggest I have ever seen, and so flavorful."

"I know, right?" Natalie said after she got done chewing. "Last night, Brian and I couldn't get over them. He bought a box for himself."

Lisa set down her cracker topped with chicken salad and gave Natalie a knowing look. Thankfully, Lisa didn't say anything else in front of the Grand Dearies. The last thing she wanted to do was talk about having a crush on Brian in front of his grandmother. Natalie didn't know if crush was even the right word, but discussing it with Charlotte wasn't high on her to-do list.

"Speaking of Brian, he should be here before too long. He's going to take Lindy and me home," Charlotte said.

Natalie already knew this, since she had been texting with him all day. She looked forward to seeing him again. Brian had become a part of her everyday routine, and she wasn't mad about that one bit.

Natalie was clearing the table when Charlotte got Brian's text that he'd pulled into the back parking lot of the building. Lindy yawned several times. While Natalie wouldn't have minded a little extra time with Brian, she wanted her great-aunt to get some rest.

Lisa answered the door when Brian knocked. "Were your ears burning?"

"Maybe. Why?" Brian asked.

"We heard you are a fan of the big grapes," Lisa answered.

Brian shook his head and looked toward Natalie. "I am. I had some for breakfast."

Natalie smiled at him before she put the last plate in the dishwasher. "I'm kicking you guys out. It's been a long day, and I think everybody is ready for bed." She closed the dishwasher.

"I know I am," Lindy said, putting her purse strap on her shoulder.

Brian held open the front door. "Okay, then. Let's get you ladies home."

All five of them got on the elevator, and Natalie stood shoulder-to-shoulder with Brian. Even though the trip down to the first floor only lasted seconds, she'd take what she could get.

Natalie gave Lindy and Charlotte hugs goodbye. "I will see you two on Monday when we start prepping for Thanksgiving. Have so much fun at the wedding this weekend." She hugged Lindy one more time.

"We will." Lindy smiled at Lisa. "It has been such a pleasure getting to know you. I hope we get to see more of you after you come back from your parents' house."

"For sure," Lisa said as she gave Lindy a hug goodbye.

Natalie escorted Lisa to the front door as Brian walked Lindy and Charlotte to the back. Natalie stood at the doorway watching Lisa get in her car before closing and locking the door. She had almost made it to the elevator when Brian ran in from the back door. He rushed up to her and pulled her into an embrace.

"I couldn't leave without telling you goodbye," he said, and kissed her.

The kiss was sweet and too short.

"Sweet dreams, Natalie." Brian gave her one more quick peck before turning around and heading back to the parking lot.

Natalie blushed as he walked away. "Sweet dreams, Brian."

Chapter 21

7 Days till Thanksgiving

After work on Thursday, Natalie went home to change for the company Thanksgiving Party. Lisa picked her up so they could arrive together. When they got to the hotel, Natalie was amazed to see so many people in the lobby. She wondered if people were already starting to arrive in the city for the holiday.

She knew there'd be a lot of people at the party, so walking into a packed ballroom was not a surprise. Craning her neck, Natalie tried to find her team.

Lisa gently nudged Natalie and pointed. "I see them. We're at the table in the corner."

"Good eyes," Natalie responded, and looked to where Lisa indicated.

There were people milling about everywhere. "I'm shocked you didn't ask Brian to join you tonight," Lisa said as she side-stepped a man backing his chair up.

Natalie acted like she couldn't hear Lisa to delay her response. She'd thought about inviting him, but inviting him meant attaching a label to whatever they were doing, and she wasn't ready for that. It was way too soon.

Lisa stepped closer to Natalie. "Why didn't you invite Brian?"

Natalie shrugged and said, "I don't know many people who'd invite their landlord to a work function."

Lisa smiled and started walking again. "Oh, okay. So we are pretending like there isn't something going on between you two."

Natalie nodded. "Yes, exactly. I feel really comfortable in that delusion, and I'd like to stay there as long as possible."

"Okie dokie, all I ask is that you let me know when you want to enter the land of reality," Lisa said as they arrived at the table.

Before Natalie could reply, Donna greeted both of them. "Welcome, ladies. I saved you two seats."

"Great," Lisa said, and put her purse down on one of the empty seats. "I am going to run to the restroom and be right back."

Natalie began to pull out the chair right next to Donna and then stopped. "Is this where your wife's sitting?"

"No, one of our corgis had their teeth cleaned today and is still loopy from being put under. So she stayed home to keep an eye on him," Donna said and pulled Natalie's chair out slightly.

Natalie took her coat off and hung it on the back of her chair before she sat down.

"This room is stunning," she said. The floral arrangements on the tables were similar to what she had ordered for her Thanksgiving. Seeing the tables decorated so beautifully made her excited for her own tablescape. So many things had fallen behind on her Thanksgiving to-do list, but she had pushed through the frustration because the centerpiece she'd ordered was stunning.

Their table was situated close to the front of the room, and Natalie took in what she could from her vantage point. The stage had a magnificent floral display. "Is that a human-sized turkey made out of flowers?" she asked.

"Yes, and after tonight it will be moved to the lobby of the hotel and installed next to a giant cornucopia. Every year, the Thanksgiving displays around town get better and better. Chicago goes nuts for St. Patrick's Day, New Orleans for Mardi Gras, and we go a little batty for Thanksgiving," Donna said.

"Before I moved here, I had no idea you guys were known for your Thanksgiving celebrations. My great-aunt has been living here for years, but she hasn't been here at Thanksgiving and didn't realize how big of a deal it was. So when I talked to her about moving here, I was truly clueless," Natalie said as she picked up her water glass.

"I've enjoyed watching how the Marv's Choice campaign has come together," Donna said.

After taking a sip of her water, Natalie put her glass back down. "It's been a lot of fun working on it. I hope it goes over well. I have two weeks' worth of content ready to go. Tomorrow

Lisa and I will automate the posts, so we don't have to worry about anything over our Thanksgiving break."

"Good. That all sounds great," Donna said, sounding sincere.

Lisa made it back to the table right as the company's owners took the stage to welcome everyone. Natalie liked hearing the recounting of the company's history. She knew it was on the website, but hearing interesting anecdotes straight from them made her feel even more like part of the company family than she already did. They talked about different family members who had made a massive impact on them, and Natalie was surprised to see how big a role Marv played in their lives. Natalie leaned over to Lisa and said softly, "Did you know Marv took the owner in and raised him after his parents died?"

Lisa whispered back, "I had no idea."

Natalie's eyes widened as the owner talked about how Marv's work ethic and moral compass were the founding pillars of their company.

Lisa looked at Natalie and mouthed, "OMG."

Natalie leaned toward Lisa again and quietly panicked. "Shit," Natalie whispered. "I hope they like what we do."

"I know. I mean, our Marv's lovable. Right?" Lisa whispered.

"I sure hope so."

Natalie knew they were past the point of no return now. If she didn't post the Marv content, there'd be giant holes in her social media strategy for the rest of the year.

CHAPTER 22

6 DAYS TILL THANKSGIVING

Natalie had forgotten to contact the florist the day before about adding a plant for the bathroom to her order. But seeing the centerpieces last night had reminded her she needed to call sooner rather than later. After walking out of her last unexpected meeting of the day, Natalie wished more people would ask themselves if their information could have been conveyed just as easily in an email. In her opinion, it should be illegal to schedule a meeting on a Friday. Especially if it's the Friday before a holiday break. But her workday was almost done, and that was what mattered most. She made her way over to Lisa's desk to say a quick goodbye before they both headed out.

"I hope you have a great time at home. And I'll bring turkey leftovers for you when we come back to work next Monday," Natalie said, and hugged Lisa.

"You're the best!" Lisa exclaimed. "I can't wait to hear all about your Thanksgiving weekend and see pictures of the bar all decorated."

"You and me both." Natalie stepped back and smiled at her new friend. "You have been such a lifesaver these past few weeks. I've got a lot left to do, but you're a big reason I still have a shot at pulling this off. I owe you big time."

Lisa blushed. "Stop it."

Natalie grinned. "I will, but only because I know you're ready to get on the road. Drive safely and have a wonderful holiday."

"You too," Lisa said.

Natalie put her coat on and set her purse on her desk before calling Flowers, Flowers, Flowers. When the florist answered, Natalie had a hard time hearing her because of all the background noise.

"Hold on, give me a second," the florist said. Natalie heard muffled movement. The background noise had quieted down when the florist returned to the phone. "There, that's better. Natalie, I am glad you called. I was just about to call you."

"Perfect timing then. I was wondering if I could add a plant to my order. Something on the smaller side that could sit on a bathroom counter," Natalie said, tapping her pen on the desk.

"Yes, we can add the plant. But I need to talk to you about your order." The florist sounded serious.

Natalie put her pen down and leaned forward.

"Last night, there was a power surge at the store, and it blew the compressors on our refrigerators. They won't be able to be replaced until after the holiday. Therefore, we will not be able to fulfill your full order. The cut flowers we have on hand will not be usable by your delivery date. The mums and pumpkins you ordered will be fine though. How would you like to proceed?"

Natalie sat in shock. After she didn't answer, the florist continued. "I understand you were not expecting this; neither were we. I can cancel your whole order or provide the nonrefrigerated flowers and pumpkins. It's your call."

"This is a nightmare for you," Natalie finally responded.

"It hasn't been our best day. We've been calling all our florist friends looking for space in their refrigerators for the flowers we need for weddings and funerals. All other orders, we're having to cancel," the florist said matter-of-factly.

In the grand scheme of things, Natalie's order was one order. This was a whole business having to pivot during one of the city's busiest weeks. She could only imagine the stress this woman was experiencing. Natalie tried to gather her senses.

"Yes, I'll take the mums, pumpkins, and small plant. I'm so sorry this happened to you." Natalie at least had the capability to call another florist, while Flowers, Flowers, Flowers's livelihood had been disrupted for the next week.

"Thank you for your understanding. I have noted the change to your order, and I need to call the next customer on the list," the florist said, and she disconnected the call.

Natalie had called seven florists by the time she walked in her front door. None of them had availability. Never in her wildest dreams would she have imagined she'd moved to the

Thanksgiving capital of the country. She thought everyone went home for Thanksgiving. Thanksgiving wasn't a destination kind of holiday.

She hung up the phone from her last inquiry of the night and felt lucky to have a space to host her family.

It wasn't until she sat down to eat dinner that it hit her—one more of her well-laid plans had gone to waste. She wouldn't be completely flowerless, but the spread she'd picked would have been stunning and so impressive. It would have added so much to the table. She envisioned her table as originally planned, and one by one, things had been removed from that picture. The chairs, tablecloths, picture frames ... and now flowers. With her mom not arriving this weekend, she didn't know if she could finish the goodie bags the way she wanted to, or even at all. Plus, the thought of all the cooking she needed to do. It seemed like everything was imploding.

She felt tears bubble up inside her. Natalie put her dishes in the dishwasher and tried to power through making a goodie bag. But when she picked up one of the bags Lindy had stuffed, she remembered she wouldn't even have the Grand Dearies' help this weekend. With that, the tears burst out of her. She sat at the table and cried for a few minutes. All her energy had washed away. She decided to call it a day and crawled into bed to cry into her pillow.

5 Days till Thanksgiving

The only thing that could cure Natalie's shitty feelings about everything were copious amounts of coffee and a fluffy pastry. She threw on clothes and walked to the bakery. Sugar and Spice was packed, which was to be expected for a Saturday morning. While she stood in line, she ran through her plan for the day. Now would not be the time to focus on what was out of her control, but rather what she could manage. If she was being honest with herself, nothing felt under control. Everything felt like it was spinning out, and she couldn't figure out how to get it all to stop.

"Number thirty-nine," a woman behind the counter called.

Natalie looked down at her number and realized she held ticket thirty-nine. She waved her hand and made her way to the woman.

"What can I get you?" the woman asked.

"What's going to drown my feelings and make my world feel less chaotic?" Natalie asked. She couldn't believe she'd actually said those words out loud, but now she wondered if the bakery might have a cure for her ails.

The woman tapped a finger on the counter and looked at the ceiling for a second. "Our chocolate croissants have been known to be helpful. I personally think a slice of Italian cream cake for breakfast can solve a lot of problems."

Natalie wished this woman wore a name tag because the nameless stranger had already made her feel better by not making her feel dumb.

"I'll take a chocolate croissant and a slice of Italian cream cake. Can I also get a large pumpkin spiced latte?" Natalie asked.

"Of course," the woman said. Natalie appreciated the tender tone she used. "I'm going to go place your coffee order, bag up your treats, and then come back here to ring you up. I'll be right back."

Natalie softly said, "Okay," and watched as the woman left to fill her order.

The counter was tall enough that she could lay her head right on it. She hadn't planned on doing it, but her head suddenly seemed too heavy to hold up on her own.

Once the employee announced her total, Natalie slowly lifted her head and opened her wallet to get out some cash. "Keep the change. I really appreciate your help this morning," she said, sliding the bills toward the employee. "And also, what's your name?"

"My name's Tori. I threw in a chocolate cupcake for you too. It seems like you might need that," she said as she finished up Natlie's transaction.

Tori's kindness made Natalie's bottom lip quiver a little as she said, "That's very sweet of you."

"We've all been there. I will bring you your coffee when it's ready," Tori said, and called the next number in line.

Natalie sat at a table while she waited for her coffee. Standing seemed too hard. She wondered how she had gotten herself into this mess. She knew Thanksgiving would happen and she wouldn't ruin it entirely. But how had she gotten here? In this exact moment, in this exact bakery?

Then she reminded herself it was because she had moved to a place where her only friends were two women in their eighties and a woman fifteen years younger than her. She lived in a place she might or might not be able to afford once it was completed—she didn't know because she and Brian had never had that conversation. As soon as the year was done, Brian would probably want someone to move in who could pay more rent.

To make it even more complicated, she had made out with her landlord and had some very inappropriate thoughts about him. Brian probably hated that she kept throwing herself at him. She doubted every single decision she had made in the past few years. Everything from her red-flag-riddled married ex-boyfriend, to taking on a crazy project at work that consisted of taking hundreds of pictures of an old man.

Natalie decided to go back to her place, dip her chocolate croissant in the cupcake icing, eat the slice of cake and call it a day.

"Here you go." Natalie looked up to see Tori gazing down with her kind eyes while holding out her coffee.

"Thank you, Tori," Natalie said, taking the coffee.

Tori patted her on the shoulder. "Things will get better."

Natalie nodded in agreement and left the store. At that moment, she didn't believe things would get better, but Tori did, and Natalie only knew her to be a truthful, honest woman because everyone knew chocolate made everything better. If Tori believed in her, maybe she could eat her frosted croissant *and* make a few goodie bags.

The weather was starting to transition from fall to winter. She didn't think to grab her gloves before she left her apartment and was glad she had the hot cup of coffee to hold on to. Thankfully, her building was only a short distance away. When she got back, she put the pastries on the kitchen counter. Finding a TV show she wanted to binge while putting the goodie packets together became her prime objective. After she ate, she'd call Lindy and tell her about the flowers. She'd thought about calling last night, but it was too much, too soon.

She had finally decided on a cozy British murder mystery when someone knocked on her door. Natalie panicked because she was supposed to be alone in the building. She looked around for her phone to see if someone had texted that they were coming over but couldn't find it. Had someone followed her back from the bakery? Had she not locked the door behind her? Was her apartment actually the murder cabin?

Whoever stood on the other side knocked again.

"Just a minute," Natalie yelled. She needed to find her phone so she could call the police in case someone was trying to kill her. And if she could find her phone, she could check the cameras out in the hallway to see who was there.

"I can hear you running around in there like a mouse. It's just me," Brian said through the door.

Natalie went to the door and looked through the peephole. She didn't know why she hadn't thought of doing that earlier. Probably because if the murderer had heard her standing at the door, he could have shot through it or slid a blade under it to try to slice her feet off. There were endless ways to kill someone.

Once she was satisfied it was really just Brian at the door and he wasn't there under someone else's coercion, she opened it.

"What are you doing here? It's basically six in the morning," Natalie said.

"It's almost ten, and I texted several times. I got a motion sensor alert when you came back from the bakery this morning, so I knew you were up. I decided to come on over."

Natalie scrunched her face up. "It's weird you have an alert for my comings and goings. That's very stalkery."

Brian nodded. "It is a little stalkery. I can turn it off it you want me to."

"I do," Natalie said as she saw her purse sitting on the bar cart. She had put her phone in there before she left earlier and then decided not to take her purse at the last minute. "Wait, maybe I don't. You'd get an alert if a murderer was knocking at my door. I need to think about this. I'll get back to you."

Natalie freed her phone from the confines of her purse, and saw Brian had texted several times. "I guess you did text."

Brian sighed. "You are so damn weird. Step back. I have a present for you."

Natalie gasped. "A present for me? You buried the lede there. You should've announced that first instead of making me think you wanted to cut my feet off," she said as she stepped out of the way for him.

"I did announce it. I texted you, a few times." Brian walked out of sight. "I don't know why you'd think I was trying to cut your feet off."

Natalie craned her neck to see where he had gone. "Listen, in order to understand the motives of a killer, you have to get inside their brain."

When Brian returned, he was carrying an oversized wooden table. Its design was simple, but the elaborate grain of the wood made the table look so elegant.

"What's that?" Natalie asked.

"It's a coffee table," Brian answered, and carried it into her apartment. He gently set it down in front of her couch.

"Where did you get it? I love it." Natalie sat on the couch and ran her hand over the top. The wood felt cool to the touch.

Brian watched her look at the table. "I made it."

She looked up at him and said, "No, you didn't. You're messing with me."

Brian shook his head. "No, it's true." He sat down next to her. "I had a couple of planks in my workshop I knew I wanted to use for something special. And when we broke your monstrosity of a coffee table, I started working on this. I made it the same size as your ugly one. I hope that's okay."

Natalie looked at him, utterly shocked. He'd made this for her. With his own two hands, he'd made her a table. "Thank you so much. I love it." She tried to think of something witty to say but couldn't. She was in total awe of her new table.

Brian squinted and looked at Natalie. "You're welcome... I'm glad you like it."

"I do, I really do. Are you hungry? I got a few things from the bakery," Natalie offered before she knew what she'd said. But after the words left her mouth, she thought it only right, since he had made her a table. Sharing her cupcake was the least she could do.

"I could be persuaded. Any coffee?" Brian asked.

"I can put a pot on."

She put her latte in the microwave to heat it back up and made a pot of coffee for Brian. She got plates and a knife to split the croissant and cupcake in half. She didn't bother trying to divide the cake — that'd simply be a free-for-all.

Brian walked over to see what all she had bought. "Someone had a sweet tooth this morning."

"I needed the healing powers only refined sugar could provide," Natalie said as she plated the pastries.

While the coffee brewed, she found the coasters Lisa picked out during their shopping spree and tossed them to Brian to place on her wooden work of art. He picked up their breakfast and headed to the living room.

Natalie placed Brian's cup of coffee on his coaster and climbed over his long legs to get to her spot on the couch. "I can't get over how this table completes the space. It's so good," Natalie said as she nestled into the couch.

Brian blushed. "I'm glad you like it so much."

"I'm still in shock you did this for me. It means a lot." The past eighteen hours had been hard, and this act of kindness added extra emotions to her already overflowing cup. She did her best to push back the tears. There were so many feelings swirling around inside of her, it was hard to process everything.

Brian tilted his head. "You okay?"

Natalie didn't realize she had been lost in thought. "Yeah. I'm just having a moment. Feeling all my feelings at once. Does that ever happen to you?"

Brian shook his head. "No."

Natalie chuckled and said, "Of course not. You are too grumpy for that to happen to you."

"I'm not grumpy. I laughed the other night, and I laugh at you frequently," he said.

She rolled her eyes. "I don't know why you laugh at me. I'm the logical one. It's just hard for you to see it because you are so blinded by your own linear perspective. I can see all aspects all at once, and you can only comprehend the one task right in front of you."

Brian opened his mouth to say something and then closed it again. There was a long pause before he responded. "There may be some truth to that. I may not be able to see the whole universe all at one time, but I can do better than just one task at a time."

"Jury's still out on that one," Natalie said, reaching for her half of the croissant.

"But joking aside. What's going on? Something's clearly up this morning." He pointed to her bakery selections. "What caused this to be your purchase?"

Natalie didn't know where to start. "I am usually very organized and think everything through. And when I say everything, I mean it. I work out every possible outcome and make accommodations for them. I'm never surprised. In fact, I hate surprises. This move has flipped my whole world upside down, and I can't seem to get my footing." She stared out the window and let the words spill out of her. Her brain had turned on a faucet she didn't want to turn off.

"You know, it's my usual life-implosion stuff. Hosting Thanksgiving seemed like the one thing I could control in my life. But I can't control it at all. Everything I had planned has fallen apart. I'm trying desperately to keep it together, but I can't. If I can't keep a dinner together, how am I going to keep my life together?" She didn't realize she had started crying until her hand unconsciously touched her face to wipe a tear away.

"I don't have any plans this weekend. So you have two options. One, I help you with whatever you are working on for Thanksgiving, or two, I distract you and get you out of the city for a bit."

She looked at Brian, and he seemed totally sincere in his offer.

"I don't know what to pick. I need both," Natalie answered.

"Then we will do both. Today, we'll work on Thanksgiving stuff, and tomorrow, I will take you on a little road trip." Brian stood up and drank the last of his coffee. "I'm going to put this in the sink, and then you put me to work."

Without hesitation, Natalie stood up too and gathered the goodie bag materials from where she'd placed them in a corner of the room. She laid them out on the coffee table and handed him a completed goodie bag to look through.

"This is what I'm putting together for everyone in my family."

Brian carefully pulled out of the contents of the bag. "Man, this is awesome." He held up one of her fun facts pages. "Did you draw this?"

"I did." She waited for him to tell her she was doing too much.

"That's so cool. This whole thing is crazy impressive."

"I know I'm doing too much and making this too hard on myself," Natalie said as she straightened the piles of pens in front of her.

Brian put a hand on her arm. "There's no way I could have come up with any of this. I think it's so thoughtful you're doing this for every member of your family. It shows how much they all mean to you."

"These weren't my idea. The bags have been part of Thanksgiving my whole life. I'm keeping the tradition alive," Natalie stated.

"I don't know why you are minimizing this. If these have been around forever, it's even more impressive you're maintaining them. It's clearly a lot of work, and I'm sure most people would've stopped doing them when it was their turn to take the holiday over. Unless you feel compelled to do them. And if that's the case, then I don't think you should make the bags. Do you feel compelled to do them?"

She took a moment to gather her thoughts before responding. "The answer to that isn't easy. It's both yes and no. I do feel compelled to make them, and I also want to make them. I know how I felt when I received these bags over the years, and I want my family to get those same warm, fuzzy feelings from them. My grandmother always said she enjoyed planning a party more than the actual party. And I think I'm the same way. I love the little details. Not everybody notices them, but when someone does, it makes it all worth it. Plus, I notice the details. I want them there."

"Then let's make some bags. What am I doing?" Brian asked.

A man had never made her feel so seen and understood in her whole life. Even her dad thought the goodie bags were a waste of time. She almost didn't know how to answer.

"Aunt Lindy stuffed them with all the coloring sheets and word searches. What would save me a ton of time is if you looked up facts for each person. I already know the topics for everyone. This is what my mom and I used to do. I'd hunt for facts, and she'd write them out and draw little pictures. Not having to do both at once would be so helpful."

"I can totally do that. What am I looking up first?" Brian said as he took his phone out.

Natalie sat on the floor and pulled the coffee table closer to her. She picked up the next bag that needed to be worked on. "Uncle Tim. He loves to fish, so give me some fishing trivia." She put the bag down on the table, took out the fun fact page, and picked out a few pens while Brian looked up the information.

"Okay, did you know fly-fishing originated in Japan?" he asked.

"I didn't, and that's perfect. Little simple stuff like that is exactly what I'm looking for." Natalie wrote on the paper.

"Here's another one. Fly-fishing lines were originally made from braided horsehair. That's actually pretty interesting."

"My hands ache just thinking about braiding fishing line," Natalie said, and reached for a different colored pen.

* * *

"If over four thousand kinds of sewing machines have been invented, I wonder how many other utilitarian machines have been developed? How many types of toasters or alarm clocks have been made? I've never looked at a blender and thought, I can make that better. But somebody else has," Brian said, and opened the truck's passenger door for Natalie.

"I know. I don't have the capacity to understand the inner workings of a machine and think I could make it function better," Natalie said, sliding into her seat. Her stomach rumbled; she was ready to eat lunch.

Brian closed her door and walked around the truck to his side. He opened the door and said, "Also, I have never thought about the transition from buttons to zippers on boots. I only deal with laces. I'd never thought about how time-consuming it must have been for women to button shoes. Did men's shoes have buttons? Or was it just women's shoes? Did military boots have buttons?"

Natalie smiled and said, "I don't know. We will have to look those questions up during lunch."

Brian started the truck. "I get why you enjoy making these bags. This morning has been fun. I learned a lot."

"I know, right? The facts spark interesting conversations about buttons on military boots. The rest of the weekend gets spent debating which family member could braid the best fishing line."

"I have so many questions about shoe buttons floating around in my head," Brian said as he backed out of the space.

"I will see if I can find you a book or perhaps a cobbler you could talk to." Natalie leaned forward to turn the heater on.

"A cobbler would be ideal. Also, cobbler sounds so good right now," Brian said.

"Drive faster then."

CHAPTER 24

4 Days till Thanksgiving

It was a beautiful Sunday morning, and when Natalie finished her breakfast, she decided to clean a few dishes as she waited for Brian to pick her up. He hadn't told her where they'd be going, only that he was taking her out of the city for the day. They had accomplished a lot the day before. Brian helped her all day long, and all but five bags were done. However, there was still so much more to do. She had barely begun the place cards, but she needed a break. Last night, after Lindy and Charlotte got back from the rehearsal dinner, Brian and Natalie took them ice cream, and Natalie finally told Lindy about the flowers. When she told the Grand Dearies about Brian giving her a day of distraction, the look the two women exchanged made Natalie blush. Lindy smiled from ear to ear as she agreed time away would be very helpful.

Brian's assistance with the bags brought her anxiety level down several notches, but it was still so high. He had picked up on her emotional distress and hadn't attempted to touch her at all. She couldn't handle the idea of adding any more feelings to her current mental state. She was barely holding herself together and felt so fragile.

She debated about waiting in her apartment for Brian, but when he texted he was on his way, she headed downstairs. En route to the back parking lot, she thought about stopping at the bar to see if she could envision what Thanksgiving would look like now. However, today was about getting her to stop thinking about what had gone wrong. So instead, she kept walking and mentally closed the door to anything related to next week until tomorrow.

Brian's instructions on what to wear for the outing had been very clear: comfortable shoes, something warm, and a raincoat or an umbrella. He knew Natalie wasn't outdoorsy and she didn't think they were going on a hike, but maybe they were going to explore an outdoor art exhibit or something. She didn't know, and at this point, didn't care. If hiking would take her mind off everything, she'd even be willing to brave nature, as long as there were bathrooms close by.

After the truck pulled into his normal spot, she waved and hopped in. "Someone is excited," Brian said, welcoming her into the cab.

Natalie buckled her seatbelt and said, "I am. I'm glad we are doing this. Even though I'm not into surprises, I am all for not making any decisions today. Plus, I'm still so new to the area, so it'll be nice to see what all's around here."

"I think you will like it." He put the truck in reverse and said, "You get to pick the radio station."

An ornery thought came to her mind. "Do you think it's too early to listen to Christmas music?" Natalie asked. She didn't want to listen to Christmas music yet, which, of course, for her only started the day after Thanksgiving, but she knew it'd rile Brian up. Messing with him was a small pleasure that needed to start early in their adventure.

"You can't be serious. If you weren't hosting Thanksgiving, would you already be decorated for Christmas? I bet you would. I bet you have your decorations up on the first of October."

Natalie rolled her eyes and swatted his arm. "You take that back. How dare you think I'd sully the good name of Halloween. That's blasphemous."

"Well, at least some part of you is sane." Brian pulled onto the highway and mumbled under his breath, "Christmas music before Thanksgiving. Where does she think she is?"

"Did you know 'Jingle Bells' is actually a Thanksgiving song and not a Christmas carol?" Natalie asked.

"What? No, it's not. It's about going through the snow. It's Christmas."

"Nope, it's right there with 'Over the River and Through the Woods.' Both Thanksgiving songs."

Brian briefly looked at her with a quizzical side-eye. "You're making this up."

"I'm not. You can ask Aunt Lindy. It was a fun fact for me one year. It was in my bag," Natalie said and rotated her body to face his a little more.

"Well, if it was in your bag, then it's fact."

"I know. That's why I said it. I only say facts. I'm like the most factual person you will ever meet." Natalie grinned.

"You're so full of shit. I bet it wasn't even in your bag." Brian smirked.

"It totally was. We can call my mom or Lindy right now and ask."

"Do you really think I'm going to fall for this elaborate ruse you're putting on? I bet you already called them and planted this information. If we were to call them, they'd only be agreeing to this preposterous lie because they're in cahoots with you."

Natalie smiled and crossed her arms. "You found me out. I've spent the last eight hours laying the groundwork to gaslight you into believing 'Jingle Bells' is a Thanksgiving song."

"I knew it. I should turn around right now," Brian joked.

"I think it's brave of you to turn the car around and be willing to witness a possible mental breakdown while I put bags together."

"It's cute you think you won't have one outside your apartment. I'm letting you know now that if you start crying on our outing, I will pretend I don't know you."

Natalie laughed at this. "Fair. I probably won't cry."

Brian tilted his head. "You probably will. You cry a lot."

Natalie scrunched up her nose and said, "I do, don't I?"

"Yeah, but it's okay. You've got a lot going on. At least if you cry today, you will be surrounded by strangers, so the odds of you seeing any of them again are slim."

His statement made her ears perk up. "So we're going to be around people. This means I can mark murder cabin off my list of possibilities."

"Yes. Take murder cabin off for this morning. I wasn't planning on taking you there until this afternoon."

Natalie leaned forward in her seat and scanned the horizon for clues. "Where are we going?"

"I can't tell you. It's a secret."

Natalie sat back. If he wouldn't tell her where they were going, she'd at least have a little more fun getting him worked up. "Want to hear another fun fact about Christmas?"

"Why would I want to hear another fun fact about Christmas? Your first fact wasn't actually fun, and it most definitely wasn't a fact. So no, I don't want to hear any more of your lies," Brian emphatically said.

* * *

Natalie was delighted when they pulled up to an outdoor market twenty minutes later. There were rows and rows of tents.

"What's this? Where are we?" Natalie asked, jumping out of the truck.

Brian retrieved a canvas bag full of reusable bags from the back seat. "This is the Restoration Market. It started out with vendors selling salvaged items from buildings being torn down, like old doorknobs and hinges. Then it kind of grew. Now there's clothes, food, books, all kinds of stuff. There is one lady here who makes the best jam you will ever eat. It's going to ruin you for all other jams."

Natalie did a little hop of excitement. She couldn't wait to explore. Her smile went from ear to ear. "I want to see it all."

Brian offered his arm and led them into the market.

Natalie couldn't remember the last time she went shopping just to browse. One of her favorite things to do used to be to go into a store and simply look at all the things they had to offer. She especially liked it if she could share the experience with someone. Her grandmother Ruth was her favorite person to go window shopping with. They'd get lunch and walk from store to store.

There were so many things to see, and Natalie wanted to take it all in. They passed a booth with a beautiful array of baskets. She stepped into the tent to get a closer look.

"Everything you see is locally made," the vendor said from behind a table. The number of talented people in the world never ceased to amaze Natalie. She admired a flat oval basket that had a tall handle.

"What are you thinking?" Brian asked.

"I'm imagining myself walking through a garden, picking flowers, and placing them in this basket," Natalie said, flipping the tag around to look at the price.

"Are you gonna get it?"

"No, I don't have a garden or the space for this basket. But it's fun to think about." Natalie turned to the vendor and said, "Thank you for letting me look around. You have beautiful things."

The vendor smiled and waved while walking off to help another customer.

"I've missed shopping," Natalie said, exiting the tent.

"We went to Sam's the other day," Brian stated, and stepped behind Natalie to make room for a family with two strollers.

"That's a different kind of shopping. This is retail therapy." Natalie stopped at a tent that had an inviting scarf display. She held up the corner of a delicate red silk scarf with gold thread details and watched the fabric float back into place as she let it go.

"That's a nice scarf. Are you gonna get that?" Brian asked.

"No, I don't think so. It's not my style. I just like knowing it exists in the world."

Natalie walked on, and Brian followed in step with her.

"So, retail therapy is just admiring things?"

"Sometimes. Right now, I'm not in a position to buy anything, so instead, I'm simply appreciating the experience. But you brought us here, and you have bags. So what are you here to buy?" Natalie nodded at Brian's bag of bags.

"On my drive home last night, I talked to my mom. I told her I was coming here, and she gave me a list of things to get from the farmers market section." Brian placed his hand on Natalie's waist to guide her away from a kid on a scooter.

Natalie liked the feel of his hand on her body. This was the first time he had touched her all weekend. "I love a list. What are we shopping for?"

Brian took his phone out of his pocket, pulled up the text from his mom, and read the list. "Millionaire Pickles, whole-grain mustard, four bags of the good rolls, two tins of cinnamon rolls if they have them, regular pecans, spicy pecans, goat cheese, and butter."

Natalie approved of everything on this list and wondered if she needed to get some of the good rolls for her Thanksgiving.

"What are Millionaire Pickles?" she asked.

"They're a sweet and spicy pickle, and so good," Brian said as he put his phone away. "I am going to get a jar for Gigi and one for myself too."

* * *

Luckily, the rain didn't start until after they ate lunch. Natalie and Brian walked under their umbrellas to the last few stands before heading back to his truck. Everything she had bought for the day fit into one small tote. While the good rolls had been tempting to buy, she knew her family would be bummed if their traditional pull-apart rolls weren't served.

"Where are you gonna put your amethyst?" Brian asked.

Natalie had bought a small geode for her apartment. "I think at the end of the counter, or maybe on the bar cart. I need all the help I can get to avoid psychic attacks."

Brian opened her door and asked, "Is that what she said it does?"

"Yes, protection is one of the many properties of amethyst." She smiled and situated herself in her seat.

Brian expertly got in the cab while closing his umbrella at the same time. "I need to run by my house to put some of these things in the fridge. Then we can head off to part two of our outing."

Natalie looked at Brian with a curious look. "I wasn't anticipating a part two. What are we doing next?"

"Well, I was planning on acting like a tour guide and driving around the city so you could see everything," Brian said, and started the truck.

Natalie was delighted by this and she sat up a little straighter. "I love this idea."

"Good."

* * *

By the time they arrived at Brian's house, the rain had turned into a monsoon. They stood at the open end of the garage, looking out at a sheet of water. Natalie held her hand out to cup some of the falling raindrops. "I feel like a rain check on the tour is an understatement of what this is."

"Maybe it's a rain delay. Come inside. I'll make us something hot to drink while we wait the weather out," Brian said, and nodded toward the door.

Natalie followed and did her best to shake her hand dry. She wiped the remaining droplets off on her pants. "So this is the infamous murder cabin?"

Brian opened the door leading to his kitchen and then hit the button to close the garage door. "I'd say this is more murder-cabin adjacent. The true murder cabin is probably my work shed in the backyard. It's where all the saws are."

"That tracks." Natalie didn't have any expectations of what Brian's house would look like. From what she'd seen of the exterior, it was a smallish single-story craftsman. The kitchen opened to the living room and front entryway. Brian had a cozy rustic style.

"I like your house." Natalie put her bag on his kitchen island and saw there were bar stools, so she took a seat.

"Thanks, I do too," Brian said. As he put the groceries away, he took stock of what he had to offer. "I've got tea, apple cider, hot chocolate, and coffee."

"You have so many beverages," Natalie said admiringly.

Brian shrugged. "It's my mom. She loves to give me little packets of drink mixes every holiday. Don't tell her, but I kind of love them."

"I'm not judging you." Natalie took a second to think about what she wanted. "I haven't had apple cider in forever, so I pick that."

"I think I pick the same." While Brian filled the kettle, Natalie stood up and walked around the room. She went over to a bookcase to take a closer look at his pictures, and found one of him and Charlotte, and another with someone she assumed to be Brian's mom. He had more books than she expected. Everything was very neat and organized.

She made her way to his wooden coffee table and wondered if he'd made that as well. Natalie took a seat on his sofa to get a better look at the table, and as soon as her butt hit the cushion, she was enveloped in the most delightful sitting situation she had ever experienced. Without thinking, she sat back and let the couch embrace her.

"Well, I live here now. This is the most comfortable couch I have ever sat on."

"I know, it's pretty great. My parents gave it to me years ago as a gift, and I'm already panicking about what I'm gonna do when it dies and I have to replace it. It's the best couch. It's changed me forever." Brian walked toward her with their cider.

He handed Natalie her drink and took a seat next to her. Talking with him was so easy. Natalie felt completely like herself when with him. Normally, she stayed on her best behavior when she met someone for the first time. However, Brian had met her when she was at her lowest. She had zero airs with him and had brought out her crazy side right away.

While Brian told her about how he remodeled his house, she finished her cider and adjusted herself to face him with her arm resting on the back of the couch. She didn't know when they had moved closer to each other, but when she looked down at her leg, it was right up against his. Had she done that when she'd switched positions, or had he moved closer?

He had been such a gentleman this whole weekend. Brian made her feel wanted without touching her at all. She watched his lips move and thought about how soft they were to kiss. Then she wondered why she wasn't kissing them. Natalie decided to fix this error and leaned forward to gently turn Brian's face to hers. His mouth gladly accepted her kiss.

Brian gently held her face in his hands and parted her lips with his tongue. The more they touched, the more she needed him. With his hands still on her cheeks, he pulled his face away from hers and looked at her with such warmth. Natalie bit her lip, and Brian instantly embraced her. He devoured her. He kissed her deeply first and then kissed her cheek and made his way to her neck.

Natalie took his hand and slid it under her shirt. Her body yearned for his touch.

"Are you sure?" he said, nibbling her ear.

"Shut up," Natalie said, and guided his hand to her breast.

Brian's hands skillfully pulled the cup of her bra down to expose her nipple. As soon as his fingers made contact, she released a sigh of pleasure. She wanted more, and now. Natalie appreciated he had been so considerate in knowing when she needed him to be present and supportive and when she needed his hands on her. Because now, she needed that connection, and she needed it immediately.

All the emotions that had been bogging her down were pushed aside by her desire, and in this moment, she felt so light. Natalie sat back and removed her shirt and bra. Watching Brian's face as her breasts were fully exposed made her want to ravish him.

She didn't have a chance to make a move because Brian attacked her first. He pushed her back against the arm rest and partially straddled her with his knee placed between her legs. One hand took hold of her hair, pulling it back, while the other cupped her breast. He kissed her like she was his antidote. She felt small and completely consumed by his desire.

Natalie grasped a handful of his shirt and tugged him closer to her. He was close, but that wasn't good enough. She needed to be skin-to-skin. She moved her mouth just far enough away from his lips to say, "Take your shirt off."

Brian sat back on his knees and unbuttoned his shirt. Natalie loved watching his chest being exposed, but that wasn't enough either. "Get up," she commanded.

Brian looked so confused as he reluctantly stood up. Natalie followed suit and stood up as well. The way he kept opening his mouth to say something but stopping and the questioning look on his face were completely charming. Natalie gripped his half-unbuttoned shirt and pulled him to her. "Which way is your bedroom?" she asked.

The relief that radiated from his smile endeared him even more to her. Brian wrapped his arms around her and kissed her gently before saying, "Are you sure?"

"Yes, which direction is it?" she replied in between kisses.

"We don't have to do this," he said.

The touch of his hand on her bare back felt so good it was hard for her to pull away. But she wanted more. Natalie walked toward the hallway off the kitchen. "Is it this way?"

Brian took her by the hips and brought her to a stop. He stood behind her and put an arm around her soft stomach while whispering in her ear, "Wrong way."

She leaned back into him as his hands traveled up her stomach to her breasts. "You never gave me an official tour, so how was I to know?" Natalie liked how hard he was. She slowly moved her hips back and forth.

Brian groaned into her ear before whispering, "That was dumb of me."

Natalie didn't want him to stop, but she also really needed him inside of her. "All right, dummy, it's going to be hard to walk like this."

Brian brushed her hair away from her neck, kissing it gently while still caressing her breasts. "Hold your damn horses." His mouth made its way to her earlobe, and her knees went weak. Thankfully, one of his arms had traveled to her stomach to hold her securely to him.

Her ability to walk had disappeared and waves of arousal washed over her body. The world around her vanished, and he was the only thing that existed. The shiver of pleasure that ran through her whole body brought her back to reality. When he finally let her turn to face him, she kissed him deeply. Her hands went to the back of his head and clutched his hair.

Natalie stopped kissing him, took his hand, and headed in the other direction. Once around the corner, she saw an open door, which led to his bedroom. As soon as she stepped in, she kicked her shoes off and undid her pants. Brian followed her lead.

She enjoyed watching him undress quickly. Being naked in front of him was not awkward at all. He made her feel completely at ease, and she even considered doing it with the lights on. In all of Natalie's years, she had yet to figure out a sexy way to take her socks off. She sat down to remove them and after yanking off the final sock, she stood up, spread her arms out, and said, "Ta-da!"

Brian threw his head back and erupted in laughter. The sound of his laugh gave her the warm fuzzies all over. "You are ridiculous," he said once he gained control of himself.

Natalie shrugged and bit her lip as he reached for her and pulled her to him.

"I've never met anyone like you," Brian said, looking in her eyes.

"Obviously," Natalie said before kissing him. She loved feeling his naked body against hers.

* * *

Natalie felt like she was under a spell. She couldn't remember getting in the bed, nor did she have any idea how long they had been exploring each other's bodies. Her brain had completely shut down, and the rest of the world had melted away.

While pressed up against Brian with his hand on her butt, he whispered in her ear, "I only had the one condom in my drawer."

Natalie sighed. "That's totally fine by me. I can barely keep my eyes open anyway." Brian stroked her hair as she closed her eyes and fell asleep wrapped in his arms.

When she awoke from her nap, Brian lay next to her reading the news on his phone. Natalie yawned and rubbed her eyes. "What time is it?" she asked.

"It's about six. I just ordered us dinner and thought we could watch a movie before you go back to your apartment," he said, and leaned over to kiss her forehead.

As soon as he brought up food, her stomach growled. Sex always made her ravenous, and she was delighted he had taken care of that need for her as well.

Brian stood up and got dressed. "I'd love for you to spend the night, but I didn't want you to think you had to. You don't have anything here, and I don't have an extra toothbrush or anything like that for you."

The offer was very sweet, but he had been correct in his assumption. Natalie wanted to go to bed surrounded by her own things. She also wanted to take a shower using her lavender-scented body wash instead of whatever boy soap he had in his bathroom. She stretched in bed and said, "No, you were right, I'd like to go home. Thanks for the offer though. What did you get us for dinner?"

Brian leaned over, gave her a quick kiss, and said, "Burgers and onion rings."

Natalie reached her hand up to his face and patted his cheek. "Good choice."

Brian left the bedroom to wait for the delivery, and by the time Natalie joined him in the kitchen, he had unpacked the food and made drinks for them. Brian took his food to the couch and called out movie options while Natalie doctored her burger. As they settled on a movie, Natalie snuggled next to Brian, ready to enjoy dinner and a blissfully quiet mind.

CHAPTER 25

3 Days till Thanksgiving

The next morning, Natalie woke with lovely images from the night before floating around in her head. But as much as she wanted to get lost in those memories, she didn't have the time. If she could get a lot of the food prepped today, when her parents showed up tomorrow, she could leave her dad in the kitchen to cook while she focused on the last of the goodie bags and place cards with her mom. So much had changed from her original vision, but disaster hadn't hit, and she was proud of herself for being able to put together what she had so far, despite all the upheaval that had happened recently.

After she had gotten home and showered the night before, Natalie lay in bed researching specialty grocery stores. Most of her groceries would be delivered from a regular store. But she had a few family members with dietary restrictions, and some of those ingredients could only be purchased at a fancier grocer.

Natalie found a store with all the brands she needed. On their website, they also showed an elaborate floral department with buckets of flowers. She hoped if she got to the store early enough, she could get her hands on some of those fresh flowers. That way, she could at least make little arrangements for the table.

Texting with Brian on her way to the store made her blush. He wasn't saying anything inappropriate, but thoughts of his body kept popping up in her mind. Sleeping with him had complicated things, but she didn't have to figure those feelings out until after Thanksgiving. Right now, she needed to focus on the task at hand. She closed out the text thread with Brian and opened her mom's thread. She replied to her mom's text about having spotty cell service during their drive. Natalie gave her a thumbs-up and asked her mom to send a proof-of-life text when they'd settled down for the night.

The store was busy but not nearly as packed as she'd expected. She got a cart and tried to get her bearings in the store. The floral section was hard to miss. It was being restocked, so Natalie decided to hit that area last, o.n her way to check out.

After crossing off the last gluten-free ingredients, she read over her list a few more times to make sure she had everything and in the correct quantities. This was her one and only time to make it to the store. Once she was sure the contents of her cart matched her list, she made her way to the flower section.

Natalie was lost in thought when she left the canned-goods aisle. An elderly man emerged out of nowhere, and she stopped just in time to prevent a head-on collision with his cart. Natalie took a beat to regain her composure and get her head back in the game. People were everywhere. Now was not the time to be thinking seven steps ahead; she needed to be present in this moment. She took a deep breath and slowly pushed her cart around the corner, checking to ensure she wouldn't hit anyone.

As she looked toward the flower section, she froze. There, standing in front of a container of gerbera daisies, was her married ex-boyfriend, along with an attractive woman she surmised was his wife. All air left her lungs, and she stood there gasping for breath. She needed to leave, and she needed to leave now.

Trembling, Natalie ditched her cart in the middle of the grocery store and walked as fast as she could to the exit. She needed to get outside. Air was outside, and outside was free of her married ex-boyfriend. Her hands shook as she pulled up the ride-share app. She stepped into the liquor store next door while she waited for the car, worried she'd run into him out in the open.

All she wanted was her bed and to be completely alone, but she couldn't go back to the apartment building because Brian was there working and had already offered to help carry up her groceries when she returned. She didn't want to go to Lindy's because she didn't want to talk. The only place she knew would be empty was her office. Since everyone had the week off, she knew she'd be alone there.

It took all her willpower not to cry in the car. The trip to her office only took ten minutes, but it felt like hours. She made her way to the building elevator lobby and pushed the call button for the lift. Natalie forgot that even though her company was off, most of the other people in the building were still working.

She focused on clenching her fists as she stepped onto the elevator with three other people. No one seemed to notice she was seconds away from imploding.

The doors opened to her floor, and she was blissfully happy to see all the lights were off. They were motion-activated, and since they were off, it meant no one else was there. She ran to her office as tears streamed down her face. The door closed behind her, and she crumbled into the fetal position on the floor behind her desk.

* * *

Natalie had no idea how long she had been crying. She sat up and leaned her head against her cool desk drawers. Logically, she'd known she lived in the same city as her married ex-boyfriend and that he lived in her general vicinity. But for some reason, it had never occurred to her she could run into him. Even though no part of her ever wanted to be with him again, seeing him with his wife felt like a betrayal of their relationship. He'd seemed happy at the store. He also had just left a three-year relationship, and there he was, completely unfazed, happily buying flowers with his wife.

She seriously doubted that if he had noticed her, it would have sent him to pieces. This fact made her hate him even more and made her start crying again. Natalie lay back down and tried to take deep breaths to stop crying. After the lights in her office clicked off, she realized she had been lying on her floor for quite some time.

Natalie decided a good first step would be to sit in her desk chair. The lights instantly came back on as she stood up. She sat in her chair, instinctively turned on her computer, and pulled up her emails. At this point, she ran on muscle memory.

With her computer on, she might as well double-check that the Marv's Choice ad was all set to be posted the day before Thanksgiving. Lisa had been more excited about the ad than she was, and told Natalie she planned on checking regularly to make sure everything loaded correctly once the ad launched.

Natalie logged in and confirmed everything was set up and ready to go.

Once done, she couldn't think of anything else she needed to do at the office, and crying under her desk didn't seem like a good idea anymore.

Natalie reached for her purse and pulled out her phone. Her crying had blocked out all incoming message dings. She had missed text messages from Lindy, Charlotte, and Brian. She sent Lindy and Charlotte a text saying she was heading back to her apartment and would call them when she got there. Figuring out how to tell them about her morning would be another thing.

Her next dilemma was Brian. She had too many emotions coursing through her to be able to see him right now. At that moment, seeing him or talking to him was too much. She decided a simple, honest text message would be her best bet.

Natalie: I saw my married ex-boyfriend at the store this morning with his wife. I need some space right now to process everything. I'm not doing great and need a minute to work through all of these feelings.

* * *

When she got home, she didn't have the brain space to order any of her groceries. She needed to do something with her hands, and she needed to do it now. So Natalie decided to start washing the Thanksgiving dishes. They had been sitting in a box in the corner of her kitchen since the day she moved in.

As she opened the first box, she saw the top dish had broken. But a few broken dishes weren't that big of a deal, because Lisa and Charlotte had picked out tons of plates. However, plate after plate were broken or chipped. Natalie couldn't believe her eyes. How could this have happened? She'd watched Charlotte and Lisa pack the dishes away so carefully. When the boxes were brought in from Henry's truck, this top box must have been dropped. Natalie moved the box aside and frantically opened the box beneath it. It was more of the same. Each plate was unusable.

Before she realized what happened, Natalie found herself on the floor again. The tears hadn't started yet, but her ability to hold her body up on her own had disappeared. She cradled a box of broken plates and stared off into space. Her phone chimed to let her know she had received a text message. She didn't know how long she had been on the floor because there were no lights turning off to provide a sense of time. Natalie rolled onto her back and read the text message.

Lindy: I know you are busy busy busy. I am letting you know Charlotte and I are planning on leaving for your apartment in about an hour.

The thought of the Grand Dearies being in her apartment did not work for Natalie. She lived on her wood floor now and didn't feel like getting evicted.

Natalie thought about texting back, but that required her to hold her phone for too long. Instead, she called Lindy, put the call on speaker, and laid the phone on her chest so she could continue to stare at the ceiling.

Lindy answered on the second ring. "You must have been one busy bee this morning," Lindy said in her usual sing-song fashion.

"Nope, not really," Natalie said in a monotone voice.

"Hold on, dear. Charlotte is here. I'm putting you on speaker," Lindy said. Natalie heard a little commotion in the background until Lindy's voice rang back through the phone. "I'm back, dear. What's going on?"

"Are you okay?" Charlotte added.

"The jury's still out on that. I, um…" Natalie didn't know how to finish the sentence. "I, um, saw my married ex-boyfriend, and I stopped being able to function in the world. I went to my office and cried under my desk. Now I'm back home and lying on the kitchen floor. Being on the floor seems like the best idea right now."

Lindy and Charlotte weren't saying anything, but Natalie knew them well enough to know they were having a whole conversation with each other by just exchanging looks.

Lindy finally broke the silence. "Here's what we're going to do. Charlotte and I are going to come over. And we'll get everything started. If you can get the groceries delivered, we'll take care of the rest."

Natalie shook her head. "I can't do that."

"It's not a problem. You go lie in bed or on the floor of your bedroom, and we'll take care of everything else," Charlotte added.

"Nope, I mean I can't order the groceries. I can't get up. I quit. Thanksgiving is canceled. This was too much for me, and I'm done. This will be the year my family eats cold cuts and bags of chips at the KOA. Jenny can tell me I told you so for the rest of my life. I am tapping out. I am done."

Lindy paused before she responded. "I understand. Charlotte and I will figure out how to order groceries, and you can go lie in your bed. We'll take care of everything else. Don't worry, we've got you."

Natalie felt herself fall off the cliff of despair. The idea of seeing anyone else today was more than she could bear. All her decisions during the last few months had led her here, to this very spot on the floor, and she felt like a fool for having made them. All the changes were too much, and Natalie felt completely and utterly alone. The only thing that would have made her feel better in that moment was if she hopped in a time machine and went back to her past self and told her to stay put in her old life.

"Stop! You both need to stop!" Natalie couldn't believe she'd raised her voice to Lindy and Charlotte, but she couldn't stop herself. She was word-vomiting all over the place. "Everything about this move was a mistake. I moved from a retirement home to my kitchen floor. I live here now. I can't handle any of this. All of my decisions have been wrong. Selling all my stuff, selling my car, sleeping with Brian, and deciding to host Thanksgiving. Once my parents get here tomorrow, I'll let Jenny take over, and it will be the gift of a lifetime for her. I'll forever go down as the family loser, and that is simply my lot in life. So I'm going to get off the phone now because I have some crying to do. I'm going to try and will myself to crawl to the living room so I can reach a box of tissues. But the odds of that happening are slim to none. I'm sorry for yelling. I love you both, and I will talk to you later."

Natalie hung up the phone and let the tears flow.

CHAPTER 26

2 DAYS TILL THANKSGIVING

The sun beamed through a break in the floral curtains and directly onto Natalie's face. She didn't know when she had moved onto the couch or what time it was. She felt around under the pile of tissues for her phone. As she sat up, her body cracked with every movement. A day of full-body sobs had left her feeling like she had done an intense workout. Natalie tried to stretch out her neck to ease the ache as she woke her phone to check the time. Her screen lit up, telling her it was 7:42 a.m. and she had several missed text messages from Lindy and Brian.

Natalie was glad that, even in her depressive state, she'd had the ability to reply to her mom's goodnight text message. She opened Lindy's thread and saw she had texted Lindy almost twelve hours ago to say she had moved from the floor to the couch, so that settled one meltdown mystery—the other one being the location of her hair scrunchy.

Lindy's response to the couch text almost made Natalie want to start crying again.

Lindy: That's good, dear. I love you and thank you for keeping me posted.

Natalie felt terrible for yelling at Lindy and Charlotte yesterday. These two women had done so much for her, and she'd treated them so poorly. The only thing she wanted was to go and see them. She wasn't as sad as she had been the day before, but Natalie knew seeing them would make the world feel like it was back on its axis.

It took a couple of tries before Natalie decided on a text to Lindy.

Natalie: I'm sorry I yelled at you. Can I come over?

Lindy's reply came in seconds after she sent her message.

Lindy: You have nothing to apologize for. Come any time.

Relief washed over Natalie. Lindy was wrong, and Natalie definitely needed to apologize in person as well.

* * *

The box of pumpkin bread sat on the seat next to Natalie in the back of the rideshare. A tasty peace offering should always go hand in hand with eating crow.

Natalie knocked on Lindy's door and didn't have time to say hello before she was swept up in her great-aunt's arms. Lindy smelled so good, like a delicate talcum powder and ivory soap. The bakery box made it difficult to hug Lindy the way she wanted to, but Natalie held onto her aunt as tightly as she could.

She didn't realize she had begun crying again until she stepped back and saw her tears had soaked into Lindy's shirt. "I'm sorry for crying on your shoulder," Natalie said as she set the box down on the dinette table.

"Shoulders were built for collecting tears," Lindy said, and walked to the kitchen for plates and napkins.

Natalie didn't wait for her great-aunt to offer a seat. She just walked over to the couch, picked up a blanket, and snuggled into it.

Lindy hollered from the kitchen, "Would you like a cup of coffee?"

Natalie thought back to a month ago when she had been under this same blanket, and Lindy had asked if she wanted coffee. It seemed like nothing and everything had changed since then.

"Yes, please," Natalie replied.

Lindy brought coffee in, and Natalie told her all about the day before. She didn't hold back and let it all spill out.

"I feel like my feet have become sandbags. Some days, I can step out of the sand, and other days, it rains, and I can't move. Yesterday was a tsunami," Natalie said, and set her coffee cup down.

"I completely get that. You remember how I was after your grandmother died," Lindy said while warming her hands on her mug.

Natalie thought about it; that whole period in her life was a blur. She remembered bits and pieces, but nothing seemed to be in the right order. "Kind of. I remember all of us being sad."

"When Ruth passed, it felt like I lost half of my being. I was a shell, walking around mindlessly. After her funeral, you brought me a plate of food, and it was like you had given me a foreign object. I didn't know what to do with it. It wasn't until your mom sat down next to us and told me to take a bite of a finger sandwich that it dawned on me to eat anything." Lindy teared up recounting her story.

"I vaguely remember that," Natalie said as she passed Lindy the box of tissue.

"If it hadn't been for your mom and dad, I don't know how I'd have gotten through any of that. I say all of this because it takes a while to recover from a big heartache. You can't snap your fingers, and it's gone. The good news is that you saw your ex, and you lived through the experience. Because while a broken heart feels like it'll kill you, it doesn't. You two live in the same city—it could happen again. And if it does, you can remind yourself that you picked yourself up off the floor once, and you can do it again."

Natalie sat up straighter. "I did pick myself up off the floor."

"Twice," Lindy said with enthusiasm.

"Oh, that's right."

"You can do this," Lindy said encouragingly.

"I can," Natalie said, and looked up at the clock on the living room wall. "Water aerobics is over now; I think I need to go over to Charlotte's apartment and apologize to her."

Lindy nodded. "Give it a few minutes. I bet she will swing by here any second to see why I wasn't down there."

Sure enough, a few moments later there was a knock on the door, followed by a sing-songy hello as the door opened. Natalie pushed the blanket aside to get up and greet Charlotte.

Natalie approached Charlotte with her arms outstretched. Without hesitation, Charlotte walked into Natalie's embrace. With Charlotte tucked securely in Natalie's arms, Natalie softly said, "I am so sorry for yelling at you yesterday."

Charlotte gave her a squeeze and said, "Don't even worry about it."

Natalie pulled back and looked between both women. "I don't know where I'd be without you two. You've been nothing but wonderful to me, and I should have never behaved that way. I owe you both so much."

"You owe us nothing," Lindy said.

"You were sad and having a hard time, and we weren't listening. You needed to raise your voice to be heard," Charlotte said as she pushed a stray lock of hair behind Natalie's ear. "If all the people I've yelled at didn't talk to me anymore, I wouldn't have anyone to talk to."

Knowing she had made amends with these two special women made Natalie feel so much better. And as much as she wanted to ignore Thanksgiving, it was happening whether she wanted it to or not. She leaned on a dining chair. She was done trying to do this all herself.

Natalie took a deep breath and said, "I need help with Thanksgiving."

"First things first, do you have a turkey?" Charlotte asked.

"No, I don't have any food purchased," Natalie said.

Lindy retrieved a notepad and sat down at the table. Charlotte and Natalie followed suit.

"So we need to go to the store. We'll divide and conquer while we're there, unless it's too soon for you to go to a grocery store," Lindy said, and looked at Natalie.

"Can we pick one that's a little farther out of town?" Natalie asked.

"Absolutely," Lindy said.

"Hold on. I'm going to call down and see if the shuttle is available. I'm sure it is since so many people have already left to visit their families," Charlotte said, heading to the living room to make the call.

Luckily, Natalie still had the whole grocery list on her phone. Lindy added a few things Natalie hadn't thought of. As Natalie and Lindy finalized the list, Charlotte joined them back at the table.

"One of the shuttles is ours, and they're even going to stay at the store while we shop, so we don't have to wait for them to come back."

"Oh, that'll save us some time. How'd you pull that off?" Lindy asked.

"I reminded them of the ruined picture frames and how waiting on us would put everything right as rain. And so many people are gone, there isn't a huge demand for the shuttles anyway," Charlotte said.

Natalie sat in awe of these two women. She wanted to be them when she grew up.

After the grocery list was checked and double-checked, it was time to head down to the front lobby. Charlotte was about to call down to tell them that they were on their way when Natalie looked down at her clothes. She still had on yesterday's outfit, and she hadn't realized how wrinkled and dirty it was. Who would have guessed lying on a floor for seven hours could do that to a shirt?

"Lindy, by chance did I leave any clothes here? I look terrible."

Lindy gazed at her and thought about Natalie's question. "I don't think so. But you can borrow something of mine if you want."

"I would. I think getting out of these clothes will make me feel better," Natalie said. She stood up and headed to Lindy's room.

"Wear whatever you like," Lindy said as Natalie went into the bedroom.

Lindy's closet was a cheerful place. Natalie was reminded that Lindy did not shy away from color. Natalie thumbed through the tracksuits because she didn't want to waste a lot of time trying to mix and match. She couldn't remember if she had ever seen Lindy wear a black tracksuit, and after scanning this section of the closet, she realized the answer to that question was a hard no. Natalie's gaze landed on a pale-pink ensemble with a flower wreath embroidered on the back. It turned out to be the closest option to a neutral color available to her.

Zipping up the jacket, Natalie marveled at how comfortable the outfit was, and the impressive range of motion it gave her. She made a mental note to forget to return it to Lindy. She popped the strawberry candy she'd found in the pocket into her mouth and left the bedroom.

* * *

Natalie had watched Lindy and Charlotte shop for her apartment at the rummage sale. She didn't know why she was so surprised by their shopping prowess at the grocery store, but she was. They each had finished their lists by the time Natalie was only halfway through hers.

What was even more impressive was how fast they organized all the groceries once they got to her apartment. By the time Natalie carried the last bags of groceries up, Lindy and Charlotte were done unpacking the others, and her apartment looked like a little bodega.

"I'm not sure where to start," Natalie said, standing at the counter.

Charlotte picked up a bag of onions and said, "I think we should do as much prep work as we can. It'll make assembling everything go a lot faster."

Lindy tied her apron on. "I can't cook, but I can chop and open cans."

"That's a great idea, Charlotte. Plus, the cutting boards take up so much counter space. Let me go light a candle so we don't cry as much while we chop onions," Natalie said.

"I thought you were supposed to hold a pencil in your mouth," Lindy said.

Charlotte placed the onions in the refrigerator and said, "I find chopping them when they're cold keeps the tears away. So let's start with the celery and bell peppers while the onions cool off. Then we will light a candle, bite pencils, and hope for the best."

Natalie had peeled her last carrot when her phone dinged, and a message popped up from her mom that they were almost at the apartment. She wiped her hands on her apron and picked up her phone.

"Mom and Dad are almost here," she said. "They don't know about any of the setbacks."

"Honey, they won't care. No one will. Just go down and have a little chat with them in the bar. Let them in on how you're really doing," Lindy said as she laid a hand on Natalie's shoulder.

Natalie nodded and took her apron off to head downstairs and meet her parents.

The wind had picked up since that morning, and it was colder outside than she anticipated. Natalie stood next to her parents' truck, shivering in the tracksuit.

"Where's your coat?" Susan asked.

"I know, I didn't think to grab it before I left my apartment," Natalie said. A cold chill moved through her body as she held open her mom's door.

Susan got out of the truck and wrapped her oversized scarf around Natalie's shoulders. "Is that better?"

Natalie pulled her mom into a hug. "You being here makes everything better." The scarf did help ward off the cold, but feeling the warmth of her mom next to her was the best. Before she knew it, her dad had joined in the hug, and Natalie was in the middle of a parent sandwich.

"It's good to see you, kiddo," Bill said.

"It's good to be seen," Natalie replied.

The three of them stayed in their embrace until Jenny cleared her throat.

Susan looked over at Jenny. "Oh dear, you must freezing too. Let's get inside."

Natalie nodded hello to Jenny and took her mom's hand to cross the street to the apartment building.

"Where's Kevin?" Natalie asked as she held the door of the building open for her family.

"He's back at the KOA, getting the RV all set up and acting as the welcome wagon for the family as they start to arrive," Bill said. "He'll join us for dinner."

"Good deal," Natalie said.

"This is lovely," Susan said as she entered the building.

"It really is," Natalie said, and closed the door behind her. She gave them the same tour Brian had given her a month ago. "The ground floor is mainly taken up by the bar. There are some storage rooms in the back, a kitchen, and the building manager's office," Natalie said, guiding them down the hallway. She stopped in front of the door to the bar. "I want to show you guys where we are having Thanksgiving."

She led them inside, and Susan and Bill gushed over the intricate bar. "This is going to be lovely," Susan said, running her hand along the clean countertop. "I know you sent pictures, but they don't do this place justice."

"This is a lot nicer than I thought it'd be," Jenny said.

Natalie did her best not to roll her eyes. She pointed to the small grouping of unbroken chairs. "Let's sit down for a minute and talk before heading upstairs. I need to fill you in on the progress so far."

Natalie's family sat around a table.

"I'm dying to hear what all you've been up to," Susan said.

Natalie rubbed her lips together and took a deep breath. "Well, things haven't gone as smoothly as planned."

"They never do. Every year we seem to have a few missteps," Susan said reassuringly.

Natalie scratched her head. "Well, it's a little more than a few missteps."

Bill tilted his head and really looked at her. "Like what? Are you okay, kiddo?"

It drove Natalie nuts how her father could read her like a book. In high school, she hadn't been able to get away with anything.

"We'll get to if I'm okay in a minute. That's a whole other conversation. But we don't have tablecloths or picture frames for the place cards, all the wooden chairs except the ones we are sitting on are broken, the floral centerpiece was canceled, the goodie bags aren't done, the place cards aren't done, we just bought most of the food today, I still need to go to another store to get all the specialty ingredients because the store we went to today had a terrible gluten-free selection, and the only cooking we've done is chopping a few vegetables right before you got here. Oh, and we don't have any plates."

Natalie sat back in her chair and crossed her arms to watch her parents take in the news. She avoided looking at Jenny. Susan moved her chair closer to Natalie, saying, "Okay, now I want to have the conversation about whether you're okay or not."

She had just told them how Thanksgiving was ruined, and they didn't have anything to say about that?

Bill leaned over and held Natalie's hand. "I want that conversation too."

Natalie lowered her chin to her chest. She didn't want to have this discussion in front of Jenny, but she couldn't think of a way out of it. "This move has been a lot harder than I ever anticipated it being. I'm not the biggest fan of change. And I haven't handled it very well."

Susan scooted even closer to Natalie and wrapped an arm around her shoulders. "Change is so hard."

"It is. And I overestimated my ability to keep everything together. I only had the brain space to keep one thing afloat, and I chose work because I like being able to afford to eat."

"Makes sense," Bill agreed.

"I really thought I could do everything all at once. But feelings got in the way, and it's fucking annoying they didn't stick to their timeline," Natalie said. She felt the tears gather behind her eyes.

"They tend to do that," Susan said.

"In normal times, putting on Thanksgiving would be nothing for me. I wanted to feel normal and do the things I normally do. I wanted to be extra like I always am. I wanted to show everyone I didn't need help and my married ex-boyfriend hadn't destroyed me. I didn't want a terrible Thanksgiving to follow me around forever, constantly being brought up," Natalie said.

"No one's going to bring this up," Susan said, patting Natalie's shoulder.

Natalie looked at her mom and then at Jenny.

"Me?" Jenny said, and her hand went to her chest.

"Come on, Jenny. You know you would," Natalie said. The filter was off, and she didn't have the energy to play pretend anymore.

Jenny looked back and forth between Susan and Bill. "I mean, I wouldn't do it intentionally."

"Really?" Natalie asked.

Jenny blushed and said, "No. Do I do that?"

Natalie threw her head back and scoffed. "All the time. Remember when I made those paper flowers for Teresa's baby shower, and they didn't turn out like I intended? You bring it up all the time."

"I just don't want you to make the same mistake again," Jenny said.

"Who cares if I do or not?" Natalie replied.

Jenny's mouth gaped open like a fish.

"Or the one Thanksgiving I forgot the dinner rolls and had to run home to get them. Now before every family gathering, you text me and say, 'do you have everything?' or 'don't forget xyz.'" Natalie leaned forward and Susan's arm dropped from her shoulders.

"I thought I was doing you a favor," Jenny said.

Natalie rubbed her eyes. "No, Jenny. It didn't feel like you were doing me a favor. It felt like you were reminding me of all the times I did a piss-poor job."

Jenny took a deep breath and blew it out. "I am so sorry if that's how I made you feel. That's how my parents make me feel, and I know how terrible it is."

There were a lot of possible responses Natalie thought she'd get, but the one Jenny gave her was not on her list. Now Natalie was the one with her mouth gaping open. "What?"

"Nothing I ever did was good enough for my parents. Like, ever. I have to be perfect around them all the time. When I said those things to you, I wasn't judging you or trying to make you feel bad. It was me trying to help you not look bad in front of your family. Because I know what that's like," Jenny said, looking at Natalie. "I'm sorry I've added to your stress."

Leaning back in her chair now, Natalie stared up at the ceiling. Thoughts swirled around in her brain. Jenny hadn't been lording things over her; she had been trying to help her.

Natalie slowly lowered her head and looked at Jenny. "I didn't know that was the case."

"Honey, I didn't know your parents did that," Bill said to Jenny.

"Jenny, sweetheart, I want you to feel free to look bad in front of us," Sussan added.

"Exactly, look at me. I look really bad, and these two"—Natalie said as she pointed to her parents with her thumb—"don't care. Like at all."

"We don't care," Susan said, and immediately looked to Natalie. "I mean, we do care about you, but we don't care about this other stuff." Susan motioned to the rest of the room.

Natalie waved her mom's comments off. "I know exactly what you mean."

Jenny wiped a tear from her eye. "My parents' love is conditional on perfection. And you guys are always perfect, so I thought it was kind of the same."

"I totally get wanting to be perfect," Natalie said, and flailed her arms about to encompass the whole room. "Trying to make everything look aesthetically pleasing makes me happy. I like it, we like it." She pointed between Susan and herself.

Susan nodded. "It's a neurosis we have."

"My grandmother was the one who came up with the phrase, 'Berry Perfect.' Making everything look like it came out of a magazine normally is not stressful and comes easily to me."

Susan put her hand on Natalie's arm. "You know your grandmother and I both had tough years and had to ask for help often during those rough patches."

Natalie shook her head. "Logically, I know that. But I didn't want any of you to know how hard it was for me to pull off a picture-perfect Thanksgiving. Everything else was out of control, and Thanksgiving felt like something I could control."

"You know, I'd be okay if 'Berry Perfect' went away," Dad said.

Natalie looked at her father. "Well, that's not going to happen. But I do promise to let you know the next time I find myself in over my head."

Natalie looked at Jenny and saw she was softly crying.

"Can I give you a hug?" Natalie asked.

Jenny nodded. The two women stood up, and Natalie wrapped her arms around her sister-in-law. Gently, Natalie said, "Fuck your parents, in, like, the nicest way. But that's not okay. You're a member of this family, and you now get all the unconditional love you can handle. Look at me. I'm the biggest basket case of them all, and they still showed up for me."

Jenny cried and squeezed Natalie. They stood that way until Jenny stopped crying. Before she ended the embrace, Jenny whispered in Natalie's ear, "I'm not trying to be judgy, but you smell a little bit."

Natalie stepped back and straightened her tracksuit. "That makes sense. I spent a lot of time on the floor yesterday."

Natalie sat back down and filled her family in on the events of the last twenty-four hours. After she had let it all out, Susan stood up and said, "Okay well, let's go upstairs and see what we can do to right this ship."

Susan and Bill got down to business. Dad went into the kitchen to help Charlotte. Lindy, Jenny, and Susan headed to the living room to finish the goodie bags and place cards, and Natalie was instructed to take a shower.

After her shower, Charlotte pulled her aside and told her she had talked to Brian and told him Natalie was fine. Natalie appreciated this, but also felt mortified because it hadn't dawned on her until that moment that she'd told Lindy and Charlotte she'd slept with Brian.

"I told him to not reach out, and you'd reach out when you were ready," Charlotte said.

"Thank you, and I will. I need to say something to him because I really want him to come to Thanksgiving still," Natalie said.

"Oh, he is. He's bringing my macaroni and cheese."

"Okay, good." Natalie let out a little sigh of relief. Charlotte had bought her more time to sort her feelings out and figure out what she would say to Brian.

CHAPTER 27

1 DAY TILL THANKSGIVING

Natalie loved having her little family over for breakfast on Thanksgiving Eve. They arrived early, ready to be put to work.

"Can we think of anything else we need to get?" Susan asked while looking over her list.

"Plates, any Thanksgiving-type decorations you can get your hands on, and the stuff we need from the fancy grocery store. I honestly can't think of anything else." Natalie added the last of the cold water to the food processor for pie dough.

"Okay, Kevin and Jenny have gone to warm up the truck. Lindy, I'm ready when you are," Susan said as she folded up the list and put it in her purse.

Lindy placed the last of the goodie bags in a sack marked *DONE*. "I'm ready. I've double-checked the bags, and they're all complete. If we have time tonight, there are a few I'd like to beef up a bit, but if it doesn't happen, no worries."

"Great!" Natalie was so relieved the goodie bags and place cards were mostly done. She agreed with Lindy it would be nice to have all of them completed to the usual level of detail, but if not, no big deal.

"Text us if you think of anything else," Susan said before holding the door open for Lindy.

"Have fun, you two," Bill said, and wiped his hands on his apron.

Natalie, Charlotte, and Bill had done so much cooking yesterday. All the dressings and casseroles were crossed off the list. Charlotte had left this morning for her daughter's house, so the only cooks left were Natalie and her dad.

"The first turkey will come out in about an hour. I'll have the second turkey ready to go in right after," Bill said.

"Tonight, during dinner, we will bake the pies," Natalie said. She dumped the pie dough on the counter to start shaping it into small discs.

Bill got two coffee mugs from the cabinet. "After the second turkey goes in, I vote we clean the folding chairs up."

Natalie wrapped a disc of dough with plastic wrap. "I think that's an excellent plan."

By the time Bill had their coffee made, Natalie had placed the last bundle of pie dough in the fridge. She followed her dad to the couch as she sipped her first cup of the day. She always loved the way her dad made coffee; he added cinnamon to the grounds.

Bill sat on the floral couch. "I like your apartment."

"Thank you, it's come together nicely," Natalie said as she took in the space. It was a sunny fall day, and light filled the room.

"Your couch is surprisingly comfortable," Bill said while pushing on the cushions.

"I know. You haven't met him yet, but there's a man working on this building named Henry, and this was his mother's couch. She was the one who gave me the matching fabric for the curtains." Natalie made a mental note to invite Henry's mother over to see the apartment soon.

"Are you feeling better today?"

Natalie appreciated that her mental well-being hadn't been a topic of conversation for the whole group. "I feel a lot better. Talking about everything yesterday helped. I even think my day on the floor helped too. I had been holding everything in and putting everything off. It all just exploded out of me, and now that it's released, I feel better."

"Good. You'll still have hard days, but the worst ones have passed," Bill said before he took a sip of his coffee.

"I think so too." Having her parents around made her apartment feel like a home. There was something about them knowing where she kept her silverware and towels that made her apartment feel real.

"Are you going to be okay when we leave?" Bill asked.

"I really do think so. But if not, I promise I'll call," Natalie assured him.

"Good. If you are up to it, I thought we could go car shopping while Mom and I are in town."

Natalie laughed because all conversations with her dad somehow led to cars or something mechanical. "I'm in. A car is most definitely the next thing for me to tackle."

* * *

Natalie got a text that the pumpkins and mums were about to be delivered. She picked up the box of candlestick holders and the baggie of dried oranges and headed down to the bar. She and Bill placed the pumpkins in a pile on the floor because until they saw what decorations had been purchased, there was no use placing them anywhere else. Natalie left her dad arranging the tables while she put the plant in the bathroom.

Susan messaged Natalie when the shopping crew pulled up to the building. As Natalie and Bill walked to the front door, she let her dad know the second turkey still had two more hours before it was ready to come out of the oven.

Bill held the door open so Natalie and Jenny could carry in all the purchases. Susan waved goodbye to Kevin as he left for the airport to pick up the cousins who were flying in.

Natalie carried the last bag into the bar and asked, "What all did you guys get?"

Susan smiled and looked at Jenny. "There weren't any Thanksgiving decorations left. The whole city seems to be completely picked over. At a party decoration store, we did find some decor with the right color scheme, so we went with it."

Natalie saw green leaves in the bags, and her mom's explanation left her very curious.

"We truly went to three different stores before we came across these decorations. I think they'll be a lot of fun and very memorable," Jenny said, and placed a bag on the table.

Natalie stood next to Jenny as she unpacked their purchases. "You see, the only things we could find that had the right colors were these jungle party decorations," Jenny said.

Jenny handed Natalie a package of plates with orange, red, and yellow stripes along the edges and an elephant's face in the middle. Natalie couldn't help but laugh.

"Every plate is a different animal. I thought this year's theme could be 'It's a jungle out there,'" Lindy said, and picked up another pack of plates.

"It is a jungle out there," Natalie acknowledged. She held up another package that looked like folded paper. "What's this?"

"Oh, this is great," Susan said, taking the package from Natalie. "You unfold this, and it becomes a jungle scene that we can use as a centerpiece. It also comes with little animals you can place around it, but we don't have to include those."

Natalie smiled. "I think we absolutely need to include the animals."

"Oh good, me too. I think it'll be fun." Susan took a plastic tablecloth out of its wrapper. "I mean, look at this. The colors of the foliage are perfect for Thanksgiving. It's Thanksgiving meets the rainforest."

"We also got the matching napkins. I know you have cloth napkins for dinner, but you know how I love a cocktail napkin," Lindy said as she sat at the table.

Natalie smiled and kissed the top of Lindy's head. "We'll add in the candlesticks, dried oranges, and a few pumpkins. I think it'll be great," she said.

Jenny walked over to the box of candlestick holders. "These are pretty. Your original vision would have been stunning."

"Thank you. We'll do it another year," Natalie said as she laid out the napkins.

Natalie's alarm went off. "It's time to baste the turkey."

"Let's leave everything where it is, and we can decorate tomorrow morning. I'm beat and ready to sit down and have a glass of wine," Susan said. She placed the jungle diorama on the table.

"I second that motion," Lindy added.

Natalie's family went up to her apartment for some wine and much-needed rest. She thought about texting Brian. As much as she liked him, she just didn't know if she was ready to start seeing someone. She composed a few texts in her head, but decided to wait to talk to him in person the following day.

Chapter 28

0 Days till Thanksgiving

Natalie woke up to the smell of coffee. She loved that her mom had asked if she could spend the night. Of course Natalie had immediately agreed. She rolled over to where her mom had slept. Her mom hadn't been up for long because her side of the bed was still warm.

After digging out a sweatshirt from a drawer, she joined Susan in the kitchen.

"Good morning and Happy Thanksgiving," Susan said and gave Natalie a hug.

Natalie buried her nose in her mom's hair and breathed deeply. She wanted to enjoy every moment of being with her parents. "Good morning and Happy Thanksgiving," she replied while hugging her mom tight.

Susan patted Natalie on the back. "Okay, we've got a lot to do." She stepped aside so Natalie could pour herself a cup of coffee.

Susan leaned against the counter and said, "Dad and Jenny have picked up Lindy and are headed here."

Natalie looked at her to-do list. She couldn't believe how much they had gotten done. The previous night, Jenny and Bill had taken all the side dishes needing to be cooked back to the KOA. All they had left to do today was carve the turkeys so they could heat up the meat easily, and decorate the bar area, which wouldn't take long with all of them working on it.

"Go turn the parade on while I open this box of muffins," Susan instructed.

"I wonder what new balloons they've added this year," Natalie said. The Macy's Thanksgiving Day parade was a tradition Natalie couldn't fathom skipping. Never in her life had she missed watching the parade with her parents. Even the year she had strep throat as a kid, she made a pallet on the floor in the hallway so she could watch the parade from afar as her family sat in front of the TV.

Natalie's phone dinged a few times before she picked up her cell. She was enjoying watching the Broadway performance on screen and wanted to wait till it was done to read her new text. Once she eventually did look at her messages, she saw Donna had sent a group text to her and Lisa.

Donna: I'm loving all the likes on your first Marv's Choice post.

Lisa: Me too!!

Donna: I also wanted to share this text I received from the owner a few minutes ago:

Donna, tell your team they've put a smile on our whole family's face this morning. My grandson showed us the first Marv's Choice ad, and we all laughed so hard. My father did love pumpkin bread. He's smiling down on us this Thanksgiving morning.

Natalie read Donna's text twice. Getting this message was better than if the post had gone viral. They'd done something meaningful, and that felt so good.

Natalie: Well, that was an amazing text!

Donna: I know, right? Happy Thanksgiving, you two!

Natalie: Happy Thanksgiving

Lisa: Happy Turkey Day!!!!

Natalie texted Lisa so they could privately gush about the news and catch up a little bit. Knowing their post had brought up happy memories for the owner's family was an unexpected outcome. She wished Lisa a Happy Duck Day and set her phone back down.

The first marching band came on screen as Natalie's front door opened. Bill set a bag of clothes for Susan to change into on one of the kitchen chairs and he said, "Man, traffic is crazy out by the KOA. We are kind of by the river, and it's a madhouse over there because of the Turkey Trot. People are parking anywhere and everywhere. You weren't kidding when you said they take this holiday seriously. I have never seen so many people dressed up as turkeys in my life."

"Who knew we were in such a prime location?" Jenny said as she picked up a muffin. "Kevin and a few of your cousins are taking the littles over to the race to participate in some of the festivities. He's already sent me a picture of him getting his face painted."

"That's amazing," Natalie said. She scooted over to make room for Jenny on the couch.

Lindy sat in the armchair. "Since I've never been in the city for Thanksgiving, I'm loving seeing all the festivities for the first time this year."

"The next time we do Thanksgiving here, I want to join the race," Bill said while taking one of the turkeys out of the refrigerator.

After the parade was over, Jenny, Susan, and Bill headed downstairs to start decorating. Natalie stayed back to brush her teeth. Before she left her apartment, she looked around the space and admired how much had changed. A month ago, where she stood had been a construction zone, and she only had three suitcases to her name. Now she had built a whole new life for herself.

As she opened the door to the bar, she saw the tablecloths had been laid, and the hodgepodge array of fall and jungle decorations were being blended together. Natalie couldn't help but laugh to herself. It wasn't what she had originally planned, but this setup would be way more memorable.

Natalie laid the cloth napkins next to the paper plates and noticed her dad carrying over one of the broken wooden chairs from where they were being stored. "Dad, remember, those are broken. We have to use the folding chairs we wiped down yesterday."

Brian walked in behind Bill, carrying a wooden chair. "They aren't broken anymore."

"What?" Natalie asked. Seeing him felt like a soothing balm had been poured over her head. Being in his presence made her immediately feel calmer.

"I fixed them for you," Brian said, and set one of the chairs down.

Natalie's heart melted. "When?"

"I started Monday," Brian said. "I knew you were having a tough time. I wanted to do something to help, and the only thing I could do was fix the chairs. So I did that."

Natalie felt a flood of gratitude for having met this man. She had pushed him away, but he hadn't gone far.

"I think I am going to go upstairs and change," Susan said. "Why don't you three come with me? Bill, don't you need to check on something?"

"Yes, I need to check on that thing," Bill said, and walked to the door.

"And I think I missed a call from Kevin," Jenny said as she quickly followed.

Lindy smiled and stood up. "I am going to give you space to talk."

Natalie and Brian watched them leave the bar. She said to him, "I don't know where to start or what to say."

"You don't need to say anything. Gigi gave me the rundown of what happened," Brian said.

"No, you deserve to be kept in the loop," Natalie said. She pushed her hair behind her ears. "I like you a lot, but I also feel really fragile still, and I don't know what that means."

Brian took a step closer to her. "I like you too. You said you needed time. So take whatever time you need."

"I don't know how much time I'm going to need."

"You're not on a timeline."

"But maybe I should be. What if you end up waiting forever? You know what? You don't have to wait for me to be ready." Natalie felt her babbling start to wind up. "If you want to date someone else while I'm getting my shit together, well, it's not great, but I'll live. And when I'm ready to date, if you realize you don't actually like me and want to kick me out of the apartment, that would suck, but you know, whatever. I just ask that you give me a little notice so I can find somewhere else to live."

Brian held his hand up. "Stop talking. Natalie, you're worth waiting for. I'm going to keep showing up. And when you're ready, you can decide if I'm someone you want."

Brian's words almost knocked her over. No one had ever said anything like that to her before. Natalie's lower lip began to quiver. "Do you mind giving me a hug?" she asked.

"Of course not." Brian pulled her into a hug.

She felt secure in his embrace. He thought she was worth the wait. He was going to keep showing up. She took several deep breaths as she wrapped her arms all the way around him. Natalie still felt jumbled, but she was so relieved he would be staying close by.

"Don't go too far," Natalie said as she laid her head on his shoulder.

"I won't. I'll be as close as you want me to be."

Natalie smiled. "Close but not too close. Close enough where I'm like aww, and not eek. Does that make sense?"

"No, nothing you say makes sense," Brian said, and rubbed her back.

"That made the most sense of all the sense. Plus, I'm the only person in your life who truly makes sense."

Brian hugged her harder and said, "That is unequivocally not true."

She smiled and let her body fully relax into his. "We need to change the subject before you ruin my Thanksgiving."

Brian kissed her forehead. "Have you heard of doors?"

Natalie laughed and held him tighter. She looked over his shoulder to take in the room. Her Thanksgiving might not belong in a magazine, but it looked picture-perfect to her.

Epilogue

Natalie tossed the special edition socks she had snagged for Henry into a kitchen drawer. She lit the candles on the kitchen table and adjusted her dress one more time. She looked around the room and couldn't decide if the Christmas tree gave off enough light or if she needed to turn on a lamp as well.

She didn't have time to decide before there was a knock at the door. Natalie adjusted her dress one last time before opening it. Brian stood there with a bouquet of flowers and a poinsettia.

"Thank you," she said as Brian handed her the flowers.

"The flowers are from me, and the poinsettia is from Gigi. Last night, as I drove her home from dinner with you, she told me she thought you might like the color over by your window." Brian walked into the apartment.

"Oh, that's the perfect place," Natalie said. She went to the kitchen to get her vase for the flowers.

Brian placed the poinsettia on the table next to the window. "Smells good in here. What did you make?"

Natalie set the flowers in the center of the counter and joined Brian. She wrapped her arms around him. "I made marry-me chicken. Not that I thought you might want to marry me, but I was wondering if you might be interested in being my boyfriend."

"Absolutely to being your boyfriend, and I believe the other thing is a given," Brian said as he pulled her closer.

Natalie giggled and looked him in the eyes. "Good."

"Now stop talking because I believe we are standing under the mistletoe." Brian hugged Natalie tighter and gave her their first official relationship kiss in what turned out to be a lifetime of kisses.

Author Acknowledgements

I have so many people to thank, I don't know where to begin. You are all my people now and are stuck with me ... sorry not sorry. When I first started my writing journey, the best decision I ever made was to force my friend India to introduce me to Ginny Myers Sain. Ginny put me on the right path. I don't know where I might have ended up if I hadn't had those coffee dates.

After going to Romancelahoma, the best writing conference in the world (totally not biased, just stating facts), I met three women who gave me my first sense of a writing community: Kristen, Jordan, and Pam. Together we started it all and got more involved in The Oklahoma Romance Writers Guild, which is free to join and happens to be the best writers guild on the planet (again not biased, all facts). With a push from my trio and the blessing of the OKRWG board, we started the Tulsa Satellite Chapter.

The Tulsa Chapter changed everything for me. All of a sudden, I felt so confident in my writing. I was surrounded by the best coven of writers a gal could ask for. I love you all deeply and am so glad to have you all in my life now. You have talked me off so many writing ledges. I will never be able to repay them for all that they have given me. Especially Gabby and Kali—you two are such amazing critique partners. I really don't know what I would do without you guys encouraging me on a daily basis.

Thanks to the writing TED talks that Lauren Smith gave us all, I was able to discover Two Birds Author Services. Andrea and Michele, you have made my book better and me a better writer. I look forward to all our future collaborations.

Last but certainly not least, there are four people who have been on this ride with me from the very beginning: my mom Missy, my cousin Elizabeth, my best friend Jamie, and my fella John. I have been a weirdo since birth and my mom has been the best mom of all the moms (not biased I swear). Mom, I won the lottery getting you as my mother. Elizabeth, you have been an amazing cheerleader throughout everything. You are also a phenomenal liar because you have read a lot of my really crappy drafts and told me they were amazing. Your reassuring words have helped me keep going. Jamie, we are more sisters than friends at this point. We will be friends for eternity. I love growing old with you, and I can't wait to haunt puzzle stores together once we're ghosts. John, our time together has been tolerable. You are moderately amazing, and I appreciate that you still want to hang out with me even though I cry a lot. You are so lucky to be stuck with me, what an honor for you.